N. DuPree-Bossie

DEDICATION

This book is firstly dedicated to my children, the real-life Wrecking Crew. They inspired the characters in this book and have provided me with a great deal of insight into the lives of today's teenagers. I love you guys and I thank you for all your support and the awesome stories that you brought home from school every day.

Also, to my significant other, who allows me to work in peace without question and is always encouraging of everything that I do. I'd also like to dedicate this book to my mother, my father and my brother who call me wonder woman. Just know that I work hard to make you proud.

This book is especially dedicated to everyone who needs a reason to stay when everything is telling them that life is too hard and not worth living. If no one has told you, they love you today please allow me to be the first. I love you. I hope that's enough of a reason to stay, because this world would be less without you.

PROLOGUE

Beginnings and Endings

The crumpled piece of paper fell to the floor next to the waste basket. Several other crumpled balls of paper had begun to breach the rim of the can.

"It isn't right." He thought to himself as he put pen to paper once again. "How do you tell them exactly how you felt? How do you say thank you and I'm sorry and all of those things in a way that explains everything?"

He crumpled the paper he'd been writing on and tossed it to the floor with the others.

Finally, he'd made up his mind. What could really be said more than those things?

So, he wrote:

I'm sorry. I love you. Goodbye.

He grabbed the list he'd made and stuffed it into his pocket.

'There had been a few scratched off and a couple new ones

added.' He recalled as he grabbed his bag from his bed and slung it over his shoulder.

He didn't look back as he shut the bedroom door behind him. It wouldn't be missed.

He wouldn't be missed. No one cared anyway.

One less problem.

One less headache.

One less bill to pay.

One less mouth to feed.

8:15 A.M.

🔥😀 **Bestie** 🥰🤣

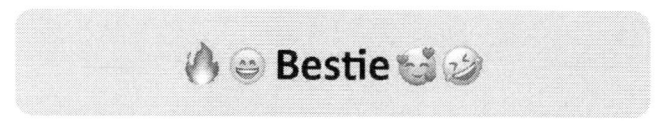

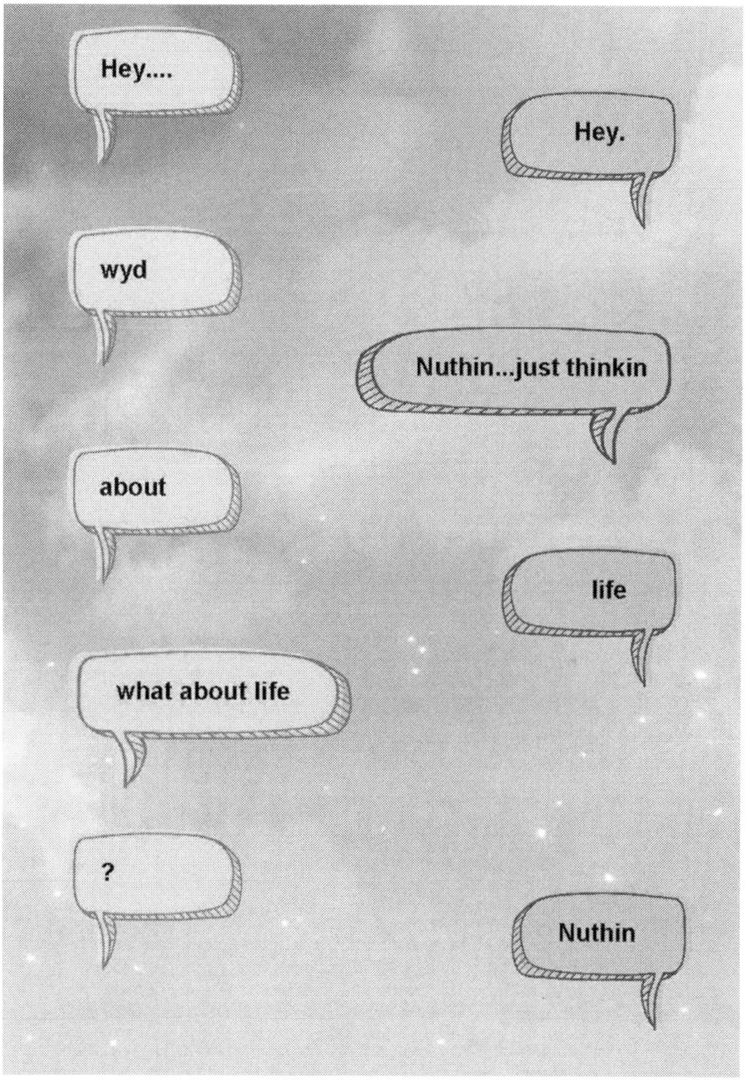
Hey....
Hey.
wyd
Nuthin...just thinkin
about
life
what about life
?
Nuthin

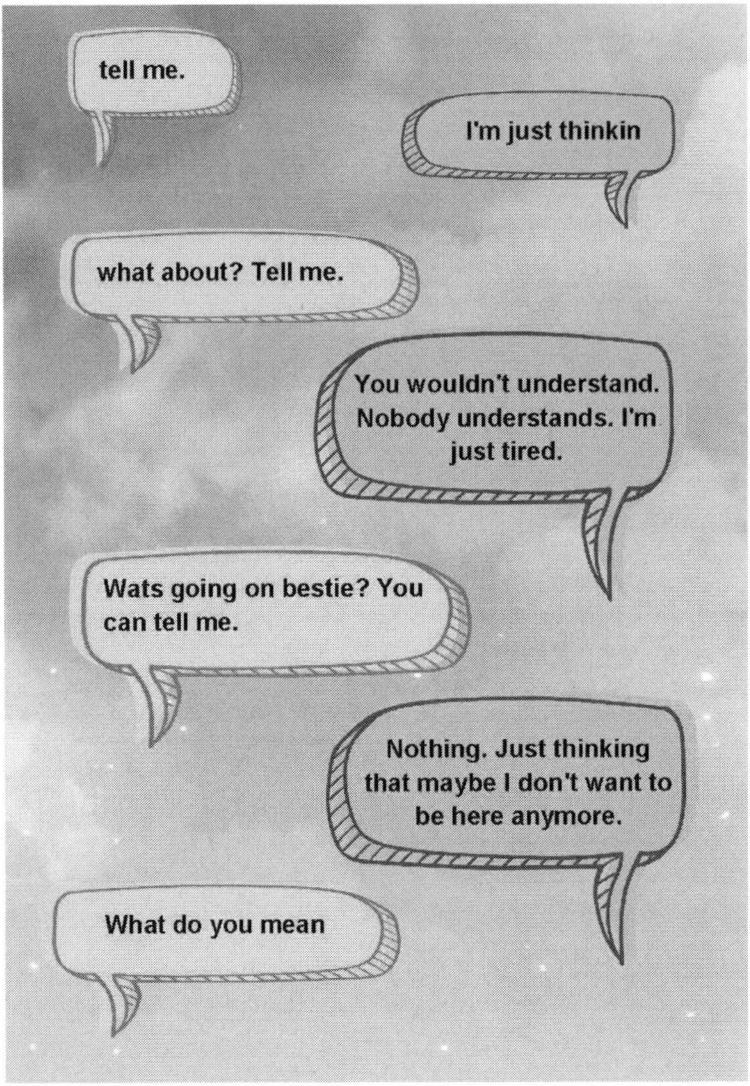

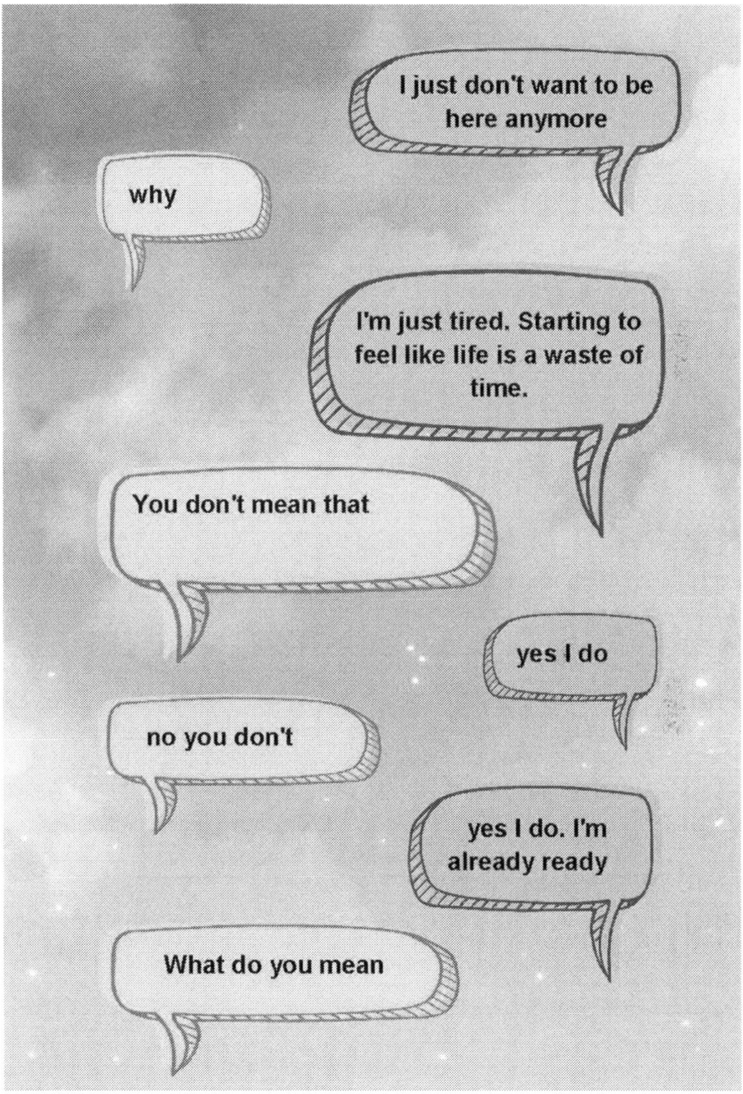

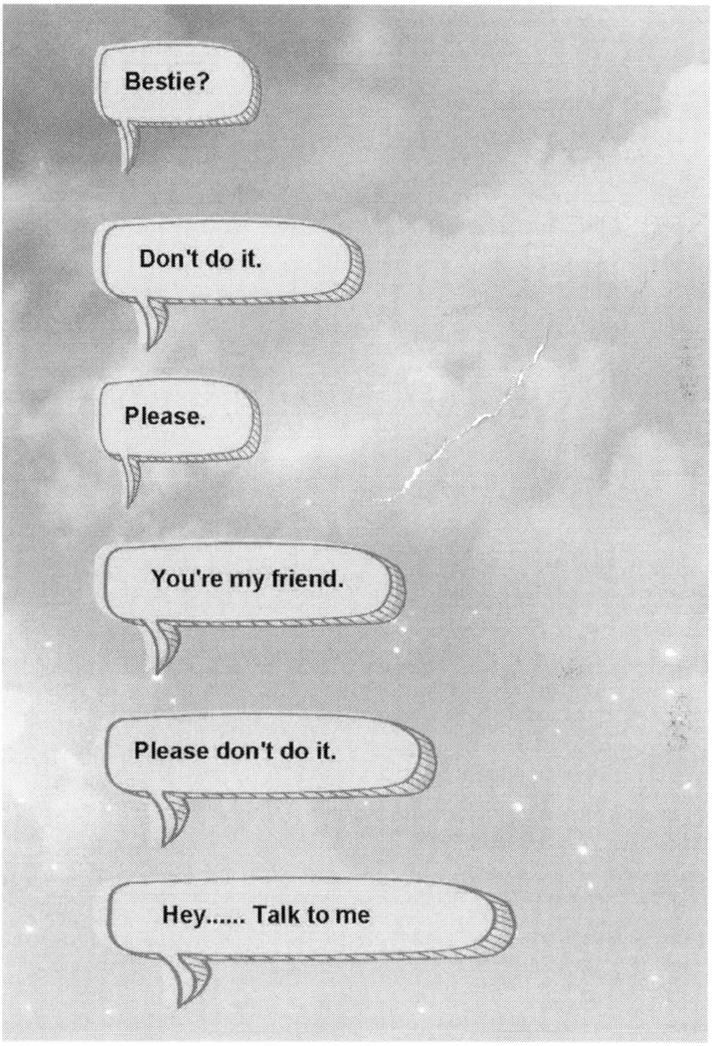

PART ONE

Reasons to Worry

Denise knew Nate was at school but the messages she was seeing concerned her. He had left his IM account open on the family computer again. She didn't mean to pry into his private conversations, but after everything that had been going on over the past few months, she was keeping a close eye on everything he did. To be honest she was scared for her son. Her once sweet, smiling, giggling little boy had somehow transformed into a dark, sulking, emotionally troubled teenager. She didn't know what to do and seeing conversations like this only caused her more concern.

This wasn't the first time she'd found out about conversations Nate had been having like this. He had a lot of friends that were concerned about him and kept in touch with her when they felt like he was having a bad day or had been sharing some dark thoughts online. Most days she noted their concerns in her mind and tried to feel him out on their rides home from school in the afternoons. For the most part she'd felt that he was fine. Perhaps a little dramatic and taking puberty and all of the emotions involved, a little hard, but other than that he was fine.

She would tell herself that Nate had a big heart and took being a friend very seriously. He defended his friends to the end, even when they were wrong, and was intensely faithful and loyal. Some people might say that she was in denial, but it was one of her worst fears to have to admit that there might actually be something wrong with him and that she had failed as a mother to see the signs.

Those messages were just another conversation in a long line of conversations that he would deny having, which was one of the reasons she wanted to believe that it was all just 'dramatic teenager' talk. Denise wanted to believe that he wasn't actually serious about what he was saying. That he had picked up the behavior from friends, who he'd personally told her, were having similar issues. She believed her son was very compassionate toward the plights of his friends and that sometimes he took some of those plights on as his own. But there were always those lingering thoughts in the back of her mind that haunted her.

What if that wasn't the case? What if she was wrong and something happened? How would she ever be able to live with herself? How would she continue to breathe if she lost her son because she hadn't believed that he was struggling and needed help?

The alarm on her phone began to sound, giving her a start. She glanced at the time and saw that it was almost 2:45. She needed to be on her way to pick Nate up from the bus stop if she was going to arrive on time. Unlike his brother and sister, Nate had to be picked up from a special bus stop in town.

He'd been attending the local alternative school since his last 'incident' at the public high school. There had been a hearing with the school board, and they had all agreed to allow him to finish out his school year rather than expelling; just, at a different school. So, every day at 2:45 p.m. she stopped whatever she was doing and went to pick her Nate up from the bus stop.

Their family had been through so much over the past few years with Nate. They were never really sure how he would be from one day to the next. On Monday he could be in a great mood; helpful and polite. Tuesday he could disappear for hours, and they would spend the evening trying to figure out where he was. Wednesday and Thursday he'd be your best friend, talkative and fun only to become sulky and quiet on Friday, hate the world on Saturday and then enjoy spending the day with family on Sunday.

He was hard to read and their fights on some of his bad days had begun to escalate into full blown wars. Through it all she had tried to be understanding of what he might be going through and show him that she supported him in every way. She fought for him and yet, she was still scared for him.

She arrived at the bus stop just as the bus was pulling up. The alternative school picked up and dropped off their students in the parking lot of a vacant office building in town. They did this to avoid having to drop students off or pick them up on school grounds, where many of them were no longer allowed to step foot. It was a bit unusual at first, but after visiting the school and getting to meet the teachers and Principal, she was confident that this school would help Nate get back on track academically. She was willing to do whatever it took to see him succeed.

The students exited the bus, single file, between the School Resource Officer and the Principal, who arrived just ahead of the bus in their personal vehicles. Having to follow such stringent guidelines didn't seem to bother any of the students the least bit. They filed off the bus with laughter, carrying on conversations and waving farewell to their friends as they went their separate ways.

Nate was no different. He and a friend were walking toward the car laughing at something that must've happened on the bus. Denise smiled; happy to see Nate seemingly in good spirits. She continued to watch as he dapped up his friend and said his goodbyes before jumping into the car.

"Hey mom." He said, sliding into the passenger seat and closing the door.

"Hey baby. How was school today?"

"It was all right." He shifted in the seat uncomfortably.

"You getting a lot of work done?" she asked, trying to encourage the conversation.

"Yeah." He mumbled.

She put the car in gear, backed out of her space and proceeded to pull out of the parking lot. She glanced over at Nate again and continued with her usual 'after-school' line of questioning.

"How are you doing with your math?"

"Still having trouble." He was gazing out the window as he said this. He'd already started sliding one of the earbuds, connected to his phone, into his right ear.

"You want me to look over it with you?" She asked. "We can work on it a little bit this evening if you want."

"Nah, I'm good." He said slipping his other ear bud in.

The drive home only took 10 minutes. They rode for eight of them in silence.

Nate stared off into the distance recalling the bus ride and discouraging any further questioning from his mother about schoolwork.

PART TWO

The Bus Ride

Nate and his friend Trevor shared a seat at the very back of the bus across from a couple of Nate's other friends. They were talking about the events of the day excitedly. Trevor had been there to witness the day's events as well, but he was happy to sit quietly and listen.

"Man, she had me messed up!" Nate was saying. "I was about to say something to her, but I was trying to be respectful."

"Why," His friend asked, "because you know your mom would kick your butt?" He laughed.

"How about I kick your butt!" Nate jumped across the aisle onto his friend, pretending to pound on him.

"Settle down back there!" The bus driver yelled from the front, watching them in her rear-view mirror.

Nate settled back into his seat.

"This guy." He nudged Trevor.

Trevor smiled appropriately and nodded.

"So, Trev," Nate turned his attention fully to Trevor now. "What's the plan for this weekend? You wanna crash at my place? Me, my brother and a couple of the guys usually game and snack all night. You down?"

"Ummm, I'd have to check and see if its ok first." Trevor said with a bit of surprise in his voice.

"That's cool, my mom's like that too but she usually says yes and then buys extra snacks and drinks. She'll probably cook breakfast too. But it's up to you. You can text me and let me know." Nate said.

"Ok. Okay cool." Trevor had actually never been invited anywhere before and didn't want to say the wrong thing. "I'll text you."

Just then a ball of paper came sailing at them. It hit Nate on the shoulder and fell to the floor.

"Oh, it's on!" Nate grabbed his book bag and pulled out a notebook. His other two friends had already started balling up paper as they prepared for war.

"Get 'em!!" Nate shouted.

Balls of paper flew from seat to seat on the bus. Kids ducked and dodged as if the paper balls were real bullets and bombs.

"Settle down back there!!" The bus driver shouted from the front once again. "Don't make me pull this bus over!"

Trevor had sunk down off the seat and to the floor, picking up the ball of paper that had hit Nate on the shoulder.

He didn't know what made him un-ball the small piece of paper and look at it, but he did. It was a note. Someone had apparently meant this note for Nate, who had mistakenly viewed it as an act of war.

The note read: 'Why are you hanging out with that lame. He looks like somebody stuck a match up his butt and set his hair on fire. LMAO!!'

This was followed by a drawing of a stick figure boy with fire for hair.

He crumpled the paper back up.

"Oh great!" Nate said looking down at him. "I was running low on ammo, let me get that."

He took the ball of paper out of Trevor's hand and sent it flying.

"Hey, grab my notebook and make some more balls. You can be my wingman." Nate had a huge devilish grin on his face. One that said, 'let's raise some hell!'

Trevor had no idea why Nate wanted to be his friend either, but he was glad he was. He took the notebook and began to tear out pages and ball them up, handing the ammunition up to Nate from his position on the floor.

"Last warning!!!" The bus driver was fuming now, but it was too late, they were already turning the corner into the parking lot of their bus stop.

All the kids on the bus knew the Principal and SRO would be waiting at the bus stop and immediately began to pick up the paper balls and stuff them into their book bags. Before the bus came to a complete stop all of the evidence of their battle had been cleared and everyone was seated and quiet.

The bus pulled to a stop and the driver spun in her seat before she opened the doors to let them out, "Y'all know I can't stand y'all, right?" She glared at them with a twinkle in her eye.

Nate stood up in the back. "But we love you though, you're like the best bus driver ever!"

"Especially you!" She added. There was the slightest hint of a smile at the corners of her mouth.

All the kids burst into laughter and began to collect their things and exit the bus when she slid the lever to open the door.

Another paper ball came flying from somewhere near the front of the bus. This one hit Trevor square in the face.

"Boom! Got'em." He heard someone say.

"Really!" Nate yelled. "Wars over man. Don't be mad cause you lost."

"Whatever Nate!" A face turned around in the line of students. "Wait till next time!"

"Who's that?" Trevor asked Nate as they stepped off the bus.

"That's just Devin's corny behind. That guy is only in school with us because he smells as corny as he actually is. Walking around like he's pimp of the year. Got caught with a girl in the bathroom. Dummy!"

They both laughed at this.

"There's my mom." Nate told him. "You need a ride?"

"Nah, I'm good. I don't live to far from here." Trevor said.

"Cool, see you tomorrow." They did a handshake that Nate had taught him; one he'd learned from his uncle and only shared with close friends.

Trevor in His Head - Interlude

Trevor watched Nate get in the car with his mom and pull off. He looked around and saw that most everyone else had been picked up as well. There was no one there to pick him up, both his parents worked during the day, and they didn't have any family nearby. So, he walked the 4 miles home every day. He didn't really mind though, except when it rained. The walk gave him time to think, and he spent a lot of time in his own head.

If he walked at a steady pace, he could usually make it home by 4:00. His mother usually made it home around 8:30-9 and his dad would roll in about 11:00. Since he was the only child, he had the house to himself until someone arrived home at night.

He went inside, dropped his bag on the floor near the door and headed into the kitchen. He opened the fridge and grabbed a soda and some lunchmeat to make a sandwich. He opened one of the cabinets near the sink and grabbed a bag of chips. His mom was sure to keep plenty of snacks and easy to make meals like Hot Pockets and lunchmeat so he could fix himself something to eat when she was too busy or too tired to cook. That seemed to be pretty often lately. So just like every other day, he fixed his food and headed to his room, stopping to grab his bag along the way.

He placed the sandwich, chips and soda on his desk and his bag on the bed. He unzipped the little top pocket of his book bag and removed the small, balled up piece of paper. He opened it and smoothed it out flat before finding a tack and pinning the paper to his bulletin board. He sat down at his desk and took a bite of his sandwich, examining the stick figure boy with the flaming hair.

"Devin. Nate said his name was Devin"

PART THREE

Nate's issues with his teachers

Nate had told his mother that his day at school had been okay, but it hadn't been. He just wasn't in the mood for another one of her lectures about making smart choices. He'd been hearing them his whole life. He knew she meant well; he just wasn't up for one today. He'd actually been sitting there thinking about his day and it hadn't been anywhere near good. He leaned back in the passenger seat and continued staring out the window. He wasn't listening to the music that was playing in his ears; he was just thinking about those stupid teachers, at that stupid school.

He hated that school and wished he didn't have to go there, but they'd already put him out of the high school, so he didn't have much of a choice. He didn't think that what he'd done had been that serious, but hey, it was what it was. He didn't care. Why should he? If that stupid school didn't care enough to keep him there, then why should he care about being there? He knew they were just trying to get rid of him anyway. They didn't care that he was upset that day. No one cared that his heart hurt. No one cared that he was in pain. All they cared about were the stupid rules and the fact that he had broken them. Today was just another day of exactly the same. He shook his head, looking down at his phone now. He guessed his mom would probably think that he was texting someone and reacting to that, but he wasn't.

Stupid school. Stupid teachers. Nobody cares.

The alternative school wasn't very much of an alternative. It was more like a place they send kids they didn't feel like being bothered with anymore. They tell you it's a chance for you to finish your schoolwork and be able to keep up with the rest of your peers and graduate on time. But really, it's just a steppingstone to nothingness. Like they want to show you exactly how they feel about you.

YOU ARE NOTHING!

Nate had been sitting in the computer lab trying to work through his online English class, when all the trouble started. The school ran on a routine schedule, and they pretty much did the same thing every single day. Though he had never actually been, he figured it was probably like jail without the bars. You came in from off the bus in the morning and had to be seated in the makeshift cafeteria, which was made up of a few round tables and chairs. They took attendance to make sure you were present and confiscated your personal belongings until the end of the day. Then gave you 'their version' of breakfast, which was usually a pack of… something. One morning it may be a pack of cereal or a pack of waffle sticks or even a packed breakfast sandwich with a rubber egg on it. After breakfast you went straight to the computer lab where you would work until the next bell rang.

Almost all of the core classes were online with the exception of one or two classes that were taught by public high school teachers who travelled to the alternative school during their planning period. Everyone else worked on class assignments online until lunch and then again until the bell rang at the end of the day. This was every day, all day, every week, for what seemed, to Nate, to be forever.

The computer lab was four long tables with six HP computers on each. They ran the length of the room, which meant that half of the seats were facing the door and half the far wall lined with windows. All of the students had to turn in their seats to face the front whenever their lab instructor, Ms. Reid, requested their undivided attention.

Nate's friend, Eric, sat a couple seats down from him at the same table. So far that had been the only upside to attending school here, he didn't feel quite so alone. Eric and Nate had only just met that year but had instantly clicked. He had been kicked out of the public high school for fighting and didn't care.

"I ain't about to let nobody disrespect my peoples." Nate recalled Eric telling him one day.

Someone had threatened to jump his brother, so he got them first. He would have gotten expelled all together, but the other kid had a knife and a reputation for being a bully. The board acknowledged that he was trying to defend his brother but also reminded him that there was a no tolerance policy when it came to fighting. So, the other kid gets expelled, and he gets to spend 45 days at the alternative school, and with it being so late in the year that basically translated into the rest of the school year.

"Hey, Nate...." Eric whispered from a few seats down. He'd leaned to the right in an effort to throw his whispered voice a little farther.

"What's up?" Nate shot him a quick nod.

"You heard about Megan?"

"Megan?" Nate sounded confused. "Heard what?

"Maaan, that girl done gone wild." Eric was wearing a huge grin as he shared his juicy news. "I heard she been with Jacob, and Darnel and now she talking to ya boy, Michael."

"Man, I don't care what that girl does." Nate was focused on his screen. "Don't really want to hear her name, for real."

"For real." Eric agreed. "I told you she was bad news, man. They should have sent her over here instead of you."

"Whatever." Nate said, waving him off.

They were interrupted by the sound of Ms. Reid, their lab teacher, clearing her throat.

"You guys are supposed to be working and not talking." Ms. Reid announced from the front of the room.

"We are working." Nate rolled his eyes as he said this.

"You don't look like you're working to me. You look like you're talking." She glared at him over the rim of her reading glasses. There was a long pause before she added. "So, stop."

Nate sucked his teeth and looked back at the computer screen. It all looked like gibberish to him. There was a whole lot of reading that he didn't want to do, but he knew that if he didn't do the work, he wouldn't pass the class. He'd have to keep retaking it and he didn't want to do that either. He hated reading and there was so much of it in his English computer lab that all of the words were beginning to run together.

The topics were so boring. Stuff about Shakespeare and Edgar Allen Poe and Marie Antoinette. He didn't care about any of those people. He didn't even know the majority of the people he was supposed to be reading about. Even with the narrator that read most of the text on the screen out loud, he found his eyes getting heavy and his head starting to nod every time he tried to make it through a section. He needed a distraction from the monotony to help keep him awake.

"Man." He mumbled under his breath. Rearing back in the blue office chair he was seated in, he stretched and yawned a wide, long yawn, sat back up and rolled the chair closer to the desk. He started clicking through the various units, bypassing all the reading to get to the questions. He didn't know what the answers were, but he planned to guess. If he failed, he would just review the ones he got wrong, ask to have the unit reset and he would try again until he passed. Ain't nobody got time for all that reading.

Stupid school. Stupid teachers.

Just then there was a knock at the door. The entire class, which was only eight students, looked up at once. They were glad for any interruption in their monotonous day, even one from the Principal, Mrs. Robinson. Mrs. Robinson was a nice enough lady for a principal, but she could also be tough. She was always stopping to talk to the students and find out how they were doing personally. Sometimes she'd sit in on a class and see what kind of progress they were making with their work, and she'd often help students if they needed assistance.

Nate had even seen her usher a few students into her office for a stern talking to and she wasn't one that was known for sugar coating the truth. If you were screwing up, she would let you know without hesitation. But no matter what the school was or how nice the teachers, everyone was always curious when the principal walked into class. They all wanted to know who she was there for and what they had done.

The last time she'd visited their class unexpectedly was to introduce a new student. That had been Trevor, who sat at the far end of their row, against the wall. He was usually pretty quiet, and no one knew what he'd done to be sent there since he didn't really talk to anyone. Nate had taken it upon himself to sit with the new kid at lunch on his first day and they had become fast friends. This had made Nate feel pretty special since Trevor treated everyone else like they were invisible.

Nate had let it be known early, to the other students, that 'Trev' was one of his friends and off limits to potential harassment and bullying unless they wanted to deal with him. Nate wasn't a bully by any means, but he did have a reputation for being fiercely protective of his friends and he hated to see other people being bullied or mistreated. It was the first time, in a long time, that anyone had stood up for Trevor this way and he appreciated Nate's genuine friendship and sincerity.

"Excuse me class." The principal addressed them from the

doorway. "Ms. Reid, can I borrow you for just a moment?"

Ms. Reid hopped up from her desk and crossed the short distance hastily.

"Alright ladies and gentlemen, this is not an invitation to talk, continue working." She gave a select few a hard look before stepping into the hallway to speak with Mrs. Robinson. The door swung shut heavily behind them.

"Oooooo." One of the girls said from the other side of the room. "Somebody's about to get in trouble." "Yeah, probably you." Another boy replied from the row across from hers.

"Probably you!" She yelled back. "You the one always doing stuff!"

"Yeah, and if you don't shut up, I'm going to do something to you." He gave her a teasing smile.

She rolled her eyes. "Whatever, boy."

The strained silence in the room had grown into a low murmuring as the students began to chat back and forth to one another. Eric and Nate were carrying on their own side conversation. Nate had minimized his class work and logged in to his Google Groups account so that he could talk to a few of his friends at the high school.

All the chairs in the lab had wheels on them and when no one was looking the students liked to glide back and forth from friend to friend carrying on conversations. Eric rolled over to where Nate was sitting and looked over his shoulder at the screen.

"Who's Bestie?" Eric asked him.

"Just ol' girl from the high school. You know her." Nate mumbled without looking away from his online conversation.

"What girl? Click on her profile picture so I can see what she looks like." Eric reached past Nate and tried to grab the mouse.

Nate shrugged him back. "It's Raina from the high school. You know her, dark hair, about my height, usually sits at the side gate before school every morning. I've been friends with her since elementary school."

"Were y'all friends?" Eric raised an eyebrow slyly. "Or were y'all 'friends' since elementary? He drew the word 'friends' out so it sounded both sexy and corny, giving Nate a couple of nudges in the side with his elbow.

"Whatever man. You crazy. She's just my friend. I can have girls as friends." He told him. He gave Eric's chair a shove with his foot, and it rolled back effortlessly.

Eric, a pretty big guy, was a blond-haired, blue-eyed country boy that loved to hunt and fish and wore a camo hat and jeans pretty much every day. He and his family had moved down south from Ohio and Nate was one of the first friends he met as a new student that year. Eric had been sent to the alternative school months before Nate and had been happy to welcome him 'to the jungle', as he called it.

"Okay, if you say so. So, what she talking about?" he asked gliding back over.

"Man nothing. She's just talking about being bored in class, boring schoolwork, her teachers getting on her nerves and her boyfriend. The usual stuff." Nate shrugged.

"So, you're over here talking to some girl about her boyfriend?" Eric said with a dramatic gasp.

"Yeah, she stay talking about some dude that she's messing with. I don't care nothing about that though. I just be saying 'mmm hmm' and 'uh huh' to everything she says. Like how I be doing my mom's, so she thinks I'm listening."

They both laughed at that.

"Yeah, I be doing that too, dawg." They slapped their hands together, raised them up high and then down low, wiggled their pinky, slid the palms across each other, and pulled back with a snap of their fingers, waving them like the snap had caused an explosion. A handshake he and his friends had been doing with each other for years.

"Nathaniel?" A voice came from behind them. "That does not look like your English work." It was Mrs. Robinson. She'd come back into the room with Ms. Reid, and they were both standing behind Nate.

"Eric, go back to your seat." Ms. Reid told him, pointing in the direction he should be moving.

Eric shrugged and pushed off with his feet, rolling across the floor until he reached his computer station.

Ms. Reid and Mrs. Robinson were standing, side-by-side, looking over Nate's shoulder.

"So, you're in here playing games and holding conversations

instead of getting your work done, knowing full well that the year is almost over, and you don't have much time left? That doesn't seem very smart at all." Mrs. Robinson shook her head.

"I was doing my work." Nate started to explain.

"Well, that doesn't look like schoolwork to me. What about you, Ms. Reid? What do you think?"

Mrs. Robinson started to take a step toward Nate to get a better look at his screen. He hit two buttons on the keyboard and immediately closed the window containing the conversation he was just having.

"Oh, so that's what we're doing now?" She said. "How about we call your mother and tell her you're not doing any work?"

"Man, I don't care. I was doing my work. I just took a quick break just like everyone else in here did." Nate said.

"Oh really." Mrs. Robinson was starting to get upset. "We'll see about that. You'll get enough of not doing any work in this class. You're not here to play games, Nate. We're trying to help you pass to the next grade and you don't seem to want to do anything to help yourself."

"Oh, my gawd! I was doing my work!" Nate turned and glared at her. "Just because you come in here for two seconds doesn't mean I wasn't working. Everybody else is in here talking, having conversations and playing games on the computer, but you jumping all over me. I was doing my work. Yeah, I stopped for a second, but I was doing it!"

"Who are you raising your voice at young man?" Mrs. Robinson said, wearing an appalled expression. She'd heard enough.

The bell rang for lunch at that moment and all the students stood and began to leave the lab, headed to the cafeteria. Nate stood to follow.

"I'm still talking to you, Mr. Williams." She stepped in front of him.

"Well, I'm done talking to you." Nate said and walked past her and out of the classroom headed to the cafeteria. He grabbed his lunch and sat down with Eric and Trevor at a table. Mrs. Robinson, Ms. Reid and now Mrs. Calhoun, the school guidance counselor, were hot on his trail.

They surrounded him at the lunch table; Ms. Reid was behind him with Mrs. Robinson and Mrs. Calhoun on each side. They weren't going to give him a chance to get away again. He would have to deal with the issue he was having.

"Nathaniel, apparently you and Eric have some trouble getting your work done when you're together. So, we are going to need you guys to separate, starting now." Mrs. Robinson told the boys sternly.

"What you mean?" Nate exclaimed, growing more and more aggravated. "It's lunch time. We're just sitting here eating lunch. I'm not bothering nobody. I'm not even doing anything."

"Nobody asked you if you were doing anything." Ms. Reid told him. "She asked you to move and have a seat at another table."

"Man, I'm not going nowhere. This ain't even fair." Nate sat back and crossed his arms.

"Nathaniel, get up now or I will be calling your parents." Mrs. Robinson exclaimed.

"Call them. I don't care." Nate said, still not moving. "I didn't do anything. It's like y'all coming in here to mess with me for no reason."

"No reason?" Ms. Reid said. "Look at how disrespectful you're being."

Nate was furious now. He was done talking. He was done trying to explain himself and trying to prove his innocence. As far as he was concerned, once again, he hadn't done anything wrong. It's like they singled him out and ganged up on him in order to make an example of him for the other students.

Stupid teachers.

"Get up, Nathaniel." Mrs. Robinson said.

Nate sat, not moving.

Mrs. Calhoun, a foreign teacher from Nova Scotia, chimed in then. She had a very heavy accent but was still a pretty nice lady based on the students' opinions of her. The guidance counselor usually tried to give the students the benefit of the doubt and work with them when they were having a difficult time; especially when they were having trouble with classroom assignments or simply just getting along and true to her nature, she tried reaching Nate with a soothing voice and logical reasoning.

"Well, it appears that this is a very frustrating situation for all of us and before we consider saying or doing anything to rash, how about we all take a moment to calm down." She said in her melodic accent. "Perhaps we just contact his mother, explain the situation, have her come and spend the day with him and go from there. How does that sound." She was looking at Mrs. Robinson now.

Mrs. Robinson considered what Mrs. Calhoun was saying for a moment and then turned her attention back to Nate.

"I'm going to ask you once more, as nicely as possible, to get up and move to another table." She told him.

"I'll Move." Trevor said, gathering up his lunch.

"Man, I'll move." Eric said, grabbing his tray from the table and getting up as well.

"I didn't ask you or Trevor to move." She said, "I asked Nate to move."

But Eric had already moved to a table across the room to avoid any further conflict and Trevor found a seat in the corner near the door to finish his frozen pizza square and juice.

Stupid, stupid, stupid teachers. Nate thought to himself.

Mrs. Calhoun said something to Ms. Reid and Mrs. Robinson that ended with something that sounded like, 'he just needs a moment to calm down…allow me to take it from here.' The other two ladies threw up their hands and headed off, happy to let Nate be someone else's problem.

Mrs. Calhoun then leaned over Nate's shoulder and spoke to him quietly so the other students wouldn't overhear.

"Finish your lunch." she said sweetly. "Then come pay me a visit in my office."

Nate shrugged his shoulders and pushed his lunch away.

"I don't even want it anymore." He said.

She could see that tears were beginning to well in his eyes. She placed her hand on his shoulder.

"Try not to upset yourself, Nate. I do have to call your mother about this interaction that we just had, but I'm sure it won't be too bad."

"Whatever." Nate said. He got up and waited to follow her to her office. When they arrived, she gestured for him to go ahead and have a seat.

He dropped into one of the big blue cushioned chairs in front of her desk.

"I shouldn't even be in here. I didn't do anything." He told Mrs. Calhoun.

"I know." She said sympathetically.

She picked up the phone and began to dial. The phone rang once, then twice before he could hear a small distant voice answering.

"Good afternoon, I'm trying to reach Mrs. Williams?"

His mother was always quick to answer the phone anytime she saw any of their schools calling. Thanks to Nate, she never knew what to expect.

There was a brief conversation. Mrs. Calhoun explained the

situation and then, in her most professional and polite voice said, "Nate's a good kid and I know he's been trying. We really want to give him an opportunity to finish up the remainder of his school year. So, we don't want to expel him for the last two weeks of the year, which is what would normally happen in a situation such as this where a student is disrespectful and belligerent with the teachers or staff, but especially the principal. So, what we're recommending is a parent shadowing. We'd like you come in tomorrow and spend the entire day with Nate in class."

He knew his mom had probably agreed quickly to that, especially because it seemed like a better option than expulsion. He heard Mrs. Calhoun say, "Yes ma'am. He's sitting right here in front of me."

Great. Now she wants to talk to him. Nate leaned forward with his head in his hands as Mrs. Calhoun handed him the phone.

"Nate?" His mother's voice came through the phone softly. "What's going on?" She asked him.

"Nothing." He answered her quietly.

"Sounds like a little more than nothing to me." She told him. "Sounds like you're jeopardizing the last opportunity this school district was willing to give you."

"Ma, I didn't do anything. They came in there and ganged up on me. First, they telling me I'm not doing the work, when most of my work is done. I just have like two classes left to do. Then they calling me disrespectful for defending myself."

"Okay well, do your teachers know that most of your work is

finished?" She asked. "Why would they be on you about your work if they can clearly see that you are doing it?"

"I can even show you that I'm doing my work." He said.

"Well, you do that when you get home." She told him. "I'll be there with you tomorrow; all day and I'll find out what's going on for myself."

"All right." Nate said solemnly and handed the phone back to Mrs. Calhoun without even a goodbye.

Ms. Calhoun put the phone back to her ear, paused for a moment, then said, "You're very welcome." and hung up.

"You can head on back to class." She told Nate. To his ears it had sounded more like 'claus', but he knew what she meant.

Stupid teachers. Stupid school. Nate thought as he rose from his seat.

"Nate?" Mrs. Calhoun called to him. "I know it's frustrating, but it's not as bad as you think. Just try to stay focused on your work. Okay?"

"Yeah, sure." Nate said as he left her office and headed back to class.

PART FOUR

'The Crew'

He shook his head again as he recalled the day's events.

Stupid, stupid, school. They didn't care. Nobody cared.

He slouched down further in the seat with his face turned toward the window.

"Well, here we are." His mom said as they pulled up to the house.

She turned off the engine and looked over, intending to try and talk to Nate about what had happened at school today. Before she could Nate was already out and, on his way up the stairs onto their porch. He waited patiently next to the door for her to come and unlock it and they walked in together. He made a U-turn for his bedroom before she could say anything to him about school, how he was feeling, or anything else for that matter. She'd wanted to talk more about what had happened at school today and her having to shadow him tomorrow, but he was clearly trying to avoid that conversation completely.

The alternative school that he attended required all of its students to wear a uniform and he was always in a hurry to get out of it as soon as he got home. As he headed back to his room his uniform fell off piece by piece. First his solid white shirt with no logos, labels or insignia came off. Then he kicked off his shoes, black with black laces. Finally went the khaki pants. It was a trail of clothes that led down the hall toward his bedroom.

His daily routine went like clockwork. He came in, stripped off all his clothes and took a shower. After that it was sweatpants and a T-shirt and into the kitchen for a snack and then onto the couch to crash and eat. Then he would throw on his jacket and shoes, no matter what the weather was outside, grab his backpack and head out. He liked to take long walks that took him through the woods that surrounded their home. His mom asked him once what he did on those walks, and he told her that he listened to music and thinks. When she asked him what it is he thinks about, his reply was simple, "Nuthin, just life."

Today was no different. Even though she'd seen his IM conversation with his friend earlier and he'd had a pretty sucky day at school, he didn't seem to be acting any stranger than usual. He came in, showered, snacked, and started to get dressed for his walk.

As 5:00PM approached, she reached for her phone to text him. They'd gotten in the habit of communicating this way, even while they were in the house together because Nate seemed to open up more through text than he did face to face.

"Hey, sweetie. I'm headed out to pick up the rest of the crew. Be right back." She typed quickly.

Nate was still in his room with the door shut.

A few moments passed and he replied, "k."

Once again, she had to stop everything she was doing to pick up her other two children, who both attended the regular high school. In all, she had three children, whom she had lovingly dubbed 'The Wrecking Crew' when they were younger and much more active. This had later been shortened to just 'The Crew', once they had all become teenagers and far less active. Nate was a middle child at 16 years old and sometimes she wondered if this had anything to do with his moodiness. His older brother, David, was 18 and a senior at the high school and his younger sister, Olivia, was 14 and a freshman. Nate was a sophomore this year but had been struggling academically as well as emotionally.

Both David and Olivia were on the high school band and practiced afterschool on most days till five. She pulled up to the high school and found the band just letting out. There was a large group of students congregating outside of the band room door that opened up behind the school and into the back parking lot. She could see David standing with a girl off to the side, having what looked to be a very intense conversation. Olivia was coming out of the building accompanied by two of her girlfriends. They were also having quite an animated conversation as they walked to the car. Olivia tapped the trunk for her mother to open it. Denise pressed the button next to her radio and there was a popping sound as the trunk sprung open. Olivia placed her instrument and her book bag into the trunk and closed it back. Denise could hear her yelling to her brother as she walked around to the driver's side and climbed into the back seat.

"Hey mom."

"Hey sweety. Did you tell your brother I was here?"

"Yeah. I don't know what that boy is doing over there with that girl, but he needs to come on." She said swinging her braids from side to side as she spoke.

"And who is the girl?" Denise asked.

"That's Savanna. She's supposed to be his girlfriend but they don't be acting like it. One minute they cool and the next minute they arguing about something stupid." She was rolling her eyes as she said this.

"I didn't even know he had a girlfriend." Her mother said.

"Yeah, some ole fat girl that's always asking him for money. That's who he's always on the phone with." Olivia explained.

Denise shook her head and beeped the car horn, gesturing for him to come on. She could almost read his lips as he told the girl he had to go, as well as hers as she mouthed, 'whatever' and turned to walk away. He headed for the car with an exasperated look on his face, but had managed to mostly shake it by the time he opened the passenger door and slid in.

"Hey mom, how you doing?" He dropped his backpack onto the floor at his feet and closed the door.

"I'm great." she said with an eyebrow raised. "How are you doing?"

"I'm great too." He said raising his eyebrows in return.

"So, I see." She smirked, "That's exactly what it looked like to me."

He made an unamused chuckling sound and then proceeded to change the subject.

"So how was your day?" He asked her.

"Awesome as always." She replied with a smile." What about yours?"

"My day was pretty good. I did my oral report on my project today and my teacher said it was one of the best in the class."

"Wow, okay. That is pretty good. Have you gotten a grade for it yet?"

"No, not yet. She said she'll let us know tomorrow."

She smiled at David, knowing exactly what he was trying to do. He wanted her off the topic of the girl he was talking to and focused on something else and any conversation about good grades was enough to change the subject.

Olivia chimed in from the back seat.

"Mom, guess what?"

"What's that?" Denise glanced back at her in the rear-view mirror.

"I got picked to do a solo in band today." Olivia said excitedly.

"Oh really?"

"Yup. I was the only one who could play the entire piece all the way through and then this girl had the nerve to get mad because she couldn't play it and the band director kept making her play it over and over again. It wasn't my fault she didn't practice. So now she has an attitude with me. Can you believe that?"

"I can believe it." David mumbled.

"That's exactly why nobody was talking to you." Olivia said rolling her eyes. A signature move that she'd been doing since before she could talk.

"Anyway." Their mother interrupted. "I tell you guys all the time that it doesn't matter what other people think as long as you are doing your best work. So let her be mad, that sounds like a personal problem."

"Yeah." Olivia said. "It's a personal problem that I'm gonna solve for her if I hear my name in her mouth again."

Denise looked at her in the rearview mirror. "You heard what I said. If she has a problem, that's her problem not yours, and it's not your job to make it your problem. But if you should choose to make it your problem, then that means I'll have to make it my problem and neither one of us wants that."

Olivia was looking back at her mom in the mirror. "I know mom. But sometimes it's hard."

"That just means that sometimes you have to try a little harder." Her mother replied. "You don't have to stoop to her level."

"Okay, I'll try to try" Olivia winked, slid back in her seat and pulled out her phone.

Both David and Olivia were now sitting silently, faces down, thumbs moving a mile a minute across the screens of their cell phones. The car was quiet, but it was okay because they were almost home. Denise turned onto the dirt road that led to their house and into the driveway. Nate was standing on the front porch. As the car passed on the driveway, he raised a hand in acknowledgment and everyone in the car waved back.

They got out of the car and headed into the house. She glanced in his direction again. He had both earbuds in and was tightening the straps on his backpack. His head was bobbing ever so slightly to the beat of the music he was listening to. She had a pretty good idea of what type of music it was, more than likely something dark and depressing about how terrible life was and how miserable living was.

She hoped not, but that was usually the case. She watched him step off the porch and head across the front yard to the dirt road. He made his way down the road and disappeared off into the distance. Denise couldn't help but wonder, once again, what it was he did in the woods on these walks of his.

PART FIVE

Something about Trevor

One of the lights over the bathroom sink flickered as Trevor examined himself in the mirror. He was definitely what some people might refer to as a 'Ginger', with his fair complexion and bright red hair. The freckles on his face didn't stand out nearly as much as the ones on his hands and arms, but they were there.

He ran his fingers through his hair. It had been quite a while since his last haircut and the amber strands slid easily through his fingers, falling back onto his shoulders and across his face. A quick shake of his head and his hair parted just enough for him to see.

"My heads on fire." He said out loud. "You look like someone stuck a match up your butt and set your stupid ass head on fire!" He was jamming his index finger into the face of the reflection in the mirror as he shouted this.

He was breathing heavily and could feel his heart beating rapidly. He wanted to punch the face that he saw there but couldn't afford the questions he would be asked in order to explain the broken mirror. There were better ways to release the pressure that had begun to build in his head. He reached under the bowl of the sink feeling for the edge of the tape that he knew he'd find there. He used his thumb nail to loosen the tape, pulling out the razor and raising it to eye level to check for rust spots. Not that it mattered; he would have still used it.

He pulled up his shirt sleeve and ran a finger along the trail of raised lines that led from just above his wrist to the bend of his elbow. In all there were a total of sixteen lines and counting, some completely healed and some only partially. The precision and order of the lines reminded him of a railroad track, one that would eventually derail as it reached the end of the line. But there was still plenty of room above his elbow and soon his right arm would match his left. There the track was forty-two lines long and ran up to his shoulder.

"Never below the wrist." He whispered as he drew the razor across his bicep. "Never below the wrist. Saving that for a special occasion."

He smiled as he repeated the words like a Mantra.

Blood began to run slowly down his arm and drip onto the white porcelain of the sink below in little circular droplets. He drew the razor across his bicep a second time.

"Burn baby, burn! Your hairs on fire! Burn baby, burn!" He sang in a haunting rendition of Disco Inferno.

The drops grew larger and more frequent now. He watched as his blood rained into the sink like a spring shower. Cleansing the world and preparing it for new beginnings. He inhaled deeply and started to pull the razor across once more.

A car door slammed.

His mother was home.

He listened as her keys jingled in the front door as she unlocked it.

"Trev, I'm home." She called out to him.

He turned on the faucet in response. She'd hear the water running and know he was in the bathroom. No need for a reply.

He watched as the water swirled and mixed with the drops of his blood in the sink, tinting it a misty pink before finally circling down the drain.

He reached over and grabbed the roll of toilet paper, wrapped it around his hand several times and then held the wadded tissue paper to his bloody arm. He'd done this enough to know that the bleeding would stop in a minute or two with applied pressure. His book bag was sitting on the toilet seat next to him. He reached in with his right hand and pulled out a roll of duct tape. Using his teeth, he started the roll and wrapped it twice around his arm over the tissue tightly. He grabbed another piece of tissue to wipe any stray drops from the sink, tossed the tape back into his bag and flushed the bloody evidence of his activities. He pulled his shirt sleeve back down, grabbed his bag and made a B-line for his bedroom just down the hall.

His mother must have been listening for the bathroom door. As soon as it opened, she peeked her head out of her own bedroom and called to him.

"Hey Tev! How was your…"

Trevor was in his room with the door closed before she could finish her sentence.

He already knew what she was going to say, just like she already knew how he was going to answer. They'd rehearsed it a thousand times.

'How was your day?'

'Fine.'

'How was school?'

'Fine.'

'How are your classes going?'

'Fine.'

'That's good. Did you eat something?'

'Yes.'

'Ok. Have you had a chance to take your medicine for today?'

'Yeah, I took it.'

'I appreciate that. Well, I had a pretty long day today so I'm going to go kick off my shoes and I'll check in on you in a bit. Okay?'

'Sure.'

It was like playing twenty questions 'Parent's Edition'. Only all the answers were basically the same. Like reading the conversation from a script called 'Things you are supposed to ask your kids to make it seem like you give a damn'. The mom says, 'How was your day?' The son replies, 'Fine.' End scene. The actors depart to their separate dressing rooms and don't speak again until their next scene together.

He could try holding his breath until she came to 'check on him' later. That would be a great way to go, self-inflicted suffocation.

He tossed his bag onto the blue comforter that covered his bed and dropped back into his desk chair. He didn't have time to talk anyway. He had his own work to do. He was only on twenty-three and there were still so many more that needed to be written down and explained.

24.

PART SIX

Nate on one of his walks

Nate stepped onto the front porch and adjusted his hood on his head, pulled the straps to tighten his backpack on his back, slipped both earbuds into his ears and hit play on his phone. Their front yard was huge. The house was set pretty far back from the road that ran in front of it, giving them a bigger front yard than backyard. On his better days, he'd usually head to the front yard and sit under one of the two trees that grew there. Today was not one of those good days. He needed to walk.

He headed across the yard and onto the dirt road. It was warm, not an unusually warm day for late May, but still far too warm for a jacket and hood. It had been in the 80's all week and today was no different at a toasty 85 degrees, but none of that mattered. Nothing mattered to Nate at the moment. He walked along the dirt road with his head down, listening to his music, headed for his usual destination.

He'd taken this walk a hundred times since they'd moved into their house a few years ago. He admitted to himself that he liked the little house in the country. It was down a dirt road that came to a dead end straight into the woods. On days like today that was where his journey began. It never started from inside his house or even when he stepped off the front porch. It was there, where the dirt road came to a dead end that his journey truly began each time.

The house itself was surrounded by trees on almost all sides and to get there you had to turn off the main road and onto a dirt road. It was like being in a completely different world. You went from a main highway, busy with cars and traffic, to a dirt road that gave you that old country home feeling, where you found what looked like a blue schoolhouse with a steeple on top. That was their house.

"Our little cottage in the woods." His mom called it. They all loved it there. It was home and it felt like home from the very beginning.

So when it came to, what he liked to call, 'his long list of personal issues', where they lived wasn't one of them. His family really didn't even bother him. It was more like life was just way too heavy. Sometimes he felt like breathing was too heavy and blinking was too heavy. His heart would race, and he would feel as though everything was coming at him all at once. His teachers were always on his case about completing assignments, telling him he wasn't doing enough or working hard enough or turning in his assignments on time. The reality was, however, that some of the work he really didn't understand and as far as he was concerned, the teachers weren't much help. It was like they didn't care how he felt. They never even asked how he felt. The only thing they cared about was the fact that he wasn't working hard enough or doing enough. He hated those teachers. Well, maybe not hated them, but he hated them.

He watched his feet as he walked down the dirt road. It was a quarter of a mile to where the road dead ends. The road itself couldn't have been more than a half-mile long from start to finish. There were other houses on it as well, not many, but a few. He glanced slightly to his left and saw an older Black woman sitting on the porch with her dog. She didn't wave or acknowledge him, and neither did he her. He didn't know her, and he didn't want to know her, neighbor or not, he kept right on walking. He knew that to her he probably looked like just another black boy in a hoodie looking for trouble, just like to him she just looked like a nosy old lady looking for a reason to call the police. He heard her dog bark once or twice and her tell the dog to hush, as he passed her house.

Where the dirt road ended there was a path that led into the woods. You could drive over it if you had the right vehicle, which is probably how it was made in the first place, hunters going into the woods in the early mornings or the late evenings, to hunt deer. Strangely enough, in the time that he had been taking this path, he'd never seen a single hunter, plenty of deer though.

When he first started making his trips into the woods and telling his mother about his walks, she would always remind him to be careful. To always be wary of snakes that can be anywhere on the ground and to watch out for other people in the woods, they might not be as kind to a young Black man, wearing a hoodie in 80° weather, wandering through the woods alone. She would remind him that not everyone loved him like she did and that some people would treat him like every other young Black man in America, disposable. He didn't always agree with her, he felt like he could handle his own, but in the back of his mind he always remained very aware of his surroundings and enjoyed his walks into the woods because they were peaceful.

The trees were full and lush this time of year and there were all types of things to see. There were birds of every color flying and singing among the treetops and a ton of rabbits, many that seemed fearless as he passed them along the trail. There was even a family of deer that lived deep in the woods that he'd seen quite often on his trips. He could always tell it was the same few and they'd recently added three fawns to the group.

He took his earbuds out and stopped his music. His headphones usually gave him an excuse for tuning people out when he didn't want to be bothered. Now that there was no one else around but him, he didn't need them. He wanted to be able to take in his surroundings, all of it, sights, sounds and smells. If he could choose any place in the world to have to spend what time he had left, this was it. This is where he'd rather be, in the woods surrounded by nature. There was no one here to yell at him, no one here to tell him he wasn't good enough, no one here to remind him that he wasn't working hard enough, no girls who loved you one minute and hated your guts the next. There were no moms to be constantly worrying or reminding or complaining. No spoiled little sisters. No annoying older brothers. Just him and the trees.

He'd been exploring here for some time, which is how he found the lake, deep in the center of the woods, before you reach the farming fields, huge and flat. The fields looked like they hadn't been used in a long time. They went for miles in every direction and were also one of his favorite places. It was just flat, open land, no houses, no people. Sometimes he would go there and stand in the middle of the field all alone.

It was like a balance of his emotions, like it finally matched. Standing in that field made him feel like he was the only person on the planet, which is how he felt on most days, alone. Today though, he was headed to the lake, more precisely, to the clearing next to the lake. He needed to think.

A hefty breeze rushed through the trees, rustling the leaves around him. He lifted his face to it, enjoying it completely. It was a bit warm, but he wore his black jacket with the hoodie because he felt like he needed to always be covered. The jacket made him feel protected; made him feel safe. The breeze had dried the sweat that began to appear on his brow and run down the side of his face. It was also a good indication of how close to the water he was. It was always cooler near to the water.

The lake was still, and the surface shimmered with the afternoon sun. Dragonflies busied themselves buzzing back and forth across the surface and landing on the tall grass that grew at the water's banks. They would take flight with each breeze as the blades swayed, rubbing against its neighbor and making a shushing sound as if it were stilling some sleeping beast.

He made his way around the bank, being sure to stay a safe distance from the water. He was a great swimmer, so drowning was the last thing he was afraid of. It was more, the being drowned while being eaten, that concerned him. He chuckled to himself as he recalled the day that he came home and told his mother about the lake.

He had found it first, and then he and a few of his friends that had stayed over, went back out there together. There were gators in the lake, real live alligators. So far, he'd counted at least three large gators and a few babies. He spent a lot of time watching animal shows and National Geographic, so he knew that those three large gators were nothing to play with and for them to have gotten as big as they had, they were eating something, and he was sure it wasn't just fish.

If the baby gators made it to adulthood without being eaten themselves, there would be a family of large predators in the woods near their home. Nate continued around the bank despite. They didn't bother him, and he didn't bother them and that's the way he planned to keep it. When his mom found out about the gators though, she wasn't happy at all.

He had been so excited he hadn't considered what he was telling his mother as he described just how big the largest of the gators was. He and his friends had run back to the house breathing heavily, pumped full of adrenaline and talking a mile a minute.

"Mom! You wouldn't believe how big that gator was we just saw. We found an old rowboat next to the lake in the woods. You know the one that I told you about?" he said excitedly.

"Oh really." She said, "I hope you didn't try to use it."

She had a sinking feeling that she knew the answer already.

"No, we didn't try to use it." His friend Kevin told her. "It had a hole in it."

Kevin and Nate had been friends for a long time, almost 10 years to be exact. He was tall, fair skinned with thick, dark hair that just brushed his shoulders and had already started growing a mustache and a little beard that made him look much older. Nate's other friend Michael; he'd been friends with since preschool. They practically grew up together. Michael was shorter than Nate by 4 inches, a little husky, and loved to joke. He had exceptional manners and was quick to use them, but Nate's mother knew better. She'd caught them plenty of times laughing at dirty jokes and swearing like sailors.

They always looked stunned when she'd ask them to repeat what they said and then quickly arrive at a word that conveniently rhymed with the assailing swear word. She couldn't tell you how many times she had caught them intensely discussing 'ships' and 'mother pluckers'. Michael wasn't fooling anyone with the 'good manners', and above the top politeness act.

However, being told that her son was in the woods with his friends battling gators is not something that she took lightly.

"No ma'am." Michael added. "The boat had a big hole in it.

"Yeah." Nate chimed in, sounding disappointed. "We did push it in the water, though, to see if it would float. That's how we figured out it had a hole in it."

"So, what you're basically telling me is you pushed it in the water trying to get into it?" Her hands were on her hips now.

"No, mom." He rolled his eyes teasingly at her and she jumped at him as if she were about to grab him and beat him up. He pretended to be startled, throwing his hands up in a mock defensive gesture.

"We were just fooling around, that's all." He assured her. "But you should've seen the gator though! It was huge! We were trying to push the boat into the water, so we didn't notice the gator sitting on the other side of the lake. Then we heard a giant splash!"

The boys replayed their reactions to the loud noise, looking at each other with shocked and amused faces.

"We must have scared it when we started pushing the boat." Michael said.

"Man," Kevin threw his hands up and stretched them as far as they would go. "That thing was a monster. It ain't scared of anything. We probably just pissed him off."

"You probably just, what?" Denise was giving Kevin a hard look.

"No, Mrs. D, I said we MISSED it off. You know, like there were more of us than him and he was probably like, 'Hey y'all makin too much noise. You can 'miss' me with that noise.' And then he splashed in the water and left."

"Yeah, well you can miss me with that lame excuse." She told him. "Watch the language."

"Yes, ma'am." Kevin replied quickly. Nate and Michael pointed at Kevin with their other hands over their mouths as though they were desperately trying to stifle their riotous laughter.

"Not funny guys." Nate's mother said sternly.

"Yeah guys." Kevin said standing next to her and putting his hands on his hips. "Cut it out or she might not cook, and I'll be darned if ya'll keep me from my spaghetti!"

They all broke out into laughter at that, including Denise. These boys were crazy, but she loved them.

"I'm serious you guys." Kevin whined at them, letting his hands fall to his sides and stomping his foot.

She shook her head, "Well I'm glad all you guys came back in one piece. I would've hated to have to call your parents and tell them you were eaten by an alligator."

"That gator wouldn't have got me." Michael said. "I'd push Kevin in and run."

"Wow really?" Kevin looked at him. "And this guy's supposed be my friend."

"Hey, it's every man for himself when it comes alligators." Michael shrugged.

All three boys were shirtless. This had actually been the first thing she'd noticed when they came bursting into the house and into the kitchen. They had been talking so fast that she never got a chance to ask them what she was reminded to ask them now.

"Soooo, where are your shirts?" She was finally able to get in.

"Oh, they got wet." Nate said with a sly little smile.

"And how did they get wet?" She asked.

"Not from going in the lake or anything, ma." He said, giving her that, 'don't worry' tone. "There are just a couple of bogs of muddy water that you can't see until you step in it and sink down. It's not dangerous or anything, you just get tripped up and end up all muddy and wet if you're not watching. We kind of got stuck a couple times while we were walking."

"Yeah, I fell." Kevin said.

"Yeah, he did." Michael added. "And then he grabbed me, trying to keep his balance and I fell."

"Okay well that explains how two of you got wet. That doesn't explain how all three of you got wet." She was eyeing the boys suspiciously.

"Oh, and our shoes are wet too." Nate said, "We took them off and left them on the porch so they could dry."

"I know those are going to stink." Denise wrinkled her nose at the thought.

"Oh yeah, big time." Nate laughed as he and his friends grabbed cold bottles of water from out of the refrigerator and headed back outside on another adventure.

Nate remembered that day fondly. It really had been an adventure and they had had fun. He guessed that sometimes life could be entertaining, adventurous and fun, but most times it was just miserable. Today had been a miserable day, so much so, he wasn't sure if he cared what tomorrow brought, if he saw it all.

When he reached his secret spot, he looked around to see if anyone else had been there. There didn't appear to be any changes that he could see. There was a stool in the clearing that he's brought there some time ago and it still stood in the exact same place as always. He climbed onto the stool letting his backpack drop off to one side. He started to slip one of the earbuds back in when he heard a rustling off to his right. He turned a bit and looked in that direction.

Just inside the tree line was the deer family, residents that roamed freely through these woods. There were four large ones and three fawns, always together whenever he'd spotted them on his walks. They had crossed paths so often that he felt like he knew them personally. He never saw a big male with them like you do on TV. You know, with the big antlers, standing back, watching over the herd. These were always a little smaller, girly looking with no antlers, so he figured they all had to be female. Today, though, there was a new little fawn. It was incredibly small and followed closely behind his mother.

"Hmm." Nate thought. "Guess there's a new kid on the block." He watched the fawn walking with the other deer for a moment. It seemed to realize it was being watched and looked in his direction curiously, its ears perking and twisting this way and that. It had a small white patch in the middle of its forehead that was shaped like a diamond and little white spots ran down its sides. Its eyes were huge and black as it stood motionless, watching him.

He adjusted his weight on the stool, knowing the rest of the troop would notice and they did. They froze in their tracks; mother deer's white tail rose in alert, and she seemed to follow her fawn's gaze to him. They had all spotted him now, sitting still on the stool in a clearing in the woods. They waited a moment to see if he would move again before reacting. He shifted his foot, and they were gone.

That was fine. He didn't need an audience, anyway. If today was the day, he'd rather be alone. He slid both earbuds back into his ears and sat looking up. He was looking up at a rope that hung lazily from a low hanging tree bow, just in front of him. A knot had been tied at one end, a kind of sloppy noose that allowed the remaining portion of the rope to loop just beneath.

"Should it be today?" he asked himself. He'd hated today. He wished it had been yesterday, but today was just as good a day as any.

The music played low in his ears as he watched the rope swing, back and forth, to the slight breeze that was still making its way through the trees.

"Should it be today?" he asked himself again. He'd felt bad but he'd had worse days. Maybe today wasn't as bad as he thought. It definitely wasn't as bad as other days he'd had. He'd wait a little longer. He'd wait until there was absolutely no doubt at all. He slid off the stool, picked up his book bag and turned to head out of the woods and back home.

It wouldn't be today.

Maybe tomorrow.

PART SEVEN

From the High School to the Alternative School

Denise had already started dinner for the evening when the phone rang. It wasn't a number that she recognized, but it was a local number, so she answered.

"Hello?" she said cautiously.

"Yes, this is Mrs. Sheppard from mental health. I'm trying to reach Mrs. Williams."

Mental health? She thought. Why would someone from mental health be calling her?

"This is Mrs. Williams." She said listening intently.

"How are you doing today Mrs. Williams?" Ms. Shepherd responded cordially.

"I guess it depends on why you're calling." There was a twinge of concern in her voice.

"Well, I was contacted by the school about Nate and the incident that occurred. I was just following up to see if you had gotten him any help considering what I've been told. I received a police report that mentioned that he told the officer that picked him up and his principal that he wanted to kill himself." Her voice echoed Denise's deep-rooted fear.

"That's not exactly what happened." She said defensively. She wasn't about to allow anyone to label her son mentally ill in any way, shape, or form. "He's been going through a lot lately emotionally and he was just having a bad day and made a poor choice. He shared with me some text messages from a young lady he had been talking to. He was just upset and needed to get away for a little while. He had no intentions of harming himself and never said that he wanted to."

"I understand." Ms. Shepherd said. "I'm just going by what the officer put on the police report."

"Well, what the officer wrote wasn't accurate. Nate has already been transferred to the alternative school and has been assigned a mentor there. He also has another mentor that comes to the house to visit and talk with him. I don't honestly feel like it's necessary to also have him signed up for mental health in addition to everything that he's already doing."

Ms. Shepherd was silent for a moment taking into consideration what Denise had just said.

"Yes ma'am. I understand, that maybe how you feel, but it's my job to follow up on cases such as this. Anytime we are told that a child is having these types of dark thoughts we like to try to get ahead of it and provide them with some type of assistance. You can take some time to think about it, but if you could come in and fill out the paperwork, we could at least get that part done."

"That's fine." Denise tried not to be offended, but somehow, she couldn't help but be just a little. She just wanted the woman who was trying to make her baby sound crazy, off her phone. She had no intention of going to the mental health office to fill out any paperwork, but if that's what the lady needed to hear then that's what she would hear.

"Great." Ms. Shepherd said. "Just give me a call as soon as you're able to do so and we will go from there."

"Okay. Thank you for calling." Denise hung up the phone and tried to push the discomfort it had caused to the deepest recesses of her mind. Try as she might her mind couldn't help but wander back to that day though. It had been an incredibly long day. An incredibly long, hard, frustrating day.

The evening before all the trouble started, she had noticed that Nate's routine had changed slightly, but she hadn't really thought anything of it. Usually, he would go out for his walk and meet up with a friend of his, a young lady who she knew he really liked. Often from her bedroom window she could see them walking together, holding hands, and sometimes hugging. Whenever she asked about the girl, he would always say that she was just a friend. She knew better though. It must be a guy thing not to want to talk to your mom about your new girlfriend.

They went on like that for some time. Every day Nate would come home and wait for her to get home after school, and they would go on their walk together. He had been the happiest she'd seen him for some time, so she didn't mind. But on that particular evening he didn't go out. He spent an hour or two sitting on the front porch texting feverishly. He'd been quiet the entire evening, barely speaking to anyone.

When he finally did come in from the porch he went straight to his room and got in the bed. She peeked in on him once or twice and asked him if he was all right. He nodded and gave her a weak smile. So, she left it alone. Her motherly instincts told her that there was more there than he was letting on, but she didn't want to pry too much or push too hard and simply reassured him that if he needed to talk, she was there.

The next morning his mood seemed to have lightened somewhat. He was up and dressed early and ready for school and even beat his siblings to the door when it was time to go. Denise eyeballed him suspiciously. There was something off about his appearance today and she was trying to put her finger on it. Finally, she figured out exactly what it was.

"Why does your book bag look so big?" She asked him. Her brow furrowed with concern.

His bag had been filled to the brim with something. It was big and pushed all the way out to its seams. It made it look like he was going hiking rather than to school.

"It's just some snacks and some water mom that's all." He assured her.

"Well must be a lot of water and snacks." She said shaking her head.

He was probably taking enough to share with his friends at school, so she didn't think anything of that either. He was always taking something to school to share with his friends. Sometimes she even bought extra snacks and drinks because she knew all of her crew like to take things to school to share.

"Well, okay let's go then." She told him, but she still couldn't quite shake the feeling that something just wasn't right.

They all jumped in the car and headed to school. When they got there something still seemed a bit off. She told them all to have a good day and that she would see them later and pulled off. She was headed for home so that she could get some of her own work done. She'd been working from home for a little over a year now, having started her own business, and it kept her pretty busy. As she was riding, she heard a text come in on her phone. At the next red light, she glanced down at the new message. It was from David.

It read, "Mom, nobody can find Nate."

She pulled over into the next gas station she saw and threw the car in park.

"What do you mean?" She texted back.

David's response was quick.

"No one knows where he is. A few of his friends said they saw him leave campus."

"On my way." She replied.

She tossed her phone in the passenger seat, threw the car into drive, swung around and was back on the road headed to the high school. When she got there David was waiting at the back fence for her. He ran over to the car and leaned into the open window.

"What the heck is going on?" She asked.

"Mom, to tell you the truth I really don't know. Some of his friends said they saw him leave campus and they went and told the principal because he was texting people telling them that he was sorry and that he didn't want to live anymore. I guess they got worried and reported it."

"I don't understand this." His mother said. "He seemed fine this morning. I knew I should've checked his book bag."

"Yeah. Well, the bells getting ready to ring, if I hear anything else I'll text you and let you know." He was watching the expression on his mother's face. It seemed to be dancing back and forth between anger, concern, and worry.

"Okay sweetie." She tried to keep her composure in front of her oldest son. "You go back in, and I'm going to ride around and see if I can see him anywhere."

"Okay mom." He rose slowly and turned to head back into the building, glancing back once with the same look of concern on his face.

She pulled off. This was her second time at the high school today and it wasn't even 8 o'clock yet. Where could he have possibly gone? Why did he leave? He seemed fine this morning. They hadn't had a fight or an argument in weeks, so she didn't understand what would compel him to leave campus immediately after being dropped off to school. Or maybe she did know. She grabbed her phone and tried calling him before she pulled back out into the street. The call went straight to voicemail, frustrating her even further.

She dropped the phone back into the passenger seat and thought back to his strange behavior the night before. She recalled the excessive texting, going to bed early without dinner and even telling her that he was fine though his face said something different. This had to be about a girl. This wasn't the first time Nate had runoff, as a matter of fact, it wasn't even the third or fourth time. But every time he had; it had involved a girl. She must've broken up with him, but even so, this was ridiculous.

Denise rode around for about an hour. She stayed close to the school at first thinking that he couldn't have possibly gotten very far so quickly. Then she expanded her search into the surrounding neighborhoods. She thought maybe he had gone through the back gate where the kids sneak off sometimes when they're cutting school. That gate leads into a cul-de-sac in a small community of cookie-cutter houses. She rode up and down each of the eight streets that made up the little neighborhood. He was nowhere to be found.

Like any mother, her mind began to present to her a million scenarios of what could've happened to her son. She saw strange cars pulling over and offering him rides that he gets into and is never heard from again. She saw him being invited into what seemed like a friendly, family home and then turned into a Jeffrey Dahmer style meal. She even pictured him being hit by a truck as he walked along the roadside and rolling into a ditch where no one could see him.

What if she rode by him in that ditch multiple times and he was too injured to reach his phone and text her? She pulled on the side of the road and tried calling him again. The call to voicemail, again, so she started texting, their usual means of communication.

"WHERE ARE YOU?!" She demanded in all caps, as strongly as possible through the text message. She hoped he could feel her anger and anxiety in those three words.

No response.

"You are supposed to be at school! Where are you!" She texted again.

Still no response.

She was starting to get desperate. He wasn't texting her back and her mind was going a mile a minute. It was time to pull out the big guns.

"Fine. Since you can't text me back and you're grown enough to leave school and go off on your own then there is no need for me to keep your phone on. So, I'll advise you to text whoever it is you need to text now because your phone will be off in a minute!"

She waited a few minutes.

Still no response.

She couldn't believe him. He really did not care about how upset she was or what she must be going through worrying about where he was. The anger that she was feeling had grown from a simmering rage into a full-blown blaze. She wanted to be understanding, but she was getting so tired of his behavior.

The first time he ran away she'd stayed up all night long worrying. It had been cold that night and he had left with no jacket, just the clothes on his back. She figured the cold would cause him to have a change of heart and he would come home, but Nate was stubborn, and it was morning before he finally showed back up. She'd been standing on the porch all night bundled in a jacket and looking up and down the road in every direction. Her husband, Terrence, Nate's stepfather, had gotten in his car and rode the streets with his big floodlight looking into yards and downside streets and dirt roads trying to find him, but if Nate doesn't want to be found, he won't be.

Denise was tired; the emotional drain alone had become almost unbearable. She wouldn't do this again. She turned the car around and headed for home, knowing that riding around would not help the situation any. When she arrived at the house there was a new text on your phone. She must've been so deep in her thoughts that she didn't hear when it came in. It was Nate. He'd sent the text to their family group chat.

"I'm sorry you guys. I'm sorry mom. I'm sorry Dave and Olivia. But I won't be coming back ever again. It's just too much and it's too hard. I'm going to miss all of you guys, but I don't want to be a burden on the family anymore. I love you."

Tears welled up in her eyes as she read the text. Then another one came in, this one from Olivia that simply read, "Wow."

Denise tried texting him directly again. She tried her best to compose herself and suppress the anger that she'd felt earlier.

"Where are you?" She tried asking again. "What's going on?"

Finally, he responded to her text. "I just can't stay at that school any longer." He texted her.

"Why?" She asked.

He replied by sending her screenshots of a text conversation he had had with the young lady he'd been calling his friend.

The conversation she read summed up to this: she didn't want to see him anymore. They had exchanged words and it was clear that they were both incredibly upset. The conversation got heated and they both said things that they knew they could never take back. By the end of the conversation, he had called her a few names and told her he hated her, and she said the only thing that mattered in the entire conversation. 'You should go ahead and kill yourself. I should have never stopped you the first time.'

"Oh my God." Denise mouthed the words silently. She had to find a way to compose herself and be strong for him. If he had attempted such a thing, she wasn't aware of it. And for this girl to tell her baby that he should go through with it pissed her off in ways she didn't think were even possible. But she was the mother and had held in tears and hidden her fears and concerns hundreds of times before. Each time one of her children had injured themselves or were afraid or sad, she had to be the strong one. She had to be the one to reassure them that everything would be alright no matter what she had to do to make it so. Denise couldn't start to count how many imaginary monsters she had killed or boo boos she'd kissed to show her crew that mommy could make anything better. She took a deep breath, wiped the tears that had begun to fall from her eyes and texted him back.

"I understand that you must be upset sweetie, but this is not the way to handle it. You have the entire school looking for you. Tell me where you are, and I'll come and get you. I'm not angry, I just want to make sure you're safe."

A few moments passed and he texted her back, "I'm at the library."

She breathed a sigh of relief, put the car back into drive and pulled out of the driveway speeding toward town. When she arrived at the library there was no sign of Nate outside of the building, so she got out of her car and went in. She looked around in a few places and still did not see him anywhere. She went up to the front desk and spoke with one of the librarians.

"Excuse me miss, did you happen to see a young man wearing a white T-shirt and sweatpants, carrying a gray book bag, come in here a few minutes ago?"

"I'm sorry." The librarian said. "Sometimes we get so busy in here that I don't get an opportunity to look up and see who's coming in. You can look around if you like."

"I did." Denise told her. "But thank you anyway."

She went back out to the car and pulled out her phone again to text Nate.

"I'm at the library. Where are you?" The text read.

Again, a few moments passed before he responded with, "I'm sitting at Walmart."

She didn't know whether to believe him or not. It felt like he was sending her on a wild goose chase, but Walmart was pretty close, so she went to check just in case. She reached her destination within a minute or two and rode through the parking lot trying to see if she saw her son anywhere. But again, he was nowhere to be found.

"Nate seriously." She texted him. "I'm at Walmart and I don't see you anywhere."

This time his response was a bit faster.

"Yeah, they got me."

"Who has got you?" She responded quickly.

"The police got me. They saw me walking and picked me up. We're headed back to the school now."

Good grief. She thought.

When she arrived at the school Nate was sitting in the office along with the principal and the local deputy Sheriff that had picked him up.

The principal explained that unfortunately Nate had received so many detentions and suspensions for his behavior, fighting, not following the school rules and a long list of other infractions and that their only option was to take the matter up with the school board and let them decide how this should be handled. She signed a couple of papers acknowledging that she'd met with the principal, and Nate was officially suspended from the high school until they received notification of the next school board meeting.

The meeting was held a week later. Denise knew most of the members on the school board and had worked with several others. Most of the board members had known Nate since he was very small and hated to see him and his mother going through such a rough time. It was decided that Nate would be allowed to finish out the school year at the local alternative school. Based on his behavior and grades there, a decision would be made at the start of the following school year about whether he'd be allowed to return.

Denise thanked them for allowing him the opportunity.

It had been about a month since the school board's decision and she feared, with today's phone calls, that he was beginning to slip again. There had to be something she could do; some way to help get and keep her boy on the right track, but what?

PART EIGHT

Shadow day

Nate returned home from his walk around seven, just in time for dinner. They sat and ate together as a family, discussing the day's events and laughing at silly jokes and 'remember whens'. Nate stayed quiet through most of the conversation, only smiling when David or Olivia took a shot at him during one of their stories.

"So, what's been going on with you, Nate?" Terrence, Nate's stepdad, asked.

"Nothing much." Nate told him, still looking at his now empty plate.

"Oh yeah?" Olivia said. "That's why mom has to go to school with you tomorrow?"

Nate shot her a look that said just enough to shut her up.

"And how do you know that little miss?" Denise asked her.

"My friend's sister goes to Nate's school. She was in his class when..."

"I'm done." Nate interrupted getting up from the table. He

dropped his dishes in the sink and retreated to his room.

Olivia looked over at her mom and mouthed the word, 'Sorry.'

"It's ok. We'll talk about that later. Just next time let's try using a bit more tact, alright?" She told her softly.

"What's tact?" Olivia asked.

"Tact is when you take people's feelings into consideration before you open your mouth and just say whatever. Right, mom?" David chimed in.

"Yeah, I guess that sums it up pretty well. Nates been having a bit of a tough time, so we want to think before we speak."

"Ok." Olivia agreed and then added. "But I was talking to mom and not 'Momma's boy'." She stuck her tongue out at David.

"Can I cut it off mom? Please? It would solve so many of our problems if you just let me cut it out of her mouth. She doesn't know how to use it right anyway." He was pleading with her mockingly as he held a butter knife in his hand pointed at Olivia.

"No, you can't cut your sister's tongue out. Now help clear the table so we can get the kitchen cleaned up." Denise got up from the table and started collecting the plates.

David and Olivia got up as well. "You can try if you want to die." Olivia told David in a hushed voice.

"Mom! Olivia just threatened to murder me. Tee heard her. Can I cut it out now?"

"I didn't hear a thing." Terrence said, giving Olivia a little wink.

"Aww that's messed up. You taking her side? It's supposed to be us against them!" He made his best pouting face.

"No sir." Terrence threw up both hands and leaned back in his chair. "I learned a valuable lesson when I was your age. Who runs the world?!" He sang.

"Girls!!" Denise and Olivia sang back in return.

"Ok, Beyonce and Beyonce's mini me." David laughed.

They cleaned the kitchen, washed, and put away the dishes and retreated to their neutral corners for the night.

By ten o'clock Denise was ready to call it a night and slid into bed next to Terrence. She sighed heavily. Terrance had been with Denise long enough to know exactly what that meant. He set aside the game he'd been playing on his phone, removed his reading glasses and looked over at her.

"You good? He asked her.

"I guess." she said, pulling the covers up around her waist and leaning back against the headboard. "It's just; sometimes I don't know what to do with him." She told her husband. She crossed her arms and stared at the patterns of triangles on the teal and brown comforter. She sighed again.

"I mean, I try to be supportive and understanding. I try to talk to him instead of yelling. I try to remind him that I love him all the time. That his entire family loves him and it's like it doesn't mean anything to him. He just doesn't care." Denise could feel herself getting worked up again. There was water just behind her eyes, but she fought it back.

Terrence knew that this had been a bad year for Nate and as a result, it had been a bad year for Denise as well. Nate had taken her on quite the emotional roller coaster with his constant issues at school, rebellion, and repeated run-away attempts. Her heart was heavy with worry for her youngest son, and you could see it in her eyes. She kept up a good, strong front for her family's sake, but he knew her better than anyone.

"He's a good kid." Terrence reminded her. "And he tries. Sometimes he could afford to try a little harder, but he does try. I see that in him."

"Yeah, he is a good kid." She repeats his words like a mantra. She turned to him then. "He just seems different somehow."

"Baby, that's just part of growing up and it's hard growing up as a young, black man, in America today; but I'll talk to him. Maybe I can get through to him, you know, man-to-man." He gave her a reassuring smile.

He had the kindest smile she'd ever seen on a man of his stature. He was a very intimidating man, muscular, build like a linebacker with a heart of gold. It was his kind nature and attentiveness to her needs that stole her heart so many years ago. He'd stepped into her life fully aware that she was a package deal with three young children and never looked back. She loved him so much more for being the father theirs hadn't been willing to be.

She reached out then and took his hand in hers. "I think that would be good." she said, giving his hand a little squeeze.

"I had an idea too." She added.

"Oh yeah?" He was genuinely interested. He gave her hand a squeeze in return. "What were you thinking?"

"Well." She paused for a moment. "I've always had a dog growing up and I know you have always had a dog as a young man, and frankly, when I was younger, you know, my dog was who I talked to about everything. At least the things I didn't want other people to know. I know it sounds a little corny or whatever, but maybe if we try getting Nate a dog…. I don't know. I was just thinking…"

"That doesn't sound corny at all." Terrence said. "It'll be nice to have a dog around the house again. What kind of dog were you thinking about getting?"

"I wasn't really thinking about any particular kind." She told him. "I was actually going to head down to the animal shelter and possibly find one there. I figured that adopting a dog would be better than going to a breeder. Perhaps it'll help Nate feel better if he knows that he helped save a dog's life or something like that. You know what I'm trying to say."

"Yeah baby. I know what you're trying to say. How is it that you are so hard and so soft at the same time?" He slid his arm around her waist and pulled her close, giving her a little poke in the side to indicate her literal softness. "You know that's one of the reasons why I love you girl."

"You are so silly." She was giggling uncontrollably. "Now stop and go to sleep. You gotta be up early in the morning for work."

He leaned forward, lips puckered, waiting patiently. Denise shook her head, still smiling, and leaned forward to meet him halfway, kissing him three times softly on the lips.

"Good night baby." She whispered to him.

"Good night." He whispered back. "I love you."

"I love you more." She recites the words to their good night like she has so many nights before, and then recalls one last part of their nightly ritual that she'd neglected and jumped out of the bed. She opened her bedroom door and shouted down the hall.

"GOOD NIGHT YOU GUYS!" She waited for the tell-tale responses from her crew. The one that says, 'we know we should be asleep and therefore unable to answer you, but we're still up and we love you, so we have to respond.'

"Nite Ma." Came a groggy 'sounding' voice from David's room.

"Nite." The next was the more alert voice of Nate, still up, watching movies in the den.

"Go to bed, boy." She called to him.

"Alright." He called back.

"Yeah right." Olivia's voice yelled from her bedroom. "He'll be up all night. I was already falling asleep when I heard you say good night."

"Thanks for all the extra info, Olive Branch." Denise called to her.

"You're welcome. Nite Ma." Olivia replied with a giggle.

She closed the door, turned out the bedroom light and climbed back into bed.

"This could be a really good thing for Nate." She said. She prayed that it would be. She needed something to help her baby boy.

PART NINE

School Daze

Denise spent the next day following Nate from the cafeteria to his computer lab. She sat and worked with him on some of his online assignments and could see where some of them could be a bit confusing. She even found her own eyelids getting heavy as she tried to read through some of the material with him.

"See." Nate said when he caught her yawning a few times. "It's hard to focus on this stuff when you have to look at it all day. I do my work, I guess I'm just not doing it fast enough for them."

"Well, I'm going to have a talk with your principal before we leave today. I understand how tedious it can all seem but it's important for you to do your best work. I'm looking forward to going to all of your graduations. Aren't you?" She asked him.

"I guess so." He said with a shrug.

"You guess so? Boy, don't make me embarrass you in front of your friends." She was wiggling her fingers with the threat of tickling him until she got the answer she was looking for. "You guess so?"

"Mom, chill…ok, I am. Dang." They were both smiling now and trying to keep their laughter hushed so they weren't disturbing the rest of the class.

She glanced up and saw Ms. Reid looking over at them wearing a smile of her own. Denise gave her a thumbs up and Ms. Reid nodded approvingly. But Ms. Reid's weren't the only eyes she felt on them. Looking around the room she spotted a couple of other students looking in their direction. Most looked away as her eyes met theirs, but one young man met her gaze and held it.

"Who's the red head?" She asked Nate.

"Oh, that's my friend Trevor. I meant to ask if him and the guys could spend the night this weekend, but I guess that's pretty much out the window, huh?" Nate asked.

"I'm glad you already know that." Denise told him. "You can have company over next weekend, depending on how your week goes."

"Ok." He didn't like it, but he understood her reasons.

At lunch Nate introduced Trevor to his mom and told him that their get together was being pushed back to next weekend.

"No prob." Trevor said quietly. "It's nice to meet you Mrs. Williams."

"It's nice to meet you too, Trevor. I love your hair. I tried to get mine that color once. Let's just say it didn't come out quite right." She smiled.

"That's an understatement." Nate added. "She looked like she had a pumpkin hat on."

They all laughed. "Wow, really Nate, a pumpkin hat. I thought I looked a bit like strawberry shortcake." she teased.

"Yeah, you did. If Strawberry Shortcake was wearing a pumpkin hat!" They all broke out into laughter once again.

"I don't really like my hair that much." Trevor confided in her. There was something about Nate's mom that made her easy to talk to. He considered Nate very lucky.

"Why?" She asked him. "Your hair is awesome! And it's natural. You know how many women go to the store to buy hair that looks like yours? You should be proud of how great your hair is. You should be proud of how great you are." She told him.

"You're probably the only one that feels that way." He said shyly.

"So, what if I was? It's not your mission in life to care what other people think about you. Before anyone else can truly see you for how great you are, you have to see those traits in yourself. It doesn't matter what other people think, if someone has an issue with you it's usually because they have an issue within themselves, about themselves." She told him, but she was speaking to all the kids that had joined them at their table during the last round of laughter that had broken out.

Mrs. Robinson, Ms. Reid, Mrs. Calhoun and the lunchroom monitor were all standing near the doorway listening as Denise spoke to Trevor and the rest of the students.

"Your only true mission in life is to be the best you that you can possibly be. I tell my kids all the time, if something someone is saying about you isn't true, then why should it upset you? Yes, words can hurt but knowing who you are and what you are capable of will take you further than any insult that you receive and respond to with the same energy. It's easy to be ugly and hateful, especially when you are hurting, but it takes a different kind of strength to stand up, brush off the insults, and shine in your own individual greatness."

"This is what I have to deal with every day you guys." Nate added.

"Well, I love your bighead behind too." Denise stuck her tongue out at her son. "And Trevor, being unique doesn't make you different, it makes you awesome and we are all unique in some way or another."

The bell rang then. The students took turns giving Nate's mom a hug or saying thank you for talking to them as they headed back to class.

Mrs. Robinson called Denise to the side as they were leaving the lunchroom.

"Mrs. Williams, I just wanted to say thank you for taking the time to talk to the students. That was really good advice you were giving them."

"I didn't tell them anything I haven't been telling my own children for years." Denise smiled. "I think that sometimes information just hits different depending on who it's coming from."

"Very true." Mrs. Robinson agreed. "How would you feel about coming back and speaking to all the students? I personally think you would be great."

"Oh, well I would be happy to help in any way I can." Denise replied happily.

"I think you especially made quite the impression on one student in particular." She nodded down the hall. Denise looked just in time to see a flash of red hair disappear into the classroom.

"Yeah, I kind of got the same vibe from him that I get from Nate from time to time. Like he needs someone that's willing to listen just a little harder and pay just a bit more attention." She felt her heart swell at the thought.

"If you and I are on the same page about the boys' emotional states then you are absolutely on the money. He and Nate have more in common then they probably even realize." Mrs. Robinson shook her head as she said this.

Denise understood all too well what she meant. "Well, just let me know what you need and when you need it and I'll be glad to participate."

She headed back to the computer lab to spend the rest of the day with Nate. They worked on his English and Math and were able to get a great deal of work done. By the time the last bell of the day rang Nate's entire mood had changed.

"See, it's not so bad with a little help, right?" She asked him.

"It's not so bad when you're here to help. The other teachers aren't going to sit down with me and help me like that." He huffed.

"Well, I ask you all the time if you want me to help you at home and you always say no."

"Mom, who wants to spend the entire day doing this at school and then have to spend the entire night doing the same boring work at home?" Nate threw his hands in the air as if he were just exhausted with the entire idea.

"You are so dramatic." she told him, throwing her arm over his shoulder as they headed out of the building.

They passed the line of students waiting to get on the bus as they made their way to the car. Nate spotted Trevor waiting at the back of the line.

"Mom, can we give Trev a ride home? There's never anybody there to pick him up in the afternoons and he has to walk like ten miles home." Nate knew he was exaggerating but he also knew it would work on his soft-hearted mother.

"He walks home every day. You should have been said something, it rained like crazy the other day. Poor thing. Tell him to come on." Nate ran over to where Trevor was waiting in line, but she was already waving him over.

She watched as Nate appropriately explained to Mrs. Robinson that they would give Trevor a ride home so he wouldn't have to walk. Mrs. Robinson looked over at Denise and smiled.

The boys came running back over to the car and jumped in.

"Thanks Mrs. Williams." Trevor said climbing into the back seat.

"No problem sweety." She told him.

They rode home talking happily and Denise listened as the boys planned for all the fun, they would have the next weekend. It was nice to see them happy and talking and planning for the future, even if the future they were planning for was only a week away.

She dropped Trevor off at home, which had been a little over four miles from their normal bus stop and not ten as Nate had exclaimed. The house appeared to be empty, and the yard was in need of a good cutting but otherwise everything appeared to be pretty normal.

"You good from here?" Denise asked Trevor as he got out of the car.

"Yes ma'am. My parents will be home a little later." He assured her.

"Alright, well I'm sure you have Nate's number, so if you need anything you call and we'll be right there, ok?"

"Yes ma'am. Thank you." Trevor could see where Nate got his good nature and kind spirit. He hadn't found it on his own, he'd inherited it honestly from her. Trevor found himself wishing Denise was his mother. Perhaps then there would be no built-up pressure needing to be released, no railroad tracks, no list.

He watched the car disappear into the distance from his doorway and then headed into the house to fix something to eat and release some pressure. Then he would go back to work on his list.

PART TEN

Mom gets Nate a dog

The next morning Denise found herself excited about the day's activities. She dropped everyone off on time to school and swung by her favorite corner market to grab a cup of coffee before making the 45-minute trip out to one of the larger animal shelters in the area. Denise had visited some of the smaller local shelters. What she found was that they had been packed full of adorable kittens and rambunctious puppies. She could easily imagine spending a lot of time there playing with all the little fur babies.

It would be fun to have a new puppy in the family, but they all had pretty active lives and a puppy might get lost in all the hustle and bustle. They were adorable, but she had something else in mind. Puppies and kittens get adopted every day and from what she could see, there were plenty of young couples and children, exploring the smaller shelters looking to bring home a new addition to their family.

She was looking for a dog that was just a bit older. Not so old that it couldn't be taught new tricks, but not a puppy either. The larger SPCA in their area had photos online of all of the dogs, cats, kittens and puppies they had available, and there were a lot of them. There were so many animals in need of a good home she wished that she could do more and considered the commercials that ran daily on network TV asking for donations. She'd been meaning to sign up to make monthly donations and it crossed her mind again at that moment. She would definitely have to do that, she thought, as she considered all the photos that she had browsed through.

"One of you guys could make a huge impact in someone's life." She'd spoken to the images. It was another mantra that she was determined to believe.

She made the 45-minute trip in 38. Traffic was great and she managed to find the shelter without issue down a dirt road a little way, tucked in a quiet little nook in the woods on a large plot of land. The land itself had more than likely been donated for the shelter's purpose. She could hear the dogs barking as she approached the building. The shelter being so far out in the country was a perfect spot for it, considering all the noise.

She pulled into the closest parking spot to the front door and sat in the car for a few minutes.

"This is a good idea." She told herself.

A good dog always helps. A good dog has a way of bringing a family together and her family had always had good dogs when she was growing up.

"This is a good idea, and it will help." She repeated that affirmation to herself multiple times and then climbed out of the car and headed to the front door.

As she approached the building, she admired the art and the

brickwork along the walkway leading to the front entrance. There were imprints of animal paws, cats and dogs with their names and the dates they were adopted. There were also metal sculptures of puppies pawing the air and kittens playing with huge crystal balls in the garden.

"They really put a lot of love into the front of this building," Denise thought. "Can't wait to see what's inside."

She pulled open the front door and was immediately welcomed by the receptionist sitting at the desk just off to her left.

"Good morning, ma'am! You're here bright and early. We are so happy to see you." An older woman with strawberry blonde hair that was graying at the roots smiled at her, waving her toward the desk.

"Yes I am." Denise said. "I guess I'm kinda here with a purpose." She smiled back.

"Oh, wonderful and how can we help you today?" the receptionists asked sweetly.

"I'm looking for a dog for my son. Not a puppy, but maybe something a little older, but not so old that we're going to be burying him in the next year or two. Not to be crass." She explained to the woman.

 "Well, we definitely have plenty of dogs in need of a good loving home and a young man to play with. If you like, I'll call Adam, one of our volunteers, and he can take you back out to the dog runs. He knows all of the dogs and their personalities and that way you get to walk around and meet all of our available adoptees." She suggested, still wearing a huge welcoming smile.

"That sounds good. Thank you." Denise replied.

"Alright, you can take a seat in our waiting area." She gestured across from the desk where a row of five chairs lined the wall. "Or feel free to browse our pet novelty area. We've got a lot of great items and 100% of the proceeds go to the shelter. Adam will be right with you."

"Thank you, again." Denise walked across to the sitting area and admired all the colorful dog collars and leashes and bandannas that the shelter had for sale. Maybe she would make a purchase if she was able to find Nate a new friend today.

Adam popped from around the corner bubbling with energy. He was a young guy in probably his mid-twenties, with brown hair neatly brushed and parted to one side. He wore a lime green polo shirt tucked into his khaki shorts with the blue letters SPCA stitch into the fabric. There was the oddest little sparkle in his eyes, like something you would see in a Disney movie. Denise found it both bizarre and delightful at the same time.

"Well, hello there, you must be the young lady who is looking for a new friend for her son." He said walking over to her with his hand extended.

"Yes, it's Denise and you're Adam, right?"

"I certainly am!" He said just as perky as can be. "Follow me; I have lots of friends for you to meet!"

"Okay great!" Denise couldn't help but find Adam's enthusiasm contagious, and her excitement grew as they headed out to take a look at a few of the dogs the shelter had available.

Adam walked her down a long line of dog runs that were situated side-by-side. It was a beautiful sunny day, and all the runs were open, allowing the dogs to come out and feel the grass beneath their feet, and the sun on their coats. Many of them had been resting with their faces turned up to the bright sunshine enjoying the day. As she and Adam turned the corner they were immediately on their feet. Some of them were bouncing two or three feet off the ground with excitement. While others spun like tops, bouncing their front paws off the gate as they did, all of them wagging their tails or nubs or bottoms with such ferocity it seemed almost manic.

Adam glanced over his shoulder at her. "Looks like the guys are super excited today." He said loudly, trying to be heard over the noise. "They've already been fed for the morning and are all worked up and ready to play. As you can see, we have a completely open construction that allows them to get plenty of sun and exercise when the weather permits, and to come in when they don't want to be outside.

It gives you an opportunity to see them in an active environment. You are welcome to wander around and take a look at these guys. They are all absolutely awesome, I can guarantee that. If you have any questions about anybody just let me know. I'll give you a few and then come around and check and see if you've met anybody that you like."

"Okay thank you." Denise said, speaking loudly to be heard. She watched as Adam seemed to practically skip away. "He is such a bubbly guy." She said to herself and turned her attention back to the dog runs.

There were so many of them. She started to walk slowly down the first set of runs that she and Adam had come to. She walked past short dogs and tall dogs, brown dogs and white dogs. She saw a few Rottweilers, which she had a personal preference for, having grown up with them as a child. She saw tons of labs and a few mixed breeds. She even saw a couple of St. Bernard puppies that had a note on their clipboard that said they'd been reported missing and were waiting for their owner to arrive. They were big fluffy cute puppies, and she was glad that their owner had been able to be reunited with them. However, she knew that even if that weren't the case they would be adopted quickly.

She continued to wander past the pens reading the various clipboards that had information about the individual dogs. One read 'Pitbull mix found tied to a dumpster on the side of the grocery store.' Another read 'frisky terrier mix abandoned at the shelter.' One of the worst she saw was a dog named Miracle.

She was a lab shepherd mix and a pretty big girl. Her clipboard read that she'd been tied up, set on fire and left on the side of the road for dead. She was found by good Samaritans and brought to the shelter where he was nursed back to health and is now a happy healthy pup gratefully waiting for her forever home.

"Who could do such a thing to a poor defenseless animal?" She thought. It was a shame how evil people could be. She crouched down so that she was more on Miracle's level. The dog's tail was a blur behind her, wagging uncontrollably, as she barked hysterically.

"Hey there pretty girl." Denise said.

"Bark bark bark bark bark bark!" Miracle replied with her tongue hanging out and drool flying everywhere.

"Okay, you're quite the frisky one, aren't you?" Denise had to back up just a bit to keep from being hit by slobber bombs.

"Bark bark bark bark bark bark!" It was almost as if she wasn't barking at Denise or because of her, but more so because there were dogs around her barking, and she was trying to out bark them. She was determined to be the loudest in the shelter and would not be outdone.

Adam appeared at her side from seemingly nowhere.

"I see you've met Miracle." He said, "I personally think Miracle may be death in one ear, but our vets are so busy that no one has had an opportunity to give it a good thorough looking into. I'm sure that would help to explain the excessive barking. She's a barker but a sweet girl when she's calm. She'd make a great pet in a single dog home." Adam explained.

"Perhaps." Denise replied.

"So have you met anybody that you have any questions about so far?" He held up both hands with his fingers crossed like a hopeful child.

"Well, not quite. I was actually reading the clipboards. Some of their stories are so sad."

"Definitely." Adam said, actually sounding down for an entire split-second. "Well, if you have any questions just let me know." He sang and floated off in another direction, probably to perform some daily tasks or check on his four-legged friends. He seemed to really love his job.

Denise looked around the big yard. It held several groups of dog runs with about six or seven dogs each and then various single pens that dotted the yard here and there. Some of these pens held families of puppies and their mother, who were probably brought into the kennel expecting and gave birth there. Others had dogs that were off on their own, perhaps due to being a bit older or not able to be kept with the rest of the adoptees.

She turned, surveying the various kennels and runs trying to figure out which way she would go next when her eyes locked with one in particular. He was literally looking directly at her.

"Weird." Denise said, mostly to herself and partially to the dog that was staring at her. He was a good-sized black dog with a white starburst shaped patch on his chest. He was sitting at the front of his pen looking over at her as though he were waiting for her to make eye contact with him. He had her attention now and appeared to be calling her over to him with his eyes.

She took a step in his direction, and he shifted his front feet eagerly. His tail wasn't wagging. He wasn't barking. He just sat, staring. She took another step in his direction, and again he shifted his front feet as though he were trying to tell her that that was exactly what he wanted her to do. She moved toward him, slowly at first. He was still holding her gaze. She wondered if he'd been watching her this entire time. There was so much personality in his face and eyes. So much character and expression and when she was standing face-to-face with him it was even clearer to see that he wasn't like the rest of the dogs here.

She reached over and picked up his clipboard, eyes still locked. She had to tear herself away from his gaze to read the information on the sheet.

Name: Blackie

Breed: Cane Corso or Pos. Mastiff mix

Color: Black

Age" Three to five years

Background: Found tied to shelter fence abandoned, seriously injured, missing left eye.

She looked down at him again. She hadn't even noticed how he was holding her gaze with only one eye. She could've sworn she saw two, but sure enough, one eye was stitched completely shut and one huge brown eye continued to stare up at her. Denise let the clipboard drop back into place and crouched down in front of the dog whose name she now knew was Blackie.

"Okay guy." She said to him. "I'm looking for a friend for my son and our family doesn't tend to discriminate against being a little different. Her gaze flickered to his missing eye. "So, what do you think?" She asked him fully expecting a response.

He raised one big paw to the fence and pressed it there. She raised her hand and placed it against his paw and felt the warmth against her skin.

"So, is that a yes to coming home with me?"

Blackie huffed out a gruff little sound of acknowledgment that she accepted as a yes.

He removed his paw from the fence, stood, circled three times, and then sat back down.

"Okay well I'll definitely take that as a yes." She said smiling.

"Awesome sauce!" Came a voice from beside her. It was Adam who had once again mysteriously appeared next to her. "I knew it would be Blackie. I just knew it. He is quite the character."

Denise looked at him. "What do you mean?"

"He is going to be really good for your boy." Adam explained with a sly little smile. "I believe he really will. It's almost like he's been waiting just for you. This is the most he's ever responded to anyone."

Adam reached over and grabbed a chain leash that was hanging on one side of the dog pen and opened the gate.

"Shouldn't you put him on the leash first, so he doesn't run off?" Denise asked.

Adam was still wearing the same sly little smile as he swung the gate wide open. Blackie walked out of the open gate, over to Denise and sat in front of her waiting patiently.

Adam handed her the leash. "Just snap that lease right to his little collar and we'll go get some paperwork started," Adam said bouncing up and down on his toes excitedly. Denise, a bit surprised, reached down, clamped the leash to Blackie's collar and slid the loop around her own wrist.

"Awesome, awesome, awesome!" Adam said. "Follow me."

They headed back to the shelter's office with Denise close behind and Blackie walking diligently at her side. She glanced down several times surprised that he was so well-trained, why would someone just abandon him at the shelter. He was calm, well-mannered, and seemed to be incredibly obedient. He never once tugged at the leash. He stopped when she stopped and moved when she moved.

"Abused and abandoned." She thought.

When they walked into the office together the woman at the front desk smiled.

"He's going to be perfect for you guys." She said, "He is an awesome dog; we hate to see him go but are happy to see him go to a loving home."

Denise was being assured more and more that she'd made an awesome choice with Blackie. She wasn't so sure about the name though, but she figured that Nate would probably change that.

She filled out the paperwork and paid a small $60 fee. They gave her his tags for the shots he'd received, which were promptly added to his collar and that was that. They had a dog and apparently an incredibly special dog, at least according to the people at the shelter, and she prayed that they were right. She hoped that Blackie would be good for Nate and that he would be a reminder to the troubled young man that he had family that loved him and would always look out for him and protect him.

She suspected that she wouldn't have to do much when it came to getting Blackie into the car and she was right. He waited patiently for the back door to be opened, climbed across the seat to the passenger side near the window and sat down. The ride home was peaceful; Blackie sat watching his surroundings fly by and looked up at Denise from time to time. She would glance back at him in the rearview mirror and find him returning her gaze. There was definitely something peculiar about this dog, but a good, peaceful peculiar.

When they got home, he obediently climbed out of the car, followed her up the steps to the porch and into the house. She walked him around the entire house, giving him an opportunity to take in the new sites, sounds and smells. She showed Blackie all the children's rooms, introducing them to him by their scents before he met them in person.

"This is David's room." She told him, opening the door. "David is my oldest son and he's a little bit messy." Blackie walked into the room, stepping over shirts and pants and sneakers thrown everywhere, taking in all the smells of left-over fried chicken, cups full of soda and juice and a pack of cookies that she didn't even know were slid up under the bed. There was lots to smell here.

"Okay." She said. Blackie took the cue and found his way back to her side. "Gonna have to have a word with him about getting this room cleaned up." She told the dog as she shut the door back.

"This is my daughter, Olivia's room." She opened the door to a whole new variety of smells. Here the smells were strong and acidic. There were little bottles all lined up on a table of various shapes and sizes and motionless animals set everywhere, staring blindly off into the distance. He nudged a few of them with his nose.

"Yeah, she's a fan of stuffed animals." Denise told him. "Let's avoid tearing the stuffing out of these please. She smiled at him as he walked back over to the table with all the little bottles. He sniffed among them and drew back sharply, blowing out a series of sneezes.

"She also has a thing for nail polish. I think she does her nails at least three or four times a week. Her world always smells like nail polish remover."

He huffed again, shaking his head and then turning and walking out the door.

"Yeah, that pretty much sums it up." She laughed as she closed the door behind them.

They turned to head back down the hall toward Nate's room.

"And this is your new buddy's room." He sat next to her and looked up into her face. "I don't know if you remember me telling you that you're going to be a new friend for my son, but this is the son that I was referring to." She opened the door to his bedroom and Blackie walked in to explore.

"Nate can be a little messy sometimes too. His mess is more of an 'I don't care', messy." She explained to Blackie as though he understood.

Nate's bed was covered in the laundry that she'd given him two nights ago to put away. It looked as though he'd been sleeping on them with no sheets on his bed. The sheets and blanket were balled up in a pile at the foot of the bed and both his pillows were thrown onto the floor. Blackie walked over and sniffed both pillows flipping them over as he did. He walked over to the bed and the blankets and then walked back to Denise at the door sitting in front of her. He looked up and whimpered.

"Yeah, it probably does feel and smell a little sad in here." she said, shaking her head and looking around mournfully. There were no pictures on the wall. No posters or artwork of any kind.

"I told him that we could decorate his room, you know, do something with it to make it more personal." She said solemnly, more to herself than to the dog. Blackie placed his paw on the front of her foot. She looked down at him, placed a hand on his head and began to rub the spot on the back of his skull behind both ears with her fingers.

"Hopefully you'll be a great distraction from those sad thoughts and feelings he has." She says directly to him this time. She slid her foot from beneath his paw and stepped to one side signaling for him to come out of the room, which he did. She closed the door behind them.

"Well guy, we brought you home and I guess it's time to get you set up and make this pace feel a little more like home for you too." She went into the kitchen and pulled a plastic Tupperware bowl from one of the cabinets and filled it with water. "We'll all go and do a little shopping for you when everyone gets home from school." She said. "This should do for now, and the shelter gave us a small bag of dog food, so I'll feed you a little later too, okay guy?" She said, patting him on the head again.

 Just then her 2 o'clock alarm went off.

" Well, there's my cue." She said, looking around the house. "So should I put you in one of the bedrooms or maybe I should put you in the bathroom, so you feel a little bit more secure about me leaving you home alone. I'd hate to come back and find my house has been eaten by a big black dog."

Blackie was looking up at her with his head cocked to the side and both ears perked up as though he had just been offended by what she said.

"I don't know if you understand but this would be your first time ever being here alone. Am I just supposed to trust you out in the open alone while I'm gone?"

Blackie walked over to the kitchen table, spun three times and then plopped down stretching his back legs completely, resting his head on is front paws and looked up at her again.

"Okay, okay I get it. You're a good dog, so I'm going to trust you. Please don't make me regret it." She pleaded with him.

He flicked his nub of a tail a few times and then stills it in acknowledgment.

"You are the most bizarre dog I think I've ever met." She tells him. "I feel like we were literally holding a conversation where I understand you and you understand me. It's weird but I like it. I'll be right back." She grabbed her keys and headed out the door.

Denise sat, tapping her thumbs on the steering wheel anxiously as she waited for Nate's bus to arrive. She was beginning to have second thoughts about leaving the family's new dog home alone and loose in the house. She can't help but wonder if she gave him too much credit when it came to being left in the house alone.

She'd had too many bad experiences trying to leave a new dog home alone, just to have it destroy everything in the house out of boredom or anxiety. Blackie just didn't seem like that kind of dog, if he was a dog at all. It was a strange thought, but people have claimed to have reincarnated as worst things. Why not a dog?

The screech of the bus's brakes pulled her from her train of thought. She watched as the students got off the bus laughing and joking as they stepped between the School Resource Officer and their Principal, saying their farewells and going their separate ways as always.

Nate hopped into the passenger seat.

"Hey mom." He said letting his book bag fall to the floor.

"Hey baby." She replied with a smile.

"What?" he asked pausing midway through fastening his seatbelt.

"Nothing. So, where's Trevor? Aren't we taking him home today?" She made a conscious effort to hide her grin and change the subject a bit.

"Nah, he wasn't in school today." Nate tells her, still eyeing her suspiciously.

"Oh, ok. So how was your day?" She asks.

Nate fastened his seatbelt and gave her a look.

"What's going on?" he asked with an eyebrow raised.

"What do you mean?" Denise checks her rear-view mirror and starts to back up.

"Well for starters, because you're smiling for no reason."

"I can smile if I want to. You're my son and I love you. You always give me a reason to smile." She tells him as they pull out of the parking lot.

He looks at her for a moment. "I didn't give you a reason to smile today."

"You give me a reason to smile every day, baby, I love you." She was using her baby-talk voice which she knew Nate hated.

"Really mom." He said, preparing to slide his earbuds into his ears.

"Well, I may have gotten you a surprise." She finally admitted.

He paused again and looked at her. "A surprise…for what, doing awesome in school?" He added sarcastically.

"Nate, come on now. I can do something nice for you if I want to." It troubled her a little that he didn't feel like he deserved anything.

"I guess so." He said and slid his earbuds in his ears.

Eight minutes of silence and they were home. Today was a bit different than usual though, he was up the steps and onto the porch in a flash and waiting for her to unlock the door as usual, but this time with an expression of anticipation on his face rather than annoyed impatience. They walked in together and he stopped as soon as he saw Blackie.

"A dog?" He said, "We got a dog?"

"Well, actually, you got a dog, but yes, I guess you can say he'd be a part of the family, so we got a dog. But I got him more for you than anything. I feel like he's going to be good for you." She explained.

"Okay, so…we got a dog." Nate repeated his former question as a statement of fact.

Denise was far more excited about her surprise than Nate appeared to be. "His name is Blackie, but you can change it if you want. That's his shelter name. I'm sure he'd be happy to have that changed now that he has a home."

"Wow." Nate said, sounding unenthused. "So…thank you?"

He didn't seem particularly excited by the idea of the dog, but she did know that he liked dogs. Maybe the entire idea would take some getting used to.

"Ok so go and say hello to him. You know, let him smell you and get to know you and all that good stuff." She said giving Nate a little nudge.

Nate walked over to the dog who sat up from his stretched-out position on the floor. He hadn't moved from that spot the entire time that Dense had been gone. This she found both impressive and once again…bizarre.

"Hey dog, or Blackie or whatever." Nate looked down at the new addition to their family.

Blackie rose up slowly from his seated position, pushing himself up with his hind legs so he was able to rest his front paws on Nate's shoulders.

"Woahhh." Nate said steadying himself. "Okay you are a big guy."

He began to pet Blackie on his head and down the side of his body. Blackie pushed off and sat back on the floor in front of him, raising one paw which Nate reached for and shook.

"Okay Blackie, I'm Nate." He looked over at his mother. "Yeah, Blackie is kind of a dumb name for a black dog."

She smiled at the spark of interest that she saw in his face. "Not dumb, just basic." She said. "But you can rename him. I'm sure he'll be happy with whatever you choose."

"Okay." Nate said. "Okay."

PART ELEVEN

Tears, Eggos and Orange Juice

Trevor glanced over at the clock. It was 7:45 AM. His alarm hadn't sounded this morning and both his mother, and the school bus were long gone by now. That was fine though, he hadn't planned to go in today anyway. His father normally had to be at work by 10 and liked to get there early, so he would be leaving soon as well. He was usually on the road by 8:30AM and pulling into his factory parking lot by 9:30. So Trevor just laid there, staring at the ceiling, waiting patiently for the time to pass.

His father rarely checked to see if Trevor was in his room or gone to school for the day, so as long as he was quiet until he left, he'd have the house to himself for the entire day and most of the night. His mother wouldn't be home until late tonight and his father would make some excuse about working late to avoid coming home all together in an effort to not have to watch his wife spend yet another year crying.

The time seemed to creep as he lay there waiting, but his patience eventually paid off and he was rewarded with the sound of his father's truck door slamming and the engine rumbling to life. Trevor listened as the truck purred like a ten-ton kitty, and then idled down as it was thrown into reverse and began to back out of the driveway. He continued listening as the truck made its way down the street and away from their house, escaping the overbearing weight of this day.

Once the truck was out of earshot, Trevor got up to go about his day. He opened his bedroom door and stood in the doorway for a moment staring across the hall at the door that was directly across from his. He felt his stomach lurch in a wave, like riding a roller coaster or hitting that bump in the road at just the right speed to give you butterflies. He planned to go in there today, just not quite yet. He needed to eat first and take his meds first, then he'd be ready.

He walked sleepily down the hall looking at the pictures that hung on the wall as he passed. There were pictures of his grandparents, his aunts, and uncles. Pictures of him as a baby, him in kindergarten and at his elementary and Jr. High school graduations. There were pictures of his parents when they were dating and from their wedding. The walls were covered on both sides with hundreds of pictures of all shapes and sizes. They'd been hung similarly in their old house except there had been several more. Those pictures were no longer hung where they could be seen.

In the kitchen he went to the freezer and pulled out a box of frozen waffles. He popped a couple into the toaster and took out two plates and two glasses. While the waffles were busy toasting, he filled both glasses with orange juice. The waffles popped and he plucked them from the toaster and placed one on the plate directly in front of him and the other on the plate next to the other glass of juice.

He found his meds in a little pill container on the counter marked 'F' for Friday. It was in the same place his mother left it every day with a little sticky note that read: 'Don't forget', in her swirly handwriting. He opened the container and turned the two pills out into his hand. One was an anti-depressant and the other was for anxiety. They appeared to be a bit of an oxymoron, but they did a pretty decent job of keeping him level.

With the end of the month quickly approaching it would be time to renew his prescription soon, but he had no intention of having to take these pills forever. Sometimes he didn't take them at all. He'd been saving them in a baggy he kept in his book bag. Today though, he took them both, washing them down with a few sips of orange juice and a couple dry bites of waffle.

When he'd had enough, he grabbed the other glass and plate and headed back down the hall. He stopped in front of the door that was directly across from his and tucked the glass in the crook of his arm so he could use his free hand to open the door. He stepped into the room and used his foot to close the door most of the way behind himself.

He was careful not to touch anything once he was inside. All of the furniture was coated in a light layer of dust, and he didn't want to disturb anything more than necessary.

"I figured you'd probably be here today, so I brought you, our favorite." Trevor said. He sat the plate and glass down on the night stand next to the bed. "Eggos and orange juice."

He picked up a picture that showed him and another smiling young man that looked quite a bit like him, holding up Eggos in a silly breakfast toast.

"Let go my Eggo." Trevor said softly, remembering the day the picture was taken.

He looked around the room which was filled with baseball

trophies, framed school certificates and picture after picture of the same smiling face everywhere. Baby pictures, first steps, milestones, graduations, family vacations, they were all here. Any picture that he was in was in this room, the smiling boy that no one talked about. The boy that looked kind of like him, or perhaps Trevor looked like the boy. Same cheekbones, bright eyes, and strawberry hair. His brother.... Jacob.

None of those pictures adorned the walls of their new house. There were no pictures of his brother outside of this shrine that had been created by their mother. None except for the small strip that he kept in his wallet from their trip to the fair a few years back.

Today would mark two full years that Jake had been gone and his parents were determined to avoid this day at all costs. His mother would go out drinking with her friends and return home too drunk to care what day it was. Yet even in her drunken stupor she would still retreat to her room and spend the rest of the night crying. If you asked her why she was crying she would stop long enough to simply reply, 'It's just too sad. So sad. So sad.' Then the tears would begin again until she cried herself to sleep.

His father would work late, or at least that's what he would call and say, and wouldn't return home until the following day once things had had a chance to calm down and go back to normal. He made the same excuse for every birthday, Christmas, special occasion and of course today of all days. So, it was left up to Trevor to remember. While his parents did everything they could to forget, it was left up to him to remember it all.

Today was one of those days that he felt especially close to his brother. Like his spirit filled the room and made it easier to communicate with him. Trevor spent the next several hours telling Jake about everything that had been going on since he spoke with him last year. He told him about the new house and how difficult the move had been. How he hadn't wanted to leave him there in the cold hard ground, but their parents and the doctors had felt that it wasn't 'healthy' for him to be spending so much time at the grave site. He told Jake about his trip to the hospital to have his stomach pumped after he'd taken their mother's entire bottle of codeine. He told Jake that he thought he'd seen him then but wasn't sure, so when he got the opportunity, he tried again because he wanted to see and talk to him. This time he'd taken sleeping pills that they thought they'd hidden from him. He'd spent three days in the hospital at that time and a month in a mental health facility. Before that it had only been a week.

He explained to Jake that when he fell asleep, he heard a voice telling him exactly what he needed to do to be with his brother again and he shared his plans with Jacob. Before he realized it hours had passed, and his stomach was growling.

"Ready for lunch?" He asked the still smiling face in the photograph.

Trevor collected the plate with the untouched waffle and glass of juice and headed back to the kitchen. In his medicated mind he saw several bites taken out of the waffle and the juice practically gone. He sat the dishes in the sink and went about making sandwiches for them to have for lunch. He grabbed two bags of chips and two sodas and headed back into Jake's room.

He put Jake's food on the nightstand and sat his on the bed next to him. They had lunch together, each completely finishing their meal, or at least in Trevor's mind, and then went on discussing his plan for them to be reunited.

Trevor pulled his feet up into the bed and leaned back against the headboard.

"You know Jake, since you've been gone it's like they don't even see me anymore. All they see is how sad they are and how much they miss you. It's like we both died in that accident when you did." He told his brother.

The emotional strain of the day had begun to wear on him and before he realized it, he had closed his eyes and dozed off.

Trevor found himself walking through thick white mist, lost in a world of his mind's own creation. In the distance he could see a figure standing.

"Hello!" He called to the figure standing in the mist.

"Hey there kiddo." The familiar voice came from behind him.

"Jake?" Trevor turned and found his brother standing behind him with arms spread wide. He looked back where he'd thought he'd seen a figure standing in the mist, but it was gone and now his brother stood smiling, arms outstretched, waiting patiently. Trevor ran into his embrace wrapping his own arms around his brother's waist, never wanting to let go.

"What are you doing here?" Trevor asked him almost choked with tears.

"I came to see you, stupid. Or to be more precise I came to talk to you. I see you every day and I'm with you everywhere you go, but I guess we don't really get to talk, at least not the way that normal people do. Oh, and thanks for the waffle and juice. That'll probably always be my favorite breakfast." Jake smiled down at his little brother.

"Yeah, mine too." They both laughed at this still held in one another's embrace. "I really miss you, Jake. I wish you were still here."

Jake placed a hand on each of Trevor's shoulders and held him back arm's length. "I just told you, I'm always with you. You talk to me all the time, and as long as you continue to remember me, I'll always be with you."

Tears began to roll down Trevor's cheeks. "It's not the same and you know it."

"I know." Jake said wiping the tears from his little brother's face. "It is also way too soon for you to be here. You're only 16 Trev, you have your entire life ahead of you. I was looking forward to seeing you graduate and meeting my nieces and nephews. All this gets better with time, you just have to be patient."

Trevor's hands dropped to his sides. "I have been patient and it hasn't gotten any better. As a matter fact it's only gotten worse. Mom and dad don't even talk anymore, and I told you it's like I died when you died. I'm just a ghost in that house so I might as well be one for real. Then they can build a shrine to me like they did you and ignore that too."

"No Trevor. You are so much more than that. I love you." Jake told him taking a step back.

"Don't leave!" Trevor shouted.

"I have to kiddo, but we'll talk again soon." He took another step back.

"Please Jake," Trevor pleaded with his brother. "Please don't leave, I can't stand to be alone anymore. It's too much."

"You're never alone little brother." Tears of blood began to run from Jake's eyes and the mist surrounding them grew thicker with each passing moment.

"Jake!" Trevor reached for his brother who had begun drifting further and further away.

The tears of blood had become a stream that now flowed heavily from his eyes, his ears and his nose. His body was washed in it as he drifted. Trevor chased after him only able to remain just out of reach of Jakes extended bloody hand. Gashes had begun to open up all over Jakes body, across his face, his neck, his chest and finally a horrifically huge gash that severed his body at the waste. His drifting stopped then and Trevor watched as his upper torso began to slide slowly off the lower half of his body until he collapsed to the ground in two halves. Trevor fell to his knees near his brother's head.

"Jake!!!!!" He screamed hysterically now. "Jake!!!!!!!!!!!!"

Jakes' eyes locked with Trevor's as he reached up and took his younger brother by the shoulders.

"What are you doing?" Jake asked him quietly.

"What?" Trevor wasn't quite sure what Jake was talking about.

Jake's grip tightened on Trevor's shoulders, and he began to shake him violently. "What are you doing?! What are you doing? You're not supposed to be here!" He shook Trevor until his brain felt as though it were rattling around in his head.

"Get out!" Jake screamed at him. "You're not supposed to be in here! Get out now!!!"

Trevor snatched away causing his eyes to fly open. The eyes that met his now were those of his mother who was still shaking him frantically and screaming, "What are you doing in here!"

Trevor sat up in the bed and looked toward the window. It was dark and if his mother was home, that meant it was also pretty late. He'd fallen asleep and she'd found him lying there in Jake's bed.

Before he could speak her hand burned fire into the side of his face with a heavy slap. "How dare you come into this room! How dare you!" She screamed; her breath hot with the scent of alcohol.

Trevor shoved her away and scrambled to his feet.

"How dare I come into my own brother's room? My dead brother who never once stepped foot in this house but somehow still has a room here that you keep like a secret shame!" He shouted back at her.

"You don't speak to me that way!" She managed to slur the words out as dignified as she could manage in her current state. "I am the mother here!"

"Some mother!" Trevor yelled. "You don't care about Jake, just like you don't care about me. You hide all of his pictures in this room with the door shut and won't even come to this end of the hall to check on the only remaining child that you have! You move us to a new house and then create this," He waves his hand around to indicate the entire room. "You create this directly across from my room so that I have to be constantly reminded that you both blame me for what happened to Jake!"

"No!" His mother screamed back. "I loved Jake and I still do. I love both of you boys! How could you even say such a thing to me?" She'd begun to cry. Trevor could tell that she'd already been crying, but none of that mattered now.

"If you love him so much then why are you hiding him? Why isn't there a single picture of Jake anywhere in this house except this one room?!" He demanded.

"Because…." His mother started.

"Because what!?" Trevor shouted, picking up the picture of him and Jake from the nightstand and holding it up to her.

"Because it hurts too much to look at his face!!" She tore the photo from his hand and threw it out of the room where it shattered against the hallway wall. "You have no idea what it's like to lose a child!" She sobbed. "It's like losing a piece of your soul that you are completely lost without! I know he was your brother, but he was also the air that I breathed and now I spend every day feeling like I'm suffocating on the same air that used to give me life."

Trevor was staring out the door at the shattered glass of the photo that had sat on the nightstand next to his deceased brother's bed. "But I'm still here and I'm your son too." He reminded her quietly.

She had no words to respond. She could only watch as Trevor

went out into the hall and began picking up the broken picture frame and photo that it had held. He turned the photo over and saw where Jake had written; 'Our favorite breakfast' and the date.

"Can you please get out of my brother's room?" He said without looking back at her.

"What?" The request had sobered her momentarily.

Trevor picked up one of the larger shards of glass and repeated himself as he stood to face her. "Can you please get out of my brother's room?"

"Or what? Or you're going to cut me?" Her words had begun to slur again and there was a slight sway to her stance that made her look like a single blade of grass in the breeze.

"No." Trevor began to squeeze the shard until blood oozed through his fingers and began to drip to the floor. "But you're drunk and I'd rather you didn't damage anything else in here that you'll regret once you're sober.

"Trev…" She started, seeing the blood dripping to the floor and the unaffected, solemn expression on his face.

"I'll clean up the mess." He told her. "You go get some rest, it's late, mom."

She looked back at his bleeding hand and agreed. "It's late. I'm going to go get some rest."

She stumbled out the door past him, using the wall for balance. "Your father called. He has to work late tonight so he won't be home." She called over her shoulder.

"Right." He mumbled.

He listened for her bedroom door closing and the soft sound of her sobbing, that she thought no one heard, before he kneeled and picked up the rest of the glass from the floor with no concern for cuts or embedded shards. When he was finished, he stood, snatched his parents' wedding photo off the hallway wall and opened the back. He removed the memory of that celebrated event from its frame and let it fall to the floor, He replaced it with the picture of 'Our favorite breakfast' before going back into Jake's room and closing the door behind him.

He placed the picture back on the nightstand, leaving a single bloody thumb print on the glass and sat back on the bed holding his bleeding hand to his chest. He had slept enough for one night to last him a good long while. He didn't believe he'd be going back to sleep again any time soon.

PART TWELVE

Blackie's Story

Nate spent the rest of the afternoon sitting outside under, what had come to be known as 'Nate's Tree', which was the largest of the two pines that sat in the center of their front yard. Despite the heat, Nate was cloaked in his jacket with his hood covering his face listening to music. Blackie sat quietly with his leash dropped off to one side next to Nate unfazed, enjoying the spring breeze. Denise figured he must have been waiting for everyone to get home so that they could meet the newest addition to the family, so he'd postponed his usual walk.

There had been no band practice today, so David and Olivia rode the bus home. As they made their way up the driveway from the bus stop, they saw Nate sitting out front with the dog, but waited until they were in the house to ask about it.

"Ma!" She could hear Olivia calling for her as soon as she stepped foot in the door. Denise had been folding laundry in her bedroom as she waited for everyone to arrive.

"Yes, little girl!" Denise called back from the bedroom.

Olivia came stumbling into the doorway. "Mom! Do you know Nate is sitting out front with some random dog?" she asked franticly.

"Yes." Denise replied with a straight face.

"Really?" Olivia sounded puzzled.

"Yes." She repeated. "You guys chill out until Terrence gets home and we'll all sit down and talk about it." She told Olivia. She kept folding as she said this.

"Ummm, ok." Olivia was still confused but she knew her mother had a thing for surprises and liked to be as mysterious as possible, so she fought the urge to go outside with Nate and opted to grab a snack and wait for her stepdad to get home.

Terrence arrived home about an hour later. He'd also seen Nate sitting in the front yard and waved as he passed him on the driveway. He saw the dog sitting next to him and smiled as he recalled their conversation from a couple nights earlier.

"That woman doesn't waste any time does she." He thought to himself.

Denise met him on the porch and gave him a huge hug.

"Did you see him?" She asked as they walked into the house together.

"Who? Nate or that big black bear he has sitting next to him out there?" Terrence smiled at her.

She had to laugh at that. "Yeah, he is a big boy. But wait until you meet him. There is just something so unique about this dog. When I saw him at the kennel it was like, he was calling my name." She told him.

"That's not creepy at all, Mom." Olivia said from behind them. David was standing next to her. "So, what's the big secret surprise besides the fact that Nate has a new girlfriend?"

"That's not funny, Olive." She scolded her." You guys have a seat and I'll go get Nate."

Everyone took a seat around the kitchen table and Denise went to the door and called for Nate. He walked into the kitchen with Blackie by his side, the chain leash dragged lazily on the floor. Nate reached down and clicked the leash off the dog's collar.

"This is pretty much useless." Nate said holding the leash. "This guy isn't trying to go anywhere."

"Yeah, he was the same way with me." She told him. "Guys, this is Blackie, or at least its Blackie for now until Nate decides what we're all going to be calling him."

"So, we got a dog." David said dryly. He never was much of an animal person. If it didn't come with controllers and bonus points, he wasn't really interested.

Denise shot him a look.

"Yes, we got a dog." She said, "He is actually more Nate's dog, but of course he will be a member of the family. So, we're all going to pull together to make sure that we take good care of him."

Olivia turned to get a better look at the dog. "Dang Ma, could you find a big enough dog?" She said taking all of him in.

Blackie was a large dog at almost 125 pounds, but Denise was used to big dogs and had raised her children to love them as well. His first impression was quite intimidating, and this was a plus as far as she was concerned. She hadn't heard him bark yet, but she was sure that was just as intimidating. No one seemed to have an issue with the fact that he was missing an eye and she was proud of her family for being so accepting. She knew it would eventually come up, but not because anyone was bothered by it, but more out of curiosity. She was more than happy to fill in the blanks so everyone would have even more of a reason to love the new addition to their family.

Olivia turned her attention to Nate, now that the newness of Blackie had begun to wear off. "I was wondering whose dog you were out there sitting with. Looks like you finally have a friend that can stand to be around your smell." she teased.

"Yeah, and he's only got one eye so he can stand to look at your face. I've got two and it's killing me." He snapped back.

"Whatever!" She stuck her tongue out at him. "So, what's wrong with his eye?"

The question she'd been waiting for, and she knew Olivia would be the one to ask it. She gestured for Nate to take a seat at the table with the rest of the family and she did the same.

"Well," She started. "While I was at the animal shelter looking at all the dogs I met this guy," She nodded toward Blackie. "When I tell you it was the most unusual experience I have ever had, I would not be exaggerating. He seemed to almost call me over to him. He was super calm. He wasn't barking and jumping and acting all frantic like the rest of the dogs were. That was the first strange thing about him. He actually only even wagged his tail when you asked him a question, like he was trying to answer back. It was super weird, but one of the shelter workers, his name was Adam, also a super weird guy, told me a lot about Blackie and where he came from…

Adam had arrived at work early as usual. He loved what he did, and he considered his ability to communicate with the animals that he cared for at the shelter to be a gift. He'd always been incredibly receptive to nature and had often been called peculiar as a child, however his mother had assured him very simply that he was special, even more special than he realized. She was the very first person to acknowledge that he had a gift, a calling from the divine, and that one day he would know exactly what it was. On this particularly rainy morning he had sensed that there was a bit more urgency for him to arrive early and he never doubted his senses.

He believed his mother without question. Every job he'd ever had had involved working with animals in some way. He'd grown up on a farm taking care of livestock, chickens, and ducks. He was the president of the FFA when he was in high school and still dreamt of becoming a veterinarian one day. He was in his early 20s and knew he still had plenty of time. There was something that he was meant to do here first. And once that was done, he would be free to pursue his goals.

The sense of urgency that he had awoken to this morning had felt to him to be divine. Something special was happening; something big, and he was beyond ready. He rode down the dirt road to the shelter with the hairs rising on the back of his neck and down his forearms.

Something divine. Something…special.

It had been raining heavily all morning, but Adam did not let that deter him in the least. As he reached the front gate he came to a stop and threw his car into park reaching into the backseat for his umbrella. The front gate had to be unlocked manually and he was usually the first to arrive. He pulled out his big ring of keys and went about his morning routine of unlocking the gate, sliding it off to the side and doing checks for abandoned animals or tampering. There were no immediate signs of tampering, but on average he was usually good at finding one out of the two.

As he slid the gate off to the side, he caught sight of a chain dangling from the fence. The handle had been tied in a loose knot securing it in place. He followed the length of the chain to a pile of wet fur lying lifeless on the ground. He took a few steps forward and a tingling began to rise from the nape of his neck and work its way down his spine.

Something divine. He thought. Something special.

The pile of fur heaved up and down with a heavy breath. It wasn't dead, but it wasn't far from it. He reached over without fear, to detach the chain from the animal's neck only to find that it wasn't connected to either the dog or the fence. It was just sort of draped across it. He knelt beside the emaciated creature, slid his hands up under its side and lifted slowly. It was barely more than a soggy bag of bones lying on an old shirt or rag, but its heartbeat was strong, and Adam could feel its rhythmic thrum against his arms through its rib cage. He carried his precious bundle, leaving the rag it had been resting its head on behind, to the back of his SUV and stuck out his foot, engaging the hatch to open. It rose slowly before him and he leaned in, laying the creature in the back of the hatch.

He reached over into a mesh bag and pulled out some old towels that he kept there. Ever so gently he rubbed the poor creature he'd just picked up out of the rain and began to dry its fur. After a few minutes of this, he laid the towels across its motionless body and closed the hatch.

He didn't waste any time jumping back into the driver's seat and speeding up the remainder of the road to the shelter. He slid into his usual parking spot with his foot laid heavy on the break. He could hear the gravel crying out in distress as he did, scattering tiny stones in every direction. He pulled out his ring of keys as he jumped out of the car and headed for the front door.

He had the alarm disengaged in seconds and was in his office in a flash. He made a call to the shelter Vets to find out how long it would be before they arrived and explained the situation.

Their regular Veterinarian was only minutes away and would be there shortly. She told him to get the animal inside and hooked up to fluids. She was sure he was probably dehydrated as well as malnourished. Adam ran back out the SUV and once again stuck out his foot to engage the hatch to open. He had tried this mid run, but he was light on his toes, always had been and didn't miss a step. The hatch rose slowly to what now had taken the shape of a large black canine. It was sitting upright, not completely, however, it was weak. Its head swayed and bobbed as it tried to hold it up.

"It's okay." Adam cooed in a soothing voice. "You're safe now, nothing can hurt you here. We're gonna take good care of you here. You're safe."

He reached out and placed a hand on one side of the dog's face with his fingers wrapped just behind its ear. It leaned the weight of its massive head against his hand as though it understood that this was a safe place to rest. Adam reached in, sliding his hands up under the dog's chest and waist and lifted what he now knew to be a 'him', out of the hatch of the SUV. He carried him through the doors, catching a quick glimpse of his reflection in the glass.

He started to pause for a second when he thought he saw a long white tail dangling from beneath the towels the dog was wrapped with, but that could be right, the dog was almost completely solid black. He shook his head and continued inside, lying the exhausted, injured animal on the examination table to begin prepping him for an IV. A quick shave of his wrist, a shot of local anesthetic and the big black dog allowed itself to let go and began to breathe just a little easier.

His coat was short and patchy, and his ribs could be seen and counted through it. His stomach was sunken into itself and appeared to almost touch his back literally. The ridges of his spine protruded down to his tailbone where a two-inch nub wagged slowly anytime Adam reached out to touch the poor creature. His legs were mere sticks, and it was no surprise that he couldn't stand on them without support. Its left hind leg appeared to be especially sensitive.

"Perhaps a fracture of some sort." Adam thought. But they'd find out once the vet got there.

The shelter's Veterinarian arrived sooner than expected but did not appear hopeful considering the dog's condition. Upon closer examination they discovered several things about the new arrival. The first thing was that X-rays taken confirmed that not only did he suffer a hairline fracture in his left hind leg, but he'd already suffered from multiple fractures throughout his body; including his pelvis, his rib cage and what appeared to be another hairline fracture in his skull that ultimately resulted in the loss of his left eye. They had tried to save it, but it had been too badly damaged. It appeared that he had been severely beaten about the head and body. His previous treatment had truly been savage.

"This dog has been severely abused." She told Adam. "Poor thing. We're going to do everything that we can to make him comfortable, but there's no guarantee that he's going to make it."

"I believe he'll be fine." Adam said.

"You are always so optimistic." The vet smiled sadly.

"Don't have to be in this particular case." He smiled back confidently.

"Well, okay, let's do this." Adams confidence had been contagious, and the vet was determined that their big furry friend would make it through the night." So, what are we calling this guy?" She asked Adam.

"I don't know." Adam pondered. "Perhaps we just keep it simple for now? We can call him Blackie." There was another electric shiver that ran down his spine at that moment.

"Sounds good to me," The vet seconded.

They patched Blackie up, put his leg in a cast and kept him partially sedated for several days. He had a constant IV drip and was intubated for feeding. Adam sat with him every evening for three days, watching over him diligently. When he arrived to check on Blackie on the third day, he was not at all surprised to see him standing on all fours, cast and all, wagging his tail excitedly with recognition.

One of the Vet Techs joined Adam in front of Blackie's kennel.

"You know." He said, "If I didn't know any better, I'd say that he'd be just fine if we took that cast off. I know it's only been a couple of days but, the rate at which he's healing is absolutely remarkable. You'd never know he was the same dog that you found tied to the fence knocking at death's door a few days ago." He said with genuine amazement in his voice.

"Yeah, I think he is definitely a pretty special dog." Adam felt the hairs on his arm rise.

"Blackie is a pretty basic name, though." The Tech added. They both laughed at this last part.

"Yeah. It is, but that just allows their new owners to personalize it when they finally find their forever home." Adam explained. The Tech hadn't been with the shelter long, but Adam was glad he was here to witness this miracle. "This guy is going to be okay. I have a feeling there is someone really special out there for him."

The Tech gave him a look. "Well, you've been right about this guy so far." He gave Adam a quick pat on the back, paused for a moment to take another look at Blackie and then quickly turned and walked off to complete his morning rounds.

He had felt it though, Adam knew he had; that strange sensation of something wonderful and peculiar happening. Something indescribable that resonated to the very soul.

Blackie's recuperation was unprecedented. Within the week he had chewed off the cast himself. By the end of the month, he was out in his own pen, eating and gaining his weight back like nothing had ever happened. He spent most of his time in his doghouse on visiting days only to appear when Adam came to see him. Blackie didn't appear to be interested in interacting with anyone else. The only other time that Adam had seen Blackie appear even remotely interested in another person was when he'd been visited by a young lady that had spent a long while talking to him through the fence. Adam watched from a distance as Blackie approached her, put his head down and allowed her to reach through the fence to stroke his fur. He only saw her once very briefly, but there was an obvious connection there.

Adam had walked over to Blackie's pen after the young lady left. "So, I see you have a friend." He said to him. "Guess there's more to your story then we will ever know, huh?"

Blackie made a huffing sound and wagged his nub a few times. Adam smiled.

"You are something else." He placed his hand on the fence and Blackie met it there with is huge black paw.

Denise looked around at her family.

Blackie got up then and walked over to her, placing his head in her lap. She put her hand on his head and gave it a little scratch.

"So, it appears that he has been through a very traumatic situation and yet you can see he is still willing to trust us and give us a chance to be his family. He's not holding grudges against people. He's not angry and hateful. We can all learn something from Blackie, but most of all, we have an opportunity to give a great dog a loving home. He deserves at least that much. So, like I said before, we're all going to pull together and make sure that we take really good care of him. Okay?"

They all looked at one another, nodding in agreement.

"Well, welcome to the family Blackie." Olivia said. "Now can we please do something about that name? Nate, I mean really? Blackie? I mean, considering we're his new family, could it be any more offensive? We have white neighbors on both sides. What if you and the dog are in the yard and I want to call him? I'm just supposed to stand outside yelling 'Come here Blackie!' I can see their faces now." She shook her head and bit her lip trying not to laugh.

"Come here Blackie!" David pointed at Nate and rocked back in his chair with laughter.

They all broke out into laughter at that. As politically correct as they may have wanted to be, they just couldn't contain it.

"You guys are a mess." Denise said, getting up from the table.

Nate was wiping his eyes as he said, "We're still working on a name, but as soon as we figure it out, we'll let you know."

"Yeah, you do that." Olivia said. She stood up and walked over to the dog, crouched down in front of him and reached out so that he could smell her hand. Blackie pushed her hand off to one side and stepped close enough to rest his head on her shoulder. She wrapped her arms around his neck and gave him a quick hug and a pat on the head.

"You are definitely an interesting dog." She was holding his head in her hands now and looking him in his face. "Never met one that liked to hug. Welcome to the family."

Blackie gave her a few acknowledging wags.

She stood up and went to stand next to Nate who was still seated. David got up than and walked over to Blackie as well.

"Well, guess there's another kid in the house. And we've all got chores so yours can be to pick up all the food that Nate drops when he eats." He told him putting his hand out to shake.

To his surprise, Blackie raised his paw and placed it firmly on his palm. David closed his hand around it as much as possible and shook it.

"Wow." He said, "Nice to meet you too." He let Blackie's paw drop and placed his hand on the dog's head and gave it a quick rub. "He's even smarter than you." David told Nate as he joined them at their end of the table.

"Really dude?" Nate gives his brother a quick punch in the shoulder.

Terrence came over to get a better look at Blackie. "So, we got a big, black, one-eyed dog." He said looking down at him. He looked over at Denise, "You really do know how to pick 'em."

She smiled. "Well, we're a uniquely awesome family; he seemed like the perfect fit."

"You are definitely right about that." He agreed. "Welcome to the family big boy."

Blackie hopped up placing his two front paws on Terrace's shoulders.

"Hey!" Terrence took a step to steady himself. "Okay, I like you too." He gave him a pat on the head.

Blackie dropped back to the floor, barked once, spun in a circle, and then sat facing his new family. They were definitely, uniquely special, just like him.

PART THIRTEEN

Always calm before a storm

Nate spent the rest of the weekend getting to know his new companion. The entire family agreed that Blackie would need some time to get acclimated to his new surroundings. Denise made a special trip to the store and returned with a huge dog bed, bowls, toys and even a new collar for him, while the crew stayed behind and kept him company. Both David and Olivia joined Nate in the yard for the rest of the afternoon, playing fetch and listening to music. They laughed and talked until it was too dark to see and then headed into the house for pizza and Sci-fi movies. They spent more time together that afternoon than they had in years, just enjoying each other's company.

"Do you see this?" Denise whispered to Terrence. "There hasn't been any yelling or name calling or fighting all evening."

"Yeah, I noticed that too." Terrence said, watching the kids as they sat together in the den sharing 'what if' scenarios about the movie they were watching.

"So, you're telling me that if that monster was in your room in the middle of the night you would just sit there? You wouldn't run or scream or anything?" Olivia was asking Nate.

"I'd be out of there." David chimed in. "But I'd call ya'll once I was outside."

"That's messed up!" Olivia threw a handful of popcorn at her brother.

"I wouldn't have to." Nate said. "Blackie would let us know way before that that thing ever got into the house."

"That's true." Olivia agreed. "Then as soon as he starts barking Mom would come out with her 'Zombie Apocalypse' knife and kill it."

They all burst into laughter at the thought.

"I heard that." Denise said, coming to join them. "Scoot over."

She squeezed between Nate and Olivia on the couch. David was seated on the floor and Terrence plopped down in the recliner facing the TV.

"So, what is it we're watching?" He asked.

"Some movie on the Sci-fi Channel," David answered. "Not sure what it's called. It was already on when we got in here."

Denise grabbed the remote. "No one thought to check?"

"It's the Sci-fi channel, mom." Olivia said in a matter-of –fact tone. "We don't care what it's called. Everything on the Sci-fi channel is good. I don't ask questions, we just watch."

"True." Denise said tapping the info button on the remote. They were watching 'The Mist', a movie based on a book by one of her favorite authors.

"You wouldn't let that monster get in here would you, Blackie?" Olivia asked him in a teasing baby voice.

Blackie, who had been stretched out on his dog bed enjoying a large bone that Terrence bought him, looked up then and gave a huge rumbling bark of agreement. The room fell silent as everyone looked in his direction at once, surprised. Blackie, unphased, went back to happily chewing his bone. Once again, they all burst into laughter.

Nate howled and fell onto the floor. "Well, there's your answer! This house is prooooootected!"

It was the best night they'd had in some time and Denise loved seeing her family happy. Blackie was helping to bring some of that joy back. She made a kissy face at Terrence, and he blew her one back in agreement. Blackie rolled over, feet in the air and let his tongue flop out to one side, enjoying the love that filled the room.

Sunday flew by and Nate found himself actually looking forward to school on Monday. He was excited to tell his friends about Blackie and get their opinion about what his new name should be. Nate was up and dressed Monday morning by 5:30 even though they didn't normally leave for school until about seven. By the time Denise was up and headed down the hall to wake everyone, he was standing on the front porch waiting patiently for Blackie to come back in from doing his business.

"Hey there." she said peeking out the door. The morning had a crispness to it, and she wrapped her robe a little tighter around herself. "You're up early."

"Yeah," Nate replied. "Had to take the dog out so I figured that I might as well go ahead and get dressed. Oh, and I already woke up Dave and Olivia." He told her.

"Wow, really?" She looked down the hall and saw that their bedroom lights were already turned on.

"Morning, mom!" David peeked his head out his door and called to her.

Olivia popped out of the bathroom still pulling her hair up into a ponytail. "Morning! Be ready in just a few."

"Umm, ok. Good morning you guys." She was pleasantly surprised. "Guess I should go throw some clothes on.

"Ok." Nate was closing the front door back and Blackie was happily trotting toward the kitchen for breakfast. "I'll feed the dog and then I'll be ready too.

Denise was smiling as she headed back to her room to get dressed. She'd already thrown on a shirt and her sweatpants when David knocked on the door for her keys. He'd recently gotten his driver's license and looked for any opportunity to be behind the wheel, including starting the car every morning. Everyone was already in the car when she finally made it outside. David was still sitting in the driver's seat when she approached the car. With so much time to spare Denise decided to let him drive them to the high school. They arrived a half an hour early.

Dave and Olivia jumped out of the car and headed off to hang out with their friends.

"Have a great day at school you, guys!" Denise called to them as she slid into the driver's seat.

"Make good choices." David said mocking her.

"And do your best work." Olivia finished.

"Funny guys." Denise leaned toward the open passenger window and called to them. "I'm glad you already know!" She stuck her tongue out at them and pulled off.

"Well, what do you expect?" Nate said. "You've only been saying it since our very first day of school."

"You're right." She replied. "And I always hope that what I say to you guys sinks in and you always do your best work and make good choices."

They arrived at Nate's bus stop with plenty of time to spare.

"Thanks mom." Nate leaned over and gave her a quick peck on the cheek. "I'm going to wait on the curb with my friends.

Denise looked into her rearview mirror and saw a few familiar faces waiting on the sidewalk for the bus to arrive. Trevor was there as well, standing off to one side by himself.

"Okay. I see your friend with the red hair over there too. Tell him I said hi." She said as he slid out of the car.

Nate stood up, grabbed his bag, and called to Trevor. "Hey Trev! Come here!"

Trevor looked up from where he was standing and made his way over to where they were.

"My mom wanted to say hey." He told him as he approached the car.

Trevor leaned down so he could look into the window. "Hey Mrs. Williams."

"Het sweety, how are you doing today." She said with a smile.

Trevor shrugged. "Ok." He started to reach up to adjust his bookbag. Decided against it and shrugged his shoulder to adjust the weight. He was trying to avoid using his bandaged hand to adjust the bag, but Denise had the eyes of a mother and spotted the bandage before he could hide it.

"What happened to your hand?" she asked concerned.

"Oh...ummm. Noth-," He started to say.

Nate interrupted.

"The bus! Gotta go mom. Talk to you later." He tugged on Trevor's shirt.

"Bye." Trevor said, turning to go.

Denise shook her head. She got a vibe from Trevor that concerned her. She watched as the boys ran over to where the rest of the kids were standing and got in line to board the school bus.

When the boys made it to their seats at the back of the bus Nate took a look at Trevor's bandaged hand.

"So, what happened?" He asked him.

"Nothing. Just cut my hand taking out the trash." Trevor told him.

"Well dang man." Nate said. "That looks like it was serious. Did you have to get stitches? Was that why you weren't at school Friday?"

"Yeah." Trevor replied, thinking about the broken picture frame and the feeling of that shard of glass cutting into his palm.

"Well next weekend we're hanging out at my house. You still down?" Nate asked him.

"Yeah. Sure." Trev turned and looked out the window watching the scenery pass in a blur as the bus whisked them off to yet another mundane school day.

Nate barely noticed his friend's solemn demeanor. He had already turned his own attention to his other friends sitting across the aisle. He was telling them about his new dog and asking them what they thought a good name would be for him.

Trevor barely heard the conversation. His mind had drifted off elsewhere. He thought about his brother and the slashes to his face and body. He thought about how his body had slid and fallen to the ground in two pieces. He thought about how he wished it had been him that died in that accident instead of Jake. It should have been him.

PART FOURTEEN

A Fight With Mom

For the next few days things were quiet in the house. You might even say things were peaceful. Blackie's arrival had proved to be a distraction not only for Nate, but the entire family. He sat with Olivia in the afternoons while she giggled and texted back and forth with friends. They had become snack buddies. Denise had caught Blackie several times with Olivia, waiting patiently for her to share a chip or a bit of her sandwich. She found this to be precious.

When the kids were gone at school for the day Blackie could also be found spending time with Terrence in the backyard, following him around the shop as he worked on various customers cars and motorcycles. Terrence, a self-employed automotive technician, worked from a shop just behind their house and clients were always arriving with various repair needs. He was good at what he did, and his reputation preceded him. If there was something wrong with your ride, he could figure it out and this kept him incredibly busy. He appeared to enjoy having Blackie around the shop and Blackie turned out to be quite the shop dog. He greeted customers as they arrived, was friendly and enjoyed all the attention. The loud revving of engines and bikes didn't bother him at all.

Even David, who normally was not at all animal sociable, couldn't help but pat Blackie on the head every time he passed him in the house on his way to raid the kitchen for snacks and drinks before returning to his gaming den of solitude.

Denise noted how much lighter things had begun to feel around the house since Blackie arrived. Everyone seemed to be in better spirits and a much happier mood. The real challenge though was Nate. He had been the reason she'd gone to the shelter to begin with. She walked across the room to one of the windows that faced the front of the house, parted the blind slightly and peeked out.

There sat Nate with Blackie by his side under the trees in the front yard. This is where he and Blackie had spent the past three days together when Nate came home from school. He hadn't been on any of his walks lately. He came in, changed clothes, grabbed a snack and out the door they went to sit in the yard, soak up the sun and listen to music. Nate had even switched from his normal earbuds to a small Bluetooth speaker so that his music could play out loud so both of them could listen as he tossed a ball and Blackie happily retrieved it. She smiled and let go of the blinds.

6:23 p.m.

"I think I'll make something special for dinner tonight." She said out loud to herself.

She headed into the kitchen and began to take out the ingredients she needed to make her famous giant stuffed shells accompanied with a fresh garden salad and some cheesy Italian bread. For dessert she would make caramel brownies with ice cream and plenty of toppings. They were going to love it.

She took two boxes of pasta from the cabinet. She always made enough for two pans, otherwise there were never any leftovers. This was one of her family's favorite meals. She went about boiling the water and preparing the meat and was just adding a few spoonful's of sugar to her sauce when Olivia shouted from behind her.

"Moms making stuffed shells!" Denise jumped, dropping her spoon and splattering sauce across the stovetop.

"Olivia, really!" She turned around with her hands on her hips. "What is wrong with you?" Denise grabbed some paper towels and began to wipe up the mess.

"My bad mom." Olivia came over and gave her mother a quick hug. "Can I help stuff the shells?"

"Yes, but my goodness, inside voice please." She rinsed the spoon and dropped it back into the measuring cup that she used to hold her cooking utensils. "You remember how to stuff the shells?" She asked Olivia.

"Uhhhh." Olivia started.

"In other words, you forgot already." Denise smiled.

"I remember. I turned it into a song." She started to do a little dance as she recited. "Cheese, meat, cheese, meat, cheese."

Denise handed Olivia a small container of Ricotta cheese and a spoon. The shells were already sorted into their individual pans, each containing three rows of about twelve shells each.

"You can start on this part." She told Olivia.

Olivia spooned a small dollop of Ricotta into each shell.

"Done." She announced after a few moments.

"All right, my turn." Denise leaned over a mixture of meat and sauce that she had just combined. She took her small spoon and followed Olivia's path, placing a spoonful of meat into each open shell.

"All right. Your turn again." She said when she was finished.

Olivia had already torn open a bag of shredded sharp cheddar cheese.

"I'm going to put a lot of this in. I love cheddar cheese." She said sneaking a taste.

"Not too much." Denise reminded her. "We still have to add the rest of the meat and cheese.

"I know." Olivia was already half-done adding cheese to the shells.

Next came another dollop of meat and sauce from Denise and Olivia finished up with a healthy helping of mozzarella.

"And for our final touch we will add a little sauce to the top and sprinkle a little bit more cheese, then into the oven for about thirty minutes." Denise announced.

Olivia did as her mother instructed and opened the oven to slide the pans in. She grabbed one and then turned to grab the other.

"Oh no you don't." Denise stopped her. "You know better than that. Second pan goes into the freezer for another day."

"But moooooom, we can make both pans and just put the ones we don't eat in the freezer." Olivia gave her mother her best puppy dog eyes.

"No ma'am." Her mother told her. "Grab that foil and stick that other pan in the freezer. We'll save it for another day."

Olivia lifted her foot and nudged the oven door shut. "Yeah, another day like tomorrow." She teasingly mumbled under her breath.

"Very funny." Denise gave her a pinch.

Olivia wrapped up the second pan and slid it neatly into the freezer.

The aroma of melting cheese and baking bread filled the house. David had joined Denise and Olivia in the kitchen.

"My nose told me to come here." He told them as he sniffed the air. They laughed.

"Well, my stomach told me to stay in here." Olivia said.

The kitchen door opened then as Terrance came in from his shop.

"Well, your stomach told you to stay here." Terrance said. "Then it called my stomach and told it to hurry up and get its tail in here too." He told Olivia playfully. "I'm going to go wash up. I'm ready for whatever that smell is coming from the oven."

"Even if it's old cat butts we found in the woods?" Olivia asked.

"Well, if old cat butts smell like that, then you can fix me a plate." They all laughed.

Denise was pouring brownie mix into a greased pan. "One of you guys go and call Nate. Tell him dinner will be ready soon."

"I'll do it." Olivia jumped up from where she'd been leaning against the counter, waiting for the brownie bowl and spoon so she could lick it. She ran to the front door and swung it open wide.

"Naaaaate!!" She yelled out the door.

"Olivia, really!" Denise called from the kitchen.

Nate didn't respond. He was still sitting with his head down, listening to his music. Blackie had heard her however and sat up in front of Nate facing the house. He followed the dog's gaze to the front door where Olivia was waving her arms frantically.

"Moms, making stuffed shells! Dinners almost ready!" She called to him.

Nate threw two thumbs up and started packing up his backpack and turning off his speaker. Blackie was already up, headed back in the direction of the house.

"You hungry or something?" Nate asked him.

"Ruff!" Blackie barked, turned, took two steps toward Nate, turned again, and began trotting back in the direction of the house.

"Okay, okay I'm coming." Nate said. He threw his backpack over his shoulder, grabbed the jacket he'd been sitting on and ran to catch up with Blackie. "Yo greedy self." He gave him a little bump with his leg. They came up the front steps together and into the house to find everyone congregated in the kitchen.

"So was there a party I wasn't invited to or something." Nate said.

"Yeah, it's the 'everybody's too greedy to wait for dinner to be done' party." David rubbed his stomach hungrily.

"You are like so totally late." Olivia said in her best valley girl voice.

Nate tossed his stuff onto the couch in the den and joined everyone in the kitchen.

"Oh no you don't. I'm going to need you to wash those." Denise pointed at his hands.

"My hands are clean." Nate said holding both hands up.

"I bet they are." She could see the dirt on them from where she stood. "They're probably as clean as the dog or the ground you were sitting on, or the last thing you ate."

"Or the last butt you scratched." Olivia added.

"Point is…" She shot Olivia a look. "I'm going to need you to wash those."

"Okay I get it. I'll go wash my hands before I give you all nature cooties." Nate walked off headed for the bathroom.

They sat down to dinner as a family, which they don't often get to do. They all lived in the same house but existed in their own worlds. It was nice when they could all come together and reconnect. Dinner turned out wonderful and everyone had healthy helpings of stuffed shells and Italian bread. Only Denise and Olivia had salad and Olivia only ate it because Denise did. She didn't want her mother to feel like she was the only one who wanted the salad.

"We can have salad any day." Nate had said when she offered it to him.

"Yeah." David added. "We've got a whole yard full of salad.

They laughed and talked for an hour and once again Denise caught Olivia slipping a hand under the table and the muffled sounds of sloppy chomping from a grateful recipient. They cleared the table still laughing and talking and then began one by one to settle in for the evening.

Nate and the dog crashed in their usual spot on the couch in front of the television in the den. He had his leg slung over one end and lay sprawled across the couch on his back, his cell phone held up in front of his face, texting feverishly. David helped load the dishwasher and then slipped away back into his gamers den of solitude and Olivia was deeply engrossed in a conversation with one of her girlfriends as she turned and headed down the hall to her own bedroom to gossip and talk about boys for the rest of the evening, so Denise assumed.

"Guess it's just me and you." Terrence said.

"I could do worse." Denise teased playfully then leaned in for a kiss.

"So, what do you want to do?" He asked.

"It's Friday, how about we pop some popcorn and find something good on TV?" She said already reaching into the cabinet for the box.

"Sounds good to me." He headed into the bedroom, and she threw a bag of popcorn into the microwave.

7:43 PM

Terrance had already positioned himself on the small loveseat that sat at the foot of their bed facing the TV in their room. He patted the space next to him as she came in with the bowl of popcorn and nodded toward the TV.

The opening credits to a familiar movie were playing.

"What we watching?" she asked, already knowing the answer.

"Friday." He said, "I thought it was appropriate considering that it is Friday."

She shook her head. "You are so silly. You better be glad this is one of my favorite movies."

She snuggled up next to him and sat the popcorn that she had just popped off to the side. She'd seen this movie a thousand times, but for some odd reason, always found it absolutely hilarious.

They were still laughing when the final credits began to roll, and the announcer excitedly reminded them to stay tuned for a Friday Marathon. The running credits minimized, and Next Friday started to play.

"Oh yeah!" Terrance jumped up from the seat letting Denise fall off to one side. She had been leaning against him as they watched the movie. She pretended to be injured as a result of being thrown from her comfortable position.

"I...I can't move. Need...more.......juice." She gasped and then pretended to faint. She peeked out of one eye mockingly.

"Well, I'm gone need about 25, 35 minutes." He said mushing his lips together like the character in the movie.

"Okay Craaaaig!" She did her best Felicia impersonation.

They laughed for a minute, then suddenly Terrance threw up a hand to quiet her.

"Mute the TV." He told her.

"What's wrong?" Denise raised the remote, muting the television.

"You hear that?" He asked her.

They both listened for a moment.

"Stop playing." Denise told him. She had sat up from her faint and was leaning forward on the loveseat.

He threw his hand up again. "Shhh. You hear it now?"

She could hear it. Someone was talking loudly, just outside of their house.

"I don't care!" They yelled.

She got up and walked over to the window to see if she could see anything. She already knew who it was, or assumed she knew. She peeked out and saw only darkness. He had turned off the front porch lights and was standing in the front yard on his phone.

Terrance glanced over at the clock.

9:53 p.m.

"Yeah, he was supposed to have been in the house since 9." She agreed, reading the expression on his face.

"Not to mention that he's out there yelling and cursing. Our neighbors aren't super close to us, but we do still have them." He turned to face her. "I'll go...." He started, but she had already slipped on her house shoes and was headed for the front door.

"Nate?" She called to him in the dark. "Nate?"

He didn't answer. She flipped on the front porch lights in order to get a better look into the darkness. Nate had apparently assumed this would be her next move and had positioned himself far enough out in the front yard that he was still cloaked.

"Nate! I know you hear me calling you boy!" She whispered as loud as she could. She didn't want to call attention from their neighbors any more than Nate already had.

"I hear you mom. What?" He called back finally.

"What do you mean what? Do you see what time it is?"

"Yeah." He answered her.

"Your curfew is 9:00 Nate. You are supposed to be in the house. All doors are locked, and this house is secure by 9:00PM." She waited for a response. There wasn't one.

"Get in this house now boy or you will be spending the night outside." She warned him.

"So." He called back.

She was shocked. Had he lost his mind or something?

"So? So! Get in here right now young man!" She shouted. "Now, Nate or I'm taking your phone!"

He stepped into the light then, as if from out of nowhere, and climbed the steps.

"No, you're not." He told her plainly and then squeezed past her into the house.

Her mouth had fallen open at that moment. She slammed the front door shut and stormed off toward her bedroom on a mission.

"Everything…" Terrance stopped mid-sentence when he saw her face. "Dang." he said shaking his head.

Denise barely heard a word. She was on a mission alright. She snatched open her dresser drawers and pulled out a pair of sweatpants.

"What are you doing?" Terrance asked her with genuine concern. He'd seen that look on her face before.

She grabbed a pair of socks to cover her bare feet and dove on the floor for her sneakers. All the while mumbling to herself. "Think he can talk to me any kind of way. I'm about to show him I'm not playing."

"Ohhh man." Terrance was still shaking his head. "Calm down baby."

"NO!" She shouted. "I feed him! I clothe him! I protect him and this is the respect I get! It's been a long time since he's been spanked, but he's about to catch this beat down today!" She grabbed Terrance's church belt that he kept hung on a hook on their bathroom door and jumped across their bed like a character from an episode of Dukes of Hazard, pivoting on her hand in the middle and sliding down the other side of their king-sized General Lee. She was out the door and headed down the hall before he could say another word, but he was hot on her heels.

He saw her lift her leg off the floor in front of Nate's bedroom and kick the door open.

"Now tell me again what I'm not gone do!" She yelled at Nate who was lying across his bed still texting. Blackie was lying on the floor next to the bed, but he rose to a seated position when Denise burst into the room.

"Man mom, do we have to do this tonight."

"Give me the phone Nate." She put her hand out and waited.

"No. I'm not giving you, my phone." He told her with a straight face.

"Give me the phone now!" This time she was pointing the belt at him.

"You can beat me if you want to. It's not going to hurt anyway, but I'm not giving you, my phone."

Terrance was standing at the door observing the interaction between the two. He leaned back and looked down the hall, appeared to be saying something and then turned his attention back to Denise and Nate.

"What is wrong with you!" She yelled at him. "First you can't follow one simple rule and now that you're being punished for it you act like the rules just don't apply to you! You are a child Nate, and yes, I said CHILD! You want to act like an adult and be treated like an adult, but you are still behaving like a child! Honestly, I don't know what else to do with you." She took a step back and put a hand on her hip. "What do you want me to do Nate?" she asked him in an increasingly choked up voice.

Blackie, who had been quietly watching this interaction stood then and moved to where Denise was standing. Nate cut his eye at the dog but remained silent as he took a seat next to Denise with is left paw just barely touching her right foot.

"Look." Terrance interjected. "Even the dog is trying to figure out what's going on." He chuckled, but no one else seemed to find the humor in his observation.

The dog had locked his eye on Nate as he sat completely still and focused. Nate raised his eyes from the phone and looked over at the dog and then up to his mother. She was still screaming about being disrespectful and ungrateful or something like that. It was all stuff he had heard before, but somehow it was different. It felt different, like being pushed by the tide when you stand waist deep in the water at the beach. Over and over again the wave crashed into him, washing over him and enveloping him in colors and sensations.

As his mother yelled at him, he could feel her pain and hurt sinking into him and ringing in his ears. It felt like tears that had yet to be cried and prayers that were slowly forming even in that moment. He could feel her rage, her disappointment and her sadness all wrapped up in a tangle of emotion. He knew these were her feelings because it was all deeply laced with a love that would be familiar to him until his last breath. A love that rang of her kisses and smelled like her skin as it whispered and could be heard clearly through all the hurt and pain and rage and confusion. Over and over, it whispered. "I love you."

"Stop!" He shouted." Mom, okay. Just please stop." There were tears in his eyes as he said this. He stood up and walked over to her, handing her the phone. "Okay."

She looked down at the phone in her hand. "Nate, I don't know if you realize this but I'm having a really hard time with all this." She spoke softly now.

His back was turned to her. "I'm tired mom. Can I go to bed now?"

"Okay." She said, turning to leave the room. She turned off the light and Terrance pulled the door shut behind them.

He climbed into bed with all of his clothes on, including his jacket, and began to sob softly. Blackie joined him, spinning twice and then fitting himself snuggly at Nate's side. Nate reached out and wrapped one arm around the dog's neck. It wasn't long before the emotional evening had taken its toll and they were both fast asleep.

PART FIFTEEN

In the Clearing

Nate woke with a start the next morning. He still hadn't quite shaken the feeling he'd experienced the night before. He remembered his mother losing her mind over how he had acted and how he had felt during their argument. It was like he could feel her feelings and he hadn't liked it at all. It made him feel as if he had been the bad guy when all he had been trying to do was have a conversation with his girlfriend. Once again, no one had asked him how he felt or what he was going through. She had just jumped on the fact that he was still outside after curfew and flown off the handle.

As far as he was concerned, he had had enough. He wasn't planning to be a burden to anyone else anymore. He jumped out of bed, still fully dressed, and glanced over at his alarm clock. It was 7:45 a.m. and based on how quiet the house was, he was the only one up so far. That was a lucky break for him, at least no one would be around to see him leave. Nate was up and headed to the door without a second thought. Blackie was hot on his trail, his leash still swinging loosely from one of the knobs of Nate's dresser drawer.

He opened the door and was surprised to see Trevor standing

there with his hand raised, mid-knock.

"Hey." Trevor said sharing Nate's surprised expression.

Nate looked down the road expecting to see a car pulling off. The road was clear with no signs that a car had been down their dirt road at all that morning.

He stepped out onto the porch and closed the door behind him. "What's up Trev? How'd you get here?"

"I walked." Trevor told him.

"What do you mean you walked? Like from the end of the road?" Nate raised an eyebrow curiously. "Like from the end of the road down here?"

"I mean from my house." He said dropping the bag he'd been carrying onto the porch.

"Dude! That's like almost twenty miles. What time did you leave?" Nate had momentarily forgotten about his own issue.

"I don't know." Trevor found himself feeling a bit embarrassed now that he'd had a chance to think about what he'd just said. "Early, I guess." He laughed uncomfortably.

"My mom would have come and got you, you know." Nate paused for a moment. "Well, at least she would have before last night?"

Trevor could see a familiar expression on Nate's face. "What happened?" He asked his friend.

"Come on." Nate said heading off the porch.

 He took the same path he always did, across the yard and down the dirt road to the dead-end with Trevor at his side and Blackie keeping pace with them. They walked along the hunter's path and into the woods in silence. Neither of them felt pressured to keep up a conversation as they walked. They'd both been in this dark place before and knew that words weren't always necessary. Nate didn't have his phone, so he had no music to listen to as they walked. He mumbled a little to himself as he listened to the sounds of their feet crunching against the dry, rocky ground.

"She's angry and she said I make her sad." He kept mumbling.

"What?" Trevor asked him. Nate had said something, but he'd been lost in his own thoughts and hadn't quite caught what he said.

"Nothing man. It's just my mom. We got into this huge argument last night and she said something stupid." He confided.

"What did she say?" Trevor asked him.

"She said I make her sad. Like, why is she sad? I'm the one that's going through things. I'm the one that nobody cares about that nobody thinks about. What does she have to be so sad about? And how was I supposed to know she was sad? The colors?" He said ranting incoherently.

"Colors?" Trevor was confused. Maybe Nate saw things in his dreams the same way he did. He knew they had a lot in common; perhaps this was one of those things.

Nate shook his head and thought about what he was saying. "I don't know Trev. Maybe I was hallucinating or something. I thought I was seeing colors last night. They had been dark bloody red when she was angry and screaming about me being disrespectful and unappreciative. Then a soft blue that felt like every tear she'd ever cried. Then there had been a pail shaky yellow that felt like it was pulsating with fear. I remember being able to see those colors while she was talking to me, well, yelling at me to be more exact. But the weird thing was, I didn't just see those colors, I felt them."

"How is that possible though?" Trevor asked him. "How is it possible to feel colors?"

"That's the thing." Nate said. "I don't think they were just colors. I think I was feeling her feelings. Weird right? It's like, how is it even possible to feel someone else's feelings."

They walked for a bit more before another thought occurred to him. Had she been able to feel his as well?

It didn't matter. He knew how she felt, and as far as he was concerned, that was what mattered. She wouldn't be so sad if he was gone. They'd all be happier if he was no longer here, and he could definitely make that happen.

"I don't know." Trevor said. "But I had a bit of a fight with my mom too."

"Oh yeah?" Nate said genuinely interested.

"Yeah. The day I wasn't in school. We went at it pretty good." He shared with his friend. "That's how this happened." He raised his bandaged hand.

"Dang," Nate eyed the bandage that was now spotted with blood. "What did she do, cut you?"

"Nah," Trevor looked at his hand and saw for himself that it had started to bleed again. "Kind of did that to myself."

Nate stopped and looked at his friend. "You cut yourself? Like on purpose?"

"I was angry about something she did; didn't realize I was even doing it until my hand started to bleed." He looked away then.

Nate pulled up the short sleeve of his shirt on the right side, revealing his arm and shoulder to Trevor. "Guess we've got that in common too." Nate told him.

Trevor looked up and saw the line of cuts that crisscrossed Nate's arm. There were even profanities carved deeply into his arm creating raised reminders of how he felt about himself. Trevor pulled up his own long shirt sleeve.

"Well, that explains why you always have on a long sleeve shirt." Nate smiled and started walking again.

Trevor stood in place for a moment longer. This had been the first time he'd ever shared his secret with anyone. He'd confided in Nate and found that not only did his friend not judge him but knew exactly how he felt. Maybe he wasn't quite as alone as he'd thought.

He picked up the pace to catch up with Nate and his dog, who were a couple of yards ahead of him now.

"So where are we going?" He asked Nate.

"Headed to my hideout. I had other plans for today before you got here, but I guess they can wait."

They rounded the curve near the open field and then headed out toward the lake. The sun had risen, and the birds were up singing their morning songs. The woods seemed full and lively today. There were rabbits hurrying off in all directions and squirrels scurrying from tree to tree. Nate found himself thinking that the energy was different somehow; like everything was more present as they made their way through the trees. He caught a glimpse of the deer that roamed these woods and pointed them out to Trevor. Their new addition had gotten taller since he'd seen it a couple of weeks ago but was still the smallest of them all.

He listened to Blackie's panting as the dog followed them into the woods, trotting dutifully by Nate's side.

"You come out here to see what I was up to?" He looked down at the dog. Blackie looked up at him briefly and continued following along.

His steps were deliberate and heavy on the path as he approached the clearing just ahead. He could see the stool, a little weather-beaten from having been out in the open for the past few weeks, but still very much there. After last night, the argument with his new girlfriend Lizzy, then getting into it with his mother; he'd made up his mind. No one needed him around. They barely even acted like they wanted him around. He wasn't sure if Trevor would understand, so he planned to ask him to take Blackie back to the house for him so he could be alone for a while. He would do it then, after they were gone.

Like his mother said, she didn't even know what to do with him. She shouldn't have to deal with that, she worked too hard to have to be so stressed by him being a handful and a burden to her and to the family. He knew he embarrassed them; he was a terrible student in school, he felt stupid all the time and even Lizzy had called him an idiot.

They'd been arguing because a friend of hers told her they'd seen Nate sitting with another girl at lunch. He usually spent his lunch period with his friends since Elizabeth was a grade below him and went to lunch earlier than he did. So, when she texted him, last night accusing him of being a cheater and a liar, it had caught him off guard. The texting got to be ridiculous, with long paragraphs full of angry words from her. They'd actually only been dating for about two weeks, but she had already told him that she loved him, and he'd told her he loved her too. So, it was only natural that he would want to talk to her and try to calm her down.

He'd stepped outside when the conversation began to get a little loud. She was yelling about comments she'd seen from the same girl on his Facebook page. Asking him why he was friends with her on Facebook and why she is liking his pictures. Nate could not believe what he was hearing. She was being irrational and wouldn't let him get a word in. It was like she'd created a laundry list of issues to justify her final decision.

"You know what, Nate?" Lizzy had said after she was finally able to compose herself; tears could still be heard in her voice. "You have got a lot of growing up to do and I ain't even feeling this no more. So…."

"So what?" He asked. "So, that's it? Somebody tells you something that ain't even true and you just run with it?"

"I saw the pictures Nate. Why can't you just tell the truth?" She yelled into the phone. "You know what. It doesn't even matter anymore. You are such an ass!"

"I knew you didn't really love me." He told her. "Nobody ever really loves me. You want to talk about being a liar? You said you would always love me. So, you're the liar. Not me! You want to break up? Fine! I don't fuckin' care!"

"Fuck you, Nate!" She screamed into the phone and clicked off.

Nate fell to his knees in the yard, tears streaming heavily down his cheeks. "Fuck you." He said more to himself than to anyone.

That was last night and today was a new day. It was his last day, and no one would ever hurt him or be hurt by him again.

"This is a good spot." Trevor said looking around and breaking Nate's train of thought.

"Yeah, I like it." He walked over to the stool and stood in front of it for a moment. He placed his hand on the seat and cleared the bit of leaf litter that had collected there. No one would ever have to deal with him again and that would be the end of that. He looked up at the rope that hung just above him. There was only the hint of a breeze, but it still managed to swing menacingly from side to side. It was as though it had been pushed for emphasis, adding suspense to the moment.

Trevor followed his gaze up to where the rope hung.

"Hmm."

Nate turned and saw his friend looking up at the rope. "You probably think I'm crazy right?"

"Nope, not at all. I have had a similar idea once but decided on a different route after I found a couple of bottles in my mom's medicine cabinet." He told Nate.

"Wow, really?" Nate said, turning to him then. "So, you've…"

"Overdosed three times. The first time was after my brother died." Trevor walked over to the stool and ran his hand across it. "I thought it would be faster than doing it this way but all three times I apparently didn't take enough and ended up getting my stomach pumped and then spending the next couple of months in a mental hospital."

"Wow." Nate said.

He hadn't known any of that about the boy he'd decided to become friends with. He wasn't sure if he should continue to ask questions or leave it alone. If it were him, he probably wouldn't want anyone all in his business, so he decided that he'd asked enough questions. He looked back up at the rope hanging from the tree limb just above his head.

His heart was racing. Why was his heart racing? He was ready for this. He'd been ready for this for so long. He stood there for some time looking up, watching the rope swing back and forth and back and forth. Blackie had taken a position off to one side watching Nate. He was doing that infamous curious dog look. Ears perked up, head tilting from side to side, as though he were trying to figure out what was going on.

"Hey Trev? Can I ask you something?" Nate started, stilling staring up at the rope.

"You just did." Trevor teased.

"Seriously."

"Sure, what's up?" Trevor had managed to pull his own gaze from the rope and turn his attention back to Nate.

"What was it like?" Nate met his gaze now.

Trevor's eyes turned to the ground.

"I mean, if you don't want to talk about it, that's cool too." Nate told his friend.

"Nah, it's cool." Trevor said. "It's just kind of a long story.

PART SIXTEEN

Jacob

The sound of Tupac's 'Dear Mama' seeped into Jake's dreams and began to lull him from his afternoon nap back into reality. He mouthed the words to his mother's ring tone as he reached clumsily for his cell phone vibrating on the nightstand next to his bed.

"Hey mom," He answered groggily.

"Don't tell me you're still in the bed." She said hearing the sleep in his voice.

He leaned up on his elbow and looked over at the clock that sat next to a framed picture of himself and his little brother enjoying a waffle breakfast. It was 2:30 PM.

"Mom, you know I had to work late last night stocking the store and I had class this morning. I was just catching a quick nap." He started to explain.

"I know Jakey bear." His mother teased. "I need you to make a run."

Jake smiled at the sound of his mom's pet name for him. He'd been her 'Jakey Bear' for as long as he could remember. Now that he was older, she usually only used it when she wanted him to do something for her.

"Sure." He said, "What did you need?"

"I need you to make a run to the grocery store for me." She continued. "We're out of flour and your brother went through an entire carton of eggs last night making egg and cheese sandwiches."

"Well, you are the one that taught him how to make them." He laughed.

"That's true." She chuckled along with him. "But I didn't teach him to use an entire carton of eggs making them."

"We're growing boys mom." Jake told her as he swung his legs off the side of the bed looking at the picture of his brother on the nightstand.

"Don't remind me." She replied. "I'm still waiting for one of you to literally start eating us out of house and home, starting with the drywall." They both laughed at the idea of this.

"I don't mind running to the store for you." He said composing himself.

He yawned a long, wide yawn and stretched.

"Thank you, sweetheart. There's some money in a jar on top of the refrigerator." She started.

"I've got it, mom." Jake interrupted. "I'll even bring home an extra carton to help soothe the savage beast of Trev's hunger."

"What would I do without you." His mother said making kissing sounds into the phone.

Jake was up and headed down the hall to take a quick shower.

"Probably be miserable knowing that there could have been an incredibly handsome, athletic, and intelligent son in your life, but instead your stuck with Trev." He laughed at this as well.

"Funny." She said, "I'm going to tell Trevor you said that too."

"Great. Now I'm going to have to beat up my little brother before he can devour all the eggs in the house." He joked.

"Gotta get back to work, honey." She said, "I'll see you guys when I get off. I'll try to be home by seven. Ok?"

"Sure thing, mom." He replied. "I'm going to go ahead and run to the store, so I'll be back before Trev gets home."

"Thanks again. Love you." She ended the call as she always did.

"Love you too mom." Jake hit the end button and jumped into the shower.

He took a quick, ten-minute shower and was dressed and out the door in fifteen. He knew Trevor would be home around 3:30 and wanted to be back in time to meet his bus. He and a few of his friends had been planning a weekend fishing trip and this would be the first time he allowed Trevor to tag along with him. With a five-year age difference, Trevor had always been the bratty little brother that Jake loved but didn't want to have to take along everywhere he went.

Now that he'd graduated, and Trevor was fifteen, Jake found that they had a lot more in common. His little brother had been super excited when he told him that he could go, and his parents were allowing him to stay home from school the next day so they could get packed for their trip and get on the road before it got too dark to head for the cabin, they'd be staying in.

He could see Trev flying off the bus, probably already ready to go.

He walked around the car to do a quick check on the tires. It wasn't the newest or the best car on the road, but it was his. His 2001 Honda Accord had been a gift from his father when he'd started school at the local Technical College this past fall. His dad had taken on extra shifts at work to save for it and had presented it as a late high school graduation gift. He'd graduated last year but with no college savings the little scholarships he had received would not have been enough to send him to an out of state college and he hated the idea of placing yet another financial burden on his already hard-working parents.

So, he started a job at the local hardware store during his summer vacation to help with some of the household bills and to pay for his school supplies and his father had gotten him the car to ensure that he at least had the ability to get back and forth to school and work.

The little blue car had come in handy and with only a few minor little issues, but it ran great. His dad had shown him how to check the fluids and change the oil in the car himself. He also explained about watching the tire pressure. The car tended to pull to the left a little even when you were steering straight, but his father had assured him that a tire alignment would correct that, and he'd have his mechanic take a look at it first chance he got.

Jake jumped in the car and headed off to the grocery store.

The after-school traffic was just starting to pick up. Jake was confident that he'd be back in plenty of time. The store was only about ten minutes away and he was familiar with a few shortcuts that would allow him to bypass any stopped school buses that might slow him down. He was careful to steer closer to the right side of the road to compensate for the car pulling a bit to the left.

When he arrived at the store, he was fortunate enough to find a parking space right in front. He made his way through the familiar isles of the store with the hand basket that he'd snagged at the entrance. He tossed in a bag of self-rising flour and headed to the dairy fridge to grab the eggs. He placed two cartons in his basket and made his way to the express lane.

"Well good afternoon young man." He heard a voice call to him. It was Mrs. McCallister, their neighbor from across the street.

"Hi, Mrs. McCallister. How are you doing today?" Jake replied politely.

"Oh, you know, my blood pressures a little high and my knees have been giving me a bit of trouble, but I manage." She told him.

"Sorry to hear that." Jake said. He glanced at his phone to check the time, 3:10 PM.

"How's that adorable brother of yours?" she asked with a huge smile.

Jake liked to tease that Mrs. McCallister had a crush on Trevor, which he hated. He couldn't wait to get home and tell Trev that he'd run into his girlfriend.

"He's good." Jake told her. "I'm headed home now to meet his bus. It should be pulling up in just a few."

"Well, isn't that nice." She dug into her change purse and pulled out a dollar. "Be sure to take him some sweets for me." She took Jakes hand and folded the dollar into it.

"I will and thank you." He returned her smile.

"Well don't let me keep you."

"It was nice seeing you." He leaned in and gave her a quick hug and then turned to run back down the snack isle.

Mrs. McCallister had reminded him that he usually brings Trev his favorite hot chips and a soda when he stops at the store, he went back to grab it.

His phone chimed with a text notification as he made his way back to the car. It was a text from Trevor.

'WYA?' It read.

'Leaving the store.' He texted back, sliding into the driver seat and placing the groceries in the passenger seat next to him.

He sat his phone in the cup holder. He'd promised his mother that he would never text and drive and had managed to keep his promise since he'd been driving. He pulled his seat belt across his chest and fastened it securely, then started backing out of the parking space.

His phone chimed again.

'Be home in a minute. Grab me some chips and a soda.' It read.

Jake pressed the brake and read the message. He smiled and started to text back.

'I'll think about it.' A car horn blared behind him before he could hit send. He glanced up into the rear-view mirror and saw there was a car waiting for the park he was pulling out of. He dropped the phone back into the cup holder. The phone missed center, as he was watching the car behind him backing up to make room for him to pull out and slid between the center console and the passenger seat.

"Shoot." Jake glanced over trying to see into the crevice. The car behind him beeped again. "Guess I'll have to dig that out when I get back to the house."

Jake swung the car out of the space and headed for home. It was too late to take the back roads back home as they would be teaming with buses dropping off the local school kids, so he turned onto the main road. There were more traffic lights on this road, but it would be clear of the slower school traffic. He waited at the light for it to turn green and was on his way, making sure to mind his speed limit and steer toward the right side of the road.

The main road carried him most of the way home with only two turns before he'd arrive. On a good day this was only a fifteen-minute ride, twenty with traffic. He could see the turn just ahead of him when he heard his phone chime again. He glanced over in the direction the phone had fallen, knowing that it was probably Trevor texting him again.

Another horn blared and there was the strained sound of tires screeching on the road. Jake looked up just in time to see the semi jacked knifed in front of him and sliding out of control in his direction. Out of the corner of his eye he could see the school bus that had just turned at the light. The driver of the semi-truck had missed seeing the school buses turn signal and had been barreling toward the bus when he tried to steer away from it. The school bus was able to turn the corner successfully preventing a collision, but the truck wasn't so lucky.

The trailer had slid around and was now coming at Jake vertical to the truck itself. He could read the word 'freight' in big black letters on the side of the container and then nothing.

Trevor's bus pulled up to the house at 3:33PM on the dot. He jumped off the bus and checked the driveway for Jake's car. He hadn't made it back from the store just yet, so Trev pulled out his phone to text him again. He saw the three familiar chat dots of a pending message and waited a moment for it to come through. He pulled out his house key to unlock the front door and heard a car door close behind him. He turned, expecting to see Jake getting out of the car and was met by Mrs. McCallister waving at him from across the street.

"Hi Mrs. McCallister!" Trevor called to her and then quickly ducked into the house to avoid any further conversation with the crazy lady from across the street.

He looked back at his phone and saw that the three dots were still waving lazily on the screen.

He texted; 'WYA' and waited for a reply.

He could hear sirens off in the distance as he dropped his backpack on a chair in the den and went into the kitchen to make himself an afternoon snack. His mom had gotten him hooked on egg and cheese sandwiches made with scrambled eggs and sharp cheddar cheese. He opened the fridge, grabbed the cheese, and looked for the eggs.

"Dang." He said to himself. "Forgot I finished those off last night."

He looked at his phone again, still no reply from Jake. He texted: 'Hey, bring back some eggs too. We're all out.'

The three dots floated and danced in place.

"His phone must have died or something." Trevor said. He decided that a regular cheese sandwich would be enough and proceeded to toast a couple of pieces of bread. He made three sandwiches, melting the cheese in the microwave. He cut one of the sandwiches in half and placed a sandwich and a half on two plates. When Jake was home, they always had their afternoon snack together so they could talk about their school day and laugh about stuff that happened. He took the plates into the den and kicked his feet up on the couch to watch tv until Jake arrived.

Trev ate his half sandwich and then scooted down in the couch to get comfortable. He looked at his phone once more, still no reply. He slid the phone onto the coffee table. His eyelids were starting to get heavy; he felt a nap coming on.

Moments later he felt the sensation of someone pulling on his foot. He looked down and saw Jake sitting on the other end of the couch smiling at him.

"Hey there buddy." Jake said.

Trev gave him a playful kick. "Man, what took you so long? It's starting to get dark, and we still have to finish getting packed for the trip."

"Yeah, I know." Jake looked away sadly.

Trevor sat up and looked at his brother. "Hey, what's up? Was it cancelled or something?" He was starting to get concerned. Jake was usually a pretty happy guy. He was super popular and had tons of friends, so it was rare to see him down.

"Looks that way buddy." He looked back at Trev now. "I need you to do something for me." He told him.

"Sure, what?" Trevor's heart had begun to race in his chest, and he didn't understand why he was so nervous now.

Jake took a deep breath and exhaled slowly. He blinked a few times as though he were blinking back impending tears and swallowed hard.

"I need you to take care of mom for me. Ok?" He told his little brother.

"Jake?" Trevor had gone from nervous to scared now. He looked into Jakes pale grey face and took notice of his greyed clothing and shoes. He wasn't sure if it was the lighting from the television in the quickly darkening room, but everything about Jake had a sickening grey hue to him. "Jake... are you ok?"

"Take care of mom." He said again. He stood then and turned toward the door.

Trevor reached out for him trying to grab the back of his shirt. "Wait! Where are you going?"

The greying material slipped mistily between his fingers. Jake paused for a moment and then said over his shoulder, "You are my favorite little brother."

"I'm your only little brother." Trevor reminded him with tears in his eyes.

Jake chuckled at that and walked to the door. He reached for the doorknob and was gone.

Trevor scrambled to his feet, tripping over himself and falling off the couch and onto the floor. The shock of falling rattled him awake and he looked around the room confused.

He'd been dreaming. He wiped a hand across his eyes to dry the moisture he knew was there. He had been crying in his sleep, but it had all been a dream. He stayed on the floor where he'd fallen and reached up onto the table for his phone. Jake still hadn't texted him back and it was 6:45, mom would be home soon.

There was a knock at the door. Trevor jumped up from the floor and vaulted over the couch, relief washing over him.

"How the heck did you forget your keys…" He swung the door open wide and was met by two officers.

"Good afternoon." The first officer said. "Are your parents' home?"

Trevor stared at them, unblinking.

"Son?" The female officer reached out for him.

Trevor took a step back just out of her reach. He's seen enough movies and shows to know there were only a few reasons why they could possibly be there standing in the doorway of his home.

"Son?" She said again. "Is anyone home with you?"

Trevor stood silent. His heart had begun to pound in his ears, and he needed to pee for some strange reason.

"How about we come in and wait with you until someone gets here?" The first officer started.

Trevor slammed the door shut and leaned against it.

"No….no….no…NO!" He screamed. He slid down the door and wrapped his arms around his knees, rocking slowly.

The officers knocked a couple more times and then decided it would be best to simply wait outside for someone to arrive home.

Moments later Trevor lifted his head to the sound of another door closing. He crawled over to the window and saw his mother speaking with the two officers that stood in the driveway. Suddenly she collapsed to the ground screaming. The female officer knelt next to her and wrapped her arm around her shoulder to console her. Mrs. McCallister, who had been standing across the street in her yard watching, came over now and his mother fell limp into her arms still screaming and crying hysterically. The older woman showed great strength despite her aching knees and pulled his mother to her feet. She took the keys from her hand and walked her to the front door with the officers following close behind.

Trevor got up from where he had been kneeling at the window

and ran into his room. He heard the door open. The sound of his mother sobbing filled the house with a sorrow like he'd never heard. The sound of her crying got him started again and he buried his face into his pillow to muffle his cries.

"Would you mind fixing her a glass of water?" He heard Mrs. McCallister ask someone.

"Certainly." It was the female officer.

"Ma'am. We are sorry that we have to bring you such troubling news…"

"If you don't mind," She interrupted him. "Perhaps this should wait until her husband gets here. I took the liberty of calling him when I saw her collapse in the yard."

"Yes, of course." The officer agreed.

"He should be here shortly." She assured him.

The other officer must have returned with the glass of water. He heard Mrs. McCallister speaking softly now.

"Take a little sip, darling. It'll help." She said.

"I sent him to the store." His mother cried. "My baby would be here if I hadn't sent him to the store! Oh God! Oh God!!"

"Shhhhh." Mrs. McCallister tried to soothe her in her grief. "It's no one's fault darling. It was an accident."

"No! I sent him!" She cried out.

He heard the sound of glass smashing. Then one of the officers sounded as if they were speaking into their mic.

"Let's get an EMT unit over here. Just to be on the safe side." He said.

The paramedics arrived a few moments later and a mild sedative was used to calm his mother. They were checking her blood pressure when his father arrived.

"What's going on here?" He said taking in the scene.

Trevor got up and tipped into the hallway. He sat down on the floor just out of sight of the adults that now filled the room. Mrs. McCallister caught sight of him and smiled weakly.

"Come take a seat over here with your wife." She said his father, waving him over to her.

His father did as he was told and took her into his arms. Mrs. McCallister stood then and went into the hallway to sit across from Trevor. It took her a moment to get down onto the floor, but she eventually did. He looked across at her, eyes red from crying. Neither of them spoke.

The female officer brought a glass of water into the den for his father and then stood next to her partner who had taken a seat across from them with his hat in his hand. He was working the brim of the hat with his fingers as he considered the best approach to break such unfortunate news. This wasn't the first time he'd had to tell parents bad news, but the degree of this particular tragedy made it that much harder.

"I am so sorry that we have to inform you of this unexpected situation. There is never an easy way to break such news to anyone, but especially to parents." He started. "There was an accident this afternoon involving a freight truck. Your son Jacob was an unfortunate causality due to no fault of his own. He was found at the scene. His vehicle was one of many that were side swiped by the jack-knifed truck as the driver swerved to avoid a turning school bus."

"Oh God…oh God…. oh God." His mother repeated over and over. It was as if all words had left her but those two.

"Did he suffer at all?" His father asked the officers. There was a strain in his voice that he barely kept a handle on.

"No, sir." The officer said softly. "He was killed on impact and didn't suffer at all from what we understand."

"Oooooooh Goddddddd." His mother had begun to sag in her seat and his father did his best to hold her in place.

"When can we see him?" He asked them.

"The coroner is at the scene now. We would prefer that you waited to be contacted to identify his body at the hospital. That would be best for both of you." The Officer explained, looking mostly at Trevor's mother as he spoke.

"What do you mean?" His father asked. "Is there something you aren't saying?"

The Officer cleared his throat. "Would it be possible for me to speak with you privately?"

"TELL US!" His mother screamed now. "My son is gone. How much worse could it possibly be? Just tell us."

The Officer cleared his throat again and looked over at his partner. She was also holding her hat in her hands with a solemn expression on her face. She stepped up then and spoke.

"The vehicle your son was driving was hit square on by the freight container the truck was hauling. As a result, the engine of the vehicle was pushed into the driver's seat, which in turn pushed the driver seat back as the car was severed in half by the container. The rear portion of the vehicle was thrown into a ditch and the front remained in the middle of the road."

"He was cut in half." His father said. "Are you trying to say that my boy was cut in half?" His face was a mixture of confusion and pain.

"We are so sorry." She replied.

"Please leave." He said pulling his bawling wife closer to him. "Please.

The officers once again gave their condolences and informed them that they would be contacted soon to identify the body, before taking their leave.

Trevor crawled across the hall floor to where Mrs. McCallister was sitting. She opened her arms and took him into them, cradling him like a baby and rocking him slowly as he cried. Jake was gone, but he'd taken the time to come and say goodbye to his favorite little brother.

Jacob AD

Nate stood staring at Trevor with a blank expression. He didn't know what he would do if anything like that happened to anyone in his family. Trevor stood still staring up at the swaying rope. He wiped his hand across his eyes and continued to watch the rope swing. Nate wasn't sure what to say at that moment. His friend's brother had not only been killed but had been severed completely in half. He was glad when Trevor spoke first.

"Yeah, so that happened." He said looking at Nate now.

"Dude." Nate said.

"I'm cool." Trevor assured him. "That was two years ago. We tried to stay in our old house, but I think it was too hard for everyone. That's why I did what I did. I know that if he hadn't been trying to check his phone, he probably would have seen the truck coming and had time to get out of the way. He was texting me back when he died. They even found the chips and soda I'd asked him to bring me in the back seat with him…well, with the upper half of him. The bottom half was still in the front of the car holding the engine in his lap, his fingers were wrapped around it like he was simply catching a football or something."

They all sat silently for a minute. Blackie panted softly as he looked from one boy to the other. Finally, as if recalling why he'd started telling the story to begin with, Trevor took a long breath and looked back up at the rope.

"The funeral was closed casket. My mom couldn't bear to look at his face after the accident. Afterwards she would spend most days in bed and my dad would stay gone during the day and come home and sit up most nights swirling an endlessly half full glass of brandy as he stared off into the dark. They basically stopped speaking all together and when they did, they yelled more than anything. Probably why they never noticed me leaving every day to go sit with Jacob at the cemetery. He was the only one I could talk to about what was going on at home. Dad was always angry, and mom was always crying. It was just too much, and I just knew every time they looked at me, they were blaming me for what happened. You could see it in their eyes." He was staring back at the ground now.

"Did they ever say that?' Nate asked.

"They didn't have to. They couldn't stand to be in the same room with me. Even now I can go days without seeing my dad or speaking to my mom. They probably haven't even noticed I left to come here." He paused for a moment and then added, "I left a note though."

He continued, "When my mom was finally up for going back to work, she just assumed that meant that I was ready to go back to school. Like nothing had happened and things were supposed to just go back to normal. Don't get me wrong, I tried. I went back for a while. Every day it felt like everyone was just staring at me. Look at the red headed freak with the dead brother. I was still going to visit Jake every day after school and that only made it worse. They started calling me zombie boy and the grave digger.

Saying I smelled lie dead people and dirt."

He looked up at Nate then, "You know, they even filled my locker with dirt and a little shovel like it was a joke or something."

"I would have helped you beat they ass." Nate grumbled at the thought.

"Yeah," Trevor could just picture his friend standing up for him and beating down the guys that had played such a sick prank. Hell, maybe his life would be just a bit different if Nate had been there at the lowest point in his life. Who knows, doesn't matter now anyway. If it had mattered, he would never be telling this story.

"Anyway," Trevor went on, "I did want to get pay back and I tried but it turned into a huge fight, I got hurt pretty good and everyone said I started it. They suspended me instead of expelling me because of my brother, they said. Whatever.

When I got back home that afternoon no one was there. I cleaned up my own cuts, got an icepack for my face and went looking for some pain medicine because my chest was killing me. Found out later I had a fractured rib from being kicked in the chest. But yeah, found a bottle of pain meds in the cabinet in my parents' bathroom. Codeine, almost a full bottle from my mom having her gull bladder removed the year before. I took two and started to leave but something told me to take the bottle with me. By the time I got back to my room I'd decided to take the entire bottle. So, I did, I took 15 codeine pills and went into my brother's room and got into his bed. The pain in my head and my chest had stopped and I could feel my heart beating. I started closing my eyes and then there was Jake, I could see him between the slits of my eyes as they were closing.

I woke up with a tube down my throat, gagging. I was in the hospital having my stomach pumped. My mom and dad came in and all they could do was yell and ask me what's wrong with me and tell me how selfish I was being for doing what I'd done. I was glad when the social worker came in and said I had to be taken to Mental Health for evaluation and that they couldn't go with me. I almost died, and they were calling me selfish. Man, I hated them after that.

I stayed at the mental health hospital for about a week. I did the counseling, I acknowledged I had a problem, I took the meds they gave me, and they let me go home. Easy as that. But what they didn't know was that I had seen Jake and I knew how to get back to that place to see him again.

The doctors had warned my parents to lock up or remove any medications from the house that could be potentially dangerous, but of course they barely listened. Too busy trying to get away from each other, and me. So, I found where my mom had stashed the sleeping pills her doctor had prescribed for her," he put two fingers up indicating air quotes, "…anxiety."

"Took that whole bottle too, I just wanted to talk to Jake. Tell him that I was sorry and that I missed him. But I didn't see Jake this time. This time there were only voices and fog. Voices that said if I wanted to be with my brother I could. They said that my parents missed him and wanted to be with him too. That there were people that hurt me that would be forgiven if they were also allowed to go with us, bad people that could be made good again and that I should write their names down so that they could be made good, in their passing on to where Jake was. To where My parents and I could be as well.

Woke up in the hospital again after that time too. I wasn't conscious when they pumped my stomach that time. I was awake when my parents agreed to have me committed though. It was only a month that time, but we had visitation during the time I was there, and no one ever came. Our neighbor from across the street picked me up when I was discharged. And SURPRISE, there was no one home when I got there.

The last time was the real reason why we moved. I couldn't go back to school, and I spent all of my time at the gravesite. My counselor told my parents that it would be in my best interest. I feel like they just didn't want to be the family in the neighborhood everyone had a story about. The family who lost one son to an accident and the other at his own hand. Worrying about what other people think instead of how your remaining son feels." Trev shook his head as though he were clearing the fog of the past and stepping back into the present.

"Damn." Nate said.

He looked over at the stool and back up at the rope. The desire to be done with this harsh cruel world was still there, but now he felt a tinge of doubt beginning to seep in. Trevor had tried to kill himself several times after his brother died. Was an argument with his girlfriend or his mom really enough of a reason? He still hated himself. He still felt like he was more of a burden to everyone and that they'd all be much better off without him, but for the first time he was considering how his brother and sister would deal with his death. Would they feel the way Trevor did and try to follow in his footsteps?

PART SEVENTEEN

Formerly Known as Blackie

"If you decide to do this," Trevor was saying to him. "I wouldn't stop you, because I understand what it feels like not to want to be here anymore. But I appreciate you being my friend, Nate."

Nate considered Trev's last words as he walked over and placed his foot on the first rung of the stool. He was still contemplating the new doubt that had managed to work its way into his psyche. As he did this, Blackie lifted his front paw, and brought it down heavily. Both Nate and Trevor stumbled back, Nate barely keeping his balance. His ears were ringing. The sound banged around in his head and spread throughout is body like a sensation that screamed 'NO!'

It was like it had been yelled at him, but rather than being able to hear the word, he felt it, like a punch in the chest that had literally sent him reeling. He looked around, placing his hand on his chest and rubbed where he imagined he'd felt the pressure.

"What the..." He said looking to Trevor. "Did you hear that?

"I didn't hear anything." Trevor said with his eyes wide. "But I definitely felt something. Like a little earthquake or something."

"Yeah." Nate agreed.

He was looking everywhere; behind him, in front of him and deep into the woods, trying to see what he'd been hit with. There were no big rocks lying around. There'd been no breeze and the leaves on the trees were still. But he was sure he'd felt it, heavy against his body, pushing him back and shouting in his mind the feeling of 'NO!'

"Okay, so apparently I'm losing my mind." Nate said out loud. He got up and dusted himself off. Stepping back over to the stool, he placed his hand on the seat for balance and began to step up again.

"NO!!!" The feeling pounded into his chest. This time he really wasn't ready and tumbled to the ground rolling, head over heels, until he was back in a seated position with his back to the stool.

"What the hell!" Nate yelled.

"I heard it that time!" Trevor said running over to Nate on the ground.

Nate jumped up and they both turned around and came face-to-face with Blackie, who was now on all fours, staring at them with his head lowered. He raised his paw again and let it fall heavily to the ground. Now both Nate and Trevor were pounded in the chest with an invisible pressure that rang in their ears with not the word, but the feeling of 'NO!'

"You?" He was looking at Blackie now. They were locked in an intense staring contest that neither was actually trying to win.

"You." He said again, this time with less of the question and with more understanding. "But how?"

Blackie took a step forward, raised his head and sat in front of them.

"It was you last night too, wasn't it? Nate asked him.

"Last night?" Trevor said.

"Yeah, remember I told you I saw colors or something?" He said without looking away from the dog.

"I didn't think you meant literally." Trevor told him.

Blackie wagged his tail and a lighter, breezier sensation washed over Nate. Words once again expressed as feelings as the feeling of yes sang in his mind and ran down his spine and out the tips of his fingers and toes like a warm glow.

"Yes." Blackie was saying in his mind. "Yessss."

"Wooooh." Nate said. "This is getting a little freaky. If this were a movie, I'd be getting ready to run. You know we're always the first to die in movies like this."

"Did he say something else?" Trevor asked watching the exchange between Nate and the dog.

"Yeah," Nate looked at Trev. "He said it was him."

Blackie wagged his tail again. "Friend." The word sang in Nate's head.

"Friend." He repeated out loud so Trevor would know what he said as well. "Yeah, I suppose we're friends." Nate said getting up onto his knees in front of Blackie.

"Doesn't change that is totally freaky. I mean, what the hell dude?" He took the dog's face in his hands. "Are you like talking to me in my head?" Blackie licked the side of Nate's face and the word 'Feel' floated through him.

"Feel. Yeah, I get it. It's like knowing what you're saying but instead of hearing you I can feel what you mean." He said.

"This is so weird." Trevor said, kneeling down next to Nate in front of Blackie. "Why can't I hear him?"

"Dude, you don't have to tell me. I'm surprised you're still even here." Nate said.

"It's going to take more than a telepathic dog to scare me." Trevor assured him. "I've been through worse, remember?"

Blackie adjusted his sitting position merrily and leaned in again to lick Trevor's face as well. "Feel."

This time both the boys were able to 'hear' him. Nate let himself fall back until he was seated on his behind. He crossed his legs in front of him.

"Wow." he said shaking his head. "Of all the dogs in the kennel mom finds the one that's the telepath." Blackie shook his head heavily and the boys could feel the sensation of 'More' dance across their minds.

"More?" He asked him. "You know you're going to have to give us 'more' than that?" Nate told him. He paused for a moment and then said. "I'm sitting in the middle of the woods talking to my dog. Now if this isn't going crazy, I don't know what is. Then again, maybe I'm already dead and don't realize it."

"Been there, done that." Trevor added sitting down next to Nate.

"More." Nate said again. "You want to clarify that for me?"

Blackie lifted his front paw again and began to paw at the air expectantly. "Hands." Sang in Nate's mind. Nate lifted his hand and Blackie's paw fell into it.

"He talks and he knows how to shake." Nate mused with an ironic chuckle to himself.

"Hands." Blackie said looking from Nate to Trevor now.

"I think he wants us to hold hands." Nate said holding his hand out to Trev.

"I don't know man. This is kind of weird." Trevor was watching Blackie with wide eyes.

"Dude, come on. Do you really think he would try to do something to us? I mean something worse than we've both already tried to do to ourselves?"

"True." Trevor took Nate's hand.

"Now what?" Nate looked back at the dog who's paw he was still holding.

"Close." The feeling pressed through their minds, and he saw an image of himself closing his eyes, so they both did. Once their eyes were closed there was a bright blue blinding light that lasted for several seconds before they were able to see again.

They saw a huge black dog and several small puppies in a large pen. Her eyes glowed a warm silver glow as she patiently tended to each of her pups. She was warm and smelled of jasmine and milk. Her love and pride for her pups radiated from her. She was protective, but also wise, knowing that each of her offspring had a destiny of their own. So, when a large, strange man approached the pen she grew anxious, fearing for her young ones all while knowing she would have to let go.

The pups couldn't see the stranger's face because it was too high up, but they could see his heavy boots, denim jeans and the heavy mustard colored work jacket that he wore. Nate saw the man pointing at him and then someone lifted him up. There was a mirror positioned on the far wall in the room they were in. The room was a garage or perhaps a kennel of some kind. The mirror hung over a utility sink and the reflection was of a small Asian man holding a healthy, fell fed little black pup. It was Blackie and both Nate and Trevor were seeing what Blackie had seen as a pup. They listened as the Asian man explained about the care of the dogs.

He assured the stranger that they were all well fed. That he expected them to go to loving homes and that they needed plenty of water and room to run. All the typical things that anyone considering getting a dog might expect to naturally be told to do. From Blackie's eyes Nate saw the man nodding and smiling. The Asian man handed Blackie over to the stranger whose face he still hadn't seen. The man held Blackie up in front of him, so they were now eye to eye.

"Good boy." The stranger said. "Let's go home." The man placed one big, heavy hand under Blackie's chest and tucked the puppy firmly under his arm. He watched as the man handed the small Asian man a hefty stack of hundreds and in return the old man handed him a sack filled with several items.

"Blackie must've been a very expensive dog." Nate thought to himself.

"Heck yeah." Trevor's voice responded in Nate's head. "Look at all that money."

Nate was surprised to hear Trevor but both boys continued to watch as the scene played out.

The man took Blackie to his truck and placed him in the kennel he had waiting on the backseat. They rode for several hours, maybe days if you based the time passing on the little pup's concept of time. He was growing weary of being stuck in the cage and needed to relieve himself. He had not been allowed to do so before they'd left.

They'd been riding for so long that Nate could feel the puppy's thirst and the rumbling of his small stomach. He felt the vibration in his chest as the puppy cried and whimpered for attention, for food, for his mother and siblings. The stranger continued to drive though, unfazed by the noise.

They arrived at a cabin in the woods where the puppy was promptly removed from the truck, still in the kennel and placed in a corner of what must have passed for the den. The cabin was not very large, the den, bedroom and kitchen were all one room with a door to the left of the kitchen table that may have been a closet, or better, a bathroom. It was no concern of the pup; he never got the chance to find out what was in that room behind the door to the left of the kitchen table.

The man brought him a small bowl of water and a bowl food that he'd gotten from a small container in the sack, the puppy ate greedily. There had been a collar in the sack as well. It was leather with something etched into it and appeared to be too large for the still small dog. The stranger tossed it aside.

"Won't be needing this." He said in a gruff voice.

Nate could see the collar through the pup's small eyes. The word that had been carved into the leather was somehow beginning to fade, fizzling out like a flame following a lit fuse. He was able to just catch what it said before the last of it fizzled into a wisp of smoke.

"Reisun." Nate whispered. "That must've been your name before he changed it. Your real name, the one the Chinese man gave you." Nate was saying this out loud in a hushed voice with his eyes still closed.

"Born with." Blackie, who's name they now knew was Reisun, added. "All born with."

They watched portions of Reisun's life playout in a kind of fast-forwarded flash of scenes and moments. He spent most of his time in the very kennel that had brought him to this cabin in the woods. Sometimes many days would go by before he was taken out to relieve himself outside and was punished severely if he ever had an accident inside the kennel. A hundred times his face had been pressed into his own urine after he'd managed to hold it for several days. And a hundred times he'd been beaten for not being able to hold it until he was let out.

He lived in that kennel until he had grown so large that he could no longer fit into it, and yet Nate cringed as he watched him squeeze himself into that same cage time and time again to please the stranger that he had come to know as his master.

Unexpectedly the man came in one day and removed the cage, placing a small rug where it had been. "There, dog." The man said to him. It had been almost a year and the only name the man had given him was 'dog', but Reisun had never forgotten the writing on the collar, or his mother and siblings left behind. Often, as he lay curled in a ball on that thinning rag of rug, in the corner of the room, he would whimper softly to himself, mourning his loss.

There was no kindness from this man. There was no petting, or tug of war. No throwing balls. He was waiting for something, and the dog was of no use to him until the something that he was waiting for finally happened.

"Come dog." The man had said to him when he had been with him for a second year. He tied a loose length of rope around the dog's neck. "You should be of age now."

He walked the dog outside through the back door and into a cool clear night. The moon was high and lit up the surrounding trees like a spotlight in the sky.

The stranger stood before Reisun holding his original collar in his hand. He took a knee in front of the dog, looking him square in the eyes. "Do you understand my words?"

Reisun whimpered and sat in front of his kneeling master.

"Good." He told him. He placed the collar he was holding around the dog's neck and stood up. The boys felt a surge of energy as the letters of Reisun's name began to reappear on his collar just as they had gone. His eyes began to glow a soft silver glow and he could feel a change in his body down to the very molecules that made him who he was. He felt…reborn!

Nate could feel the familiar push from the dog to the man as he communicated with him through sensations, he knew the man felt in his mind.

"Good." The stranger said again. "Show me my power."

There was a pushing again from the dog's body, but this time it was heavier and more intense. There was a flash of images of the man beating him and punishing him for messing in his crate after being locked in it for several days. Flashes of heavy boot kicks and punches, of being alone and hungry. Reisun stood his ground as he pushed against the man's request, against his so-called master. He saw the man brace himself against the amplified sensation of 'NO!!'

The man scoffed at him. "I am your master and your breeder assured me that your powers would be passed to me! I demand that you do as I say!" He roared at Reisun.

The adolescent dog pushed back again. He had never felt so confident and powerful before and he was no longer afraid of this man who had treated his with such harshness. His master was not a good person, not worthy of being called master and Reisun would not submit.

"Not worthy!" He lowered his head and took a step forward.

The man stumbled backwards, steading himself, quickly regaining his composure. He reached into his pocket and pulled out a pair of black gloves made from some type of animal hide.

"Okay. We'll do it your way." He slid the gloves on and began to approach Reisun, his eyes filled with intent.

"NO!" Reisun pushed against the man with all his newly found strength only to have the man swat his attempt away like an annoying fly.

"See these here gloves dog? Taken from the backside of one of your very own kind." He snatched the collar from around the dog's neck.

"Still a stupid pup, what were you going to do, fight me?" He held the collar up and began to slap Reisun across the muzzle with it. "You -- don't – even – know – how to use – this!"

He made a choking sound that could have been a chuckle or a cough. Reisun only whimpered solemnly.

The man grabbed him by the scruff and re-tied the rope around Reisun's neck dragging him back through the cabin, out the front door and down the steps.

You don't submit, you don't eat! Seems to me that you need to be taught some respect!"

Reisun struggled desperately, pulling back with all his might, but he was still young and had much to learn about his newly awakened abilities. The stranger snatched at the rope causing it to tighten around Reisun's throat, strangling him. He planted all four paws in the dirt and reared back, thrashing violently from side to side trying to free his head from the rope. The stranger reeled the rope in, pulling the terrified animal closer to him and kicked him several times in the side, knocking the air and the fight out of him.

The rope had begun to unravel during their struggle, fraying just above the knot tied in it. Seeing this only angered the stranger more. He stopped at his truck and grabbed a length of chain from the truck bed dropping it in front of Reisun on the ground as he struggled to catch his breath and get back to his feet. The stranger reached into the truck then and pulled out a familiar sack. From that he removed an ornately engraved padlock. He had a flash of the old man saying that young powerful pups were often curious and mischievous. The lock was enchanted and could not be removed by the dogs, only by a person.

He reached down to remove the rope tied around the dog's neck. Reisun jerked his head back at that moment and sank his teeth deep into the strangers' hand, drawing blood.

"Son of a bi..." The stranger drew his hand back quickly, examining the injury.

"You ungrateful..." He reached down and grabbed the length of chain then, standing back up right and raising the chain over his head, he shouted, "I am your master, and you will do as I say!" He brought the chain down heavily, smashing it against Reisun's head and body until the dog screamed in pain.

Both Trevor and Nate flinched and cringe with every blow.

"That asshole!" Nate exclaimed. There were tears brimming in his eyes.

"Dammit." Trevor added and then quieted again.

Reisun lay lifeless on the ground, bruised and bleeding.

The man grabbed the limp animal by the scruff of its neck and replaced the rope he'd tied around the dog's throat with the truck chain, wrapping it tightly so that it bit into his neck. He secured it with the enchanted lock, then dragged him the rest of the way across the yard, through the trees and to a fence about 500 yards away. He attached the other end of the chain there with another lock that already hung from the fence.

"Since you're so outspoken, how about we discuss this another day? Perhaps a week from now." He told the dog and turned to leave.

The next mental push was far weaker and filled with hurt and betrayal.

"Never", came the sensation from Reisun, "Never, never, never, never!"

The man was being pushed forward, but not over. He hadn't tumbled the way Nate had. He was big and country strong from years of living off the grid and from the land. He turned then to face Reisun.

"Nevers a long-time black dog." He said to him. "We'll see how you feel after you've gone a week without food or water. You might find that you've had a change of heart." He turned and walked away.

When he returned to the cabin he climbed into his truck and sped off down the driveway past the dog he'd chained there, making sure to kick up as much dirt and rocks as possible on his way by. Reisun lay there in a ball mourning his family, whimpering softly to himself, knowing that this could not be home.

Both boys were released from the vision then.

"Reisun." Nate said leaning back onto his hands. "So, your name is Reisun. Like the word 'reason', right?"

Reisun wagged his tail happily and Nate could feel humored agreement.

"Humored? So, what's so funny about what I said?" Nate asked. He recalled the way it was spelled R-E-I...S-U-N, like the sun in sky. Maybe it meant something else, or maybe he was pronouncing it wrong, but it looked like 'reason', so he said 'reason'.

"Well, nice to make your acquaintance, Mr. Reisun." Trevor said, putting his hand out as if they were meeting for the first time. Reisun, formally Blackie, raised his paw in compliance and they shook.

"Well, Reisun." Nate said. "Looks like we're not the only ones who've had a hard childhood."

Reisun turned his head to one side, wearing a confused expression.

"Yeah, you probably don't understand." Nate said. "Sometimes life is hard, and I guess you get that part. But I mean...me personally, I just get so down sometimes I feel like I don't want to be here anymore." He confided. "Like school. It's so hard and it's like no matter what I do, I fail. My mom is always on my case about something; either I'm not clean enough, or I'm not doing enough or not helping enough. I'm either not acting my age, or not using my head. I'm always not doing something right. I can't remember the last time she told me I did anything right."

There was a soft rustle of leaves and Nate was washed in images of his mother. He could hear her voice as she talked about how she believed in him and knew he was going to grow up to be incredibly successful. He watched as she bragged about how he was so smart and that she believed that he could do anything if he put his mind to it.

Nate shook his head to clear his mind. "Well, you may have overheard her say something like that, but she's never said it to me." He told Reisun.

Trevor, who had been watching the interaction between his friend and the dog, chimed in then. "I know how that is. My mom barely speaks to me anymore and when she does it's always the same rehearsed line of questioning."

They both sat silently contemplating how different and yet the same their situations were. Though Trevor's dark thoughts and depression had been brought on by the loss of his brother and Nate's appeared to be the result of low self-esteem and anxiety they both lived each day wishing that it had been their last. The cause of the depression may be different, but the pain experienced as a result was the same.

Trevor took it upon himself to break the silence.

"You know what Reisun, you're a pretty cool dog." He said with a genuine smile.

Reisun wagged his tail happily and Nate could feel the sensation of 'home' wash over him like fresh-baked cookies and scented candles.

"Yeah, sounds good." Nate said. He stood and extended his hand for Trevor to take it, pulling him up as well. They began to brush the dirt, leaves and debris from their clothes.

Reisun nodded toward the stool and again impressed the word 'home'. He stood then and trotted over to where the stool was. He jumped up placing his front paws on the seat of the stool and then pushing off, knocking it over and onto its side.

"What are you doing?" Nate asked.

'Home'. The word sang in his head. Reisun grabbed the stool in his strong jaws and began to trot in the direction of the house.

"Should I even keep asking how any of this is even possible?" Trevor threw his hands in the air.

"Are you really taking my stool?" Nate said shrugging at Trevor's query simultaneously.

Reisun paused mid-step, wagged his backend, and began trotting, once again, for home.

Trevor and Nate jogged to catch up with him.

PART EIGHTEEN

A Talk with Dad

It had only taken them a few minutes to make it back to the hunter's trail. Reisun continued to trot merrily in front of Nate carrying the stool as though it were no more than a small bone or rubber ball. Nate was still somewhat in shock at the new information he'd discovered from this random dog that his mother had chosen at the animal shelter. He was also staring down the road in the direction of home, dreading what he would have to face when he arrived there. He could just imagine his mother waking up and finding him gone after last night's fight. He knew exactly what she'd be thinking; he ran away again.

Everyone in the house would be looking for him frantically. He was surprised that he hadn't seen the car pulling out of the driveway kicking up dirt as it sped down the dirt road to the highway. Despite this, Reisun's newly discovered talents were at the forefront of his thoughts. He'd deal with his mother, but this, this was big.

Nate replayed his experience in the woods over and over again in his mind. Seeing Reisun as a puppy, the collar with his name on it, learning that Reisun could communicate telepathically by simply expressing the sensation of words on a person; all of it was crazy.

"So, how'd you get away from that scary big dude?" Nate asked Reisun.

"Yeah, he didn't really seem like the type to feel bad about how he treated you and drop you off at the shelter." Trevor agreed.

Reisun continued to trot happily along as he expressed to the boys, "Friend,", in an array of brilliant colors that smelled of flowers and were warm like the first rays of sunshine on a cool morning.

"Must have been really good friend." Nate smiled down at his most unusual four-legged friend.

"Yes…good friend." Reisun turned to cut across the neighbors' yard and into theirs heading for the front porch.

Trevor gave Nate a nudge and whispered, "So do you think he's like, magic or something?"

Nate hadn't had a chance to really consider how Reisun had done what he'd done. Was he a magic dog? What else would explain it?

"Not quite sure yet." Nate said. "Maybe it's a natural ability or mutation of some type. But whatever it is, let's keep it our secret for now."

"I agree." Trevor nodded. "Besides, who would believe us?"

"Right." Nate laughed. He thought again about what he'd seen in the visions as they walked. Reisun had been with his mother and her eyes had glowed like his did, so obviously he wasn't the only one like him. There was so much more he needed to know, so much more he wanted to know.

"That creep in his visions had said something about passing the abilities onto the owner." Trevor went on.

"Yeah, like he was trying to take it from him or something." Nate said.

"I wonder what else Reisun can do. I mean he's obviously strong." Trevor motioned as they watched him carrying the stool.

"Yeah, I mean don't get me wrong, the stool isn't super heavy, but shoot, I got kinda tired of carrying it down the road when I brought it from the house. Reisun is carrying it in his mouth like its light as a feather." Nate saw.

First chance he got, Nate planned to sit down with Reisun and find out what else he was capable of. He had a feeling that communication was just the tip of the iceberg, but he was glad that Trevor had been there to share that experience with him. He wasn't sure he would have been quite as brave if he had been alone.

As they approached the yard they cut from the dirt road into the grass, heading for the front door. Terrence was seated there, patiently waiting, as though he had anticipated Nate showing up at any moment.

"You and the dog have a nice walk?" he asked as they reached him on the steps.

"Yeah." Nate said dropping down next to him on the porch. "I just needed to get some air and I didn't want to wake anybody."

"I can understand that. Last night was kinda hectic." Terrence gave him a sympathetic pat on the back.

"I just don't ..." Nate started.

Terrence remained silent as Nate composed his thoughts. He had never been the type to impose his will on anyone, to be overbearing or judgmental. As long as Nate had known him, he had always kind of been the buffer that had saved them from their mother's full loving wrath, when she was upset. Instead, he turned his attention to Trevor.

"Hey there." He said.

"Hi." Trevor answered warily.

"Oh, my bad." Nate looked over at his friend. "This is my dad, Terrence or Mr. Williams I guess you can call him. This is my friend Trevor from school. He's staying the weekend with us."

"Nice to meet you." Terrence shook Trevor's hand. "Your mom know you have company?" He asked Nate.

"Yeah, she said it was alright for him and the guys to stay over. But she may have forgotten though since it was like last week when she said that." He explained. "But she knows Trev, so she'll probably be cool with just him being here".

"Hey, would it be cool if I used your bathroom?" Trevor asked Nate.

Terrence answered, "In the house and it'll be the first door on your right. His moms on a bit of a warpath though so you may want to tread lightly."

"No problem." Trevor slid by and grabbed his bag from next to the door.

"My rooms the next door when you come out of the bathroom." He told him. "You can just throw your stuff in there.

"Cool." Trevor opened the front door, looked inside to ensure the coast was clear and then headed for the bathroom.

Nate waited a moment and started again. "I just don't understand why she can't just listen sometimes. It's like she only hears what she wants to hear and when I try to tell her what's really going on, she's already so upset that she doesn't even care."

Terrence let out a long breath. "Yeah, your mom is a strong lady. And the crazy thing about that is that the only reason she's so strong is to try to hide how scared she is for you guys."

"Scared?" Nate rolled his eyes. "Scared of what? We joke about what we would do to somebody if they ever tried to break into our house. She's probably more prepared for a zombie apocalypse than anybody in this town." They both laughed at that.

It was kind of their family thing to talk about what they would do if there was ever a zombie apocalypse. Nate had gotten really into the Walking Dead series when it was on TV and from that had moved on to the Z-Nation series. When the shows were really good, he would tell his mother about something that happened and ask her what she would do if it were her.

"Mom, you should've seen this episode. Everyone was trapped inside the house, and you could see the zombies coming from out the woods. You know me, I was like ya'll better run, but instead they stayed to fight and all they had to fight with was like sticks and gardening tools." Nate was explaining the episode to her in vivid detail with extremely animated hand gestures. "I was telling my friend that if that was my family them zombies wouldn't have had a chance."

His mother had laughed and walked over to her desk, reaching underneath it and behind the sliding drawer that held the keyboard. She pulled out a large black sheath with a titanium handle sticking out. She unbuttoned a snap and exposed a 6-inch serrated black blade. "They can try if they want to." She said smiling. "But they aren't going leave the same way they showed up."

"I know that's right." Nate found himself mouthing the words from this brief clip of flashback.

"What was that?" Terrence asked.

"I just wish she'd listen sometimes." Nate went on as if he hadn't heard the question.

Terrence considered this for a long time before he said anything else.

"You in a hurry to go in the house?" He asked Nate.

"If you were me, would you be in a hurry to go in the house?" He asked Terrence in return.

"So that's a no. How about I tell you a little story and maybe that'll help open your eyes some." He turned to face Nate, leaning on one elbow as he did.

"I got a whole Saturday of not being allowed to do anything, so why not." He shrugged.

Reisun had quietly slipped up the steps behind Terrence and sat the stool straight up next to the front door before coming to sit on the porch beside Nate. His ears were perked as though he were just as interested in the story that Terrence was preparing to tell. Terrence had only cut the slightest eye at the dog and stool, but he fully intended to ask about it later.

"I know you've heard bits and pieces about your mother's childhood." He started. "Most of the stories are about her and your uncle and how she used to tease and pick on him. It is only when your mother's extremely upset that she opens up about some of the harder things that she had to go through as a child. You see, your mother was a foster child for a long time, and she spent so much time bouncing from house to house that she never really had the opportunity to get attached to anything or anyone.

Everything around her changed so often that she kind of built a wall around herself so she wouldn't need to get attached to anyone. She didn't need to remember names or faces, teachers from when she was younger, schools that she went to; they're all a blur to her. To this day she has the hardest time remembering people's names and sometimes even their faces, because forgetting had become second nature to her. She would just let the memories slip away as though they'd never happened.

She and your uncle were separated from her brother and sisters when they were all very young. There had been five of them then. This happened after they'd all been found left alone in a house with no electricity and no food. She and her younger brother literally scavenged for food by knocking on neighbors' doors and giving them excuses for why they needed to 'borrow' things like food or milk. This is what she had to do to make sure her siblings stayed fed before they were split up. She told me about the day it all happened.

She said that their mother had gone out and left them with a friend, a man that your mom wasn't familiar with. Your mom made it her business to stay up to make sure that her brothers and sisters were safe. I'm sure you can see how that behavior from when she was younger translated into who she is now as your mother. She's very protective of you guys." He paused here for emphasis.

Nate nodded in agreement.

Terrence continued. "She told me that the man that her mother had watching them left in the middle of the night without a word. He may have assumed that they were all asleep and wouldn't notice that he had gone. Their mother was supposed to be back soon, but she never showed up. Your uncle, the one you know, was just a baby then and had been sick for a very long time. He'd been born during a time when their mother was using drugs heavily and suffered some side effects as a result.

He'd woken up early that morning, while it was still dark and began vomiting everywhere. Your mom did the best she could with the situation. There were no clean towels or rags they could use to clean the mess, so they covered it up by flipping the couch cushions that he'd gotten sick on or laying old newspaper over it. She'd wrapped him in an old T-shirt because there weren't any diapers in the house and made him a bottle of warm water to try to settle his stomach but that only seemed to make things worse. He continued to cry and scream and vomit.

Your mother and her younger brother took turns going out on their bikes to look for their mother, your grandmother. This way one of them would be home with their sick baby brother and younger sisters. They visited a couple of the bars they knew she frequented and knocked on the doors of a couple of the houses that she had often taken them to when she was out taking part in 'recreational activities.'"

He made air quotes with his fingers as he said this.

"They did this for about three hours. She made sure to be back before all her siblings were up and wanting to eat.

Their mother had a rule that she'd recite to them anytime she left their little apartment. The rule was, if it wasn't her, they were not to open the door for anyone. Your mother knew this rule because she had heard it a thousand times before, so when she got back, they brought their bikes inside and locked the door behind them.

She told me her baby brother had started to cry again, at the time your uncle was maybe ten months old, but the size of a four-month-old. The only thing they had in the house to eat was raw rice and powdered milk. So, she made him a bottle using the powdered milk and cooked the rice for your other uncle and aunts to eat. She tried to make enough so that it would last the entire day and she served it to them for breakfast, lunch and dinner for two days.

For breakfast she would add a little sugar to it to make it sweet so that they wouldn't complain that it was the same old thing. For lunch she would add butter to it so it would at least taste a little different and for dinner she added a little salt and a little pepper.

To be only seven or eight years old, your mother was a pretty crafty little girl." He told Nate.

Trevor stepped back onto the porch then and Terrence continued his story. He joined them, sitting next to Reisun and placing a hand on the dog's head stroking it gently.

Terrence went on, "The third morning was a Tuesday and, in the projects, where they lived there was a truancy officer that went door to door to make sure that all the children were in school. On this particular morning, when the truancy officer knocked on the door to their little apartment; your mother was so anxious that she ran to the door thinking it was her mother. By the time she realized it wasn't, it was too late.

The truancy officer had already started asking them questions about where their mother was and who was home with them. Before too long the entire parking lot was filled with police cars and she and her brothers and sisters were taken down to the police station. Within hours the police found and arrested her mother for child neglect.

That's how she ended up in the foster care system and that's why she's so protective of you guys. She just wants you to understand that no matter what you're going through she will always be there for you, even if she has to kill a few zombies to do so." They both chuckled dryly.

"Wow." Nate whispered. "I never knew all that."

"I'm not finished." Terrence said. "There are so many twists and turns to your mother's story that we could sit here all day. I just wanted to give you the gist of what drives her. You see, as a result of her mother's actions it was years before she saw her brothers and sisters again. They were mostly grown and had started to have children of their own, at least her sisters had. Her brother on the other hand, not the uncle that you know, but the one that you never got the chance to meet, he died before she ever got to see him again."

Trevor looked up then. He'd been listening quietly, but that last statement had piqued his interest.

"What happened to him?" Trevor asked and then immediately regretted intruding on this obviously private conversation.

Terrence gave him a reassuring smile and continued, "Well, he'd gone into the military right out of high school and had later found himself overseas in Iraq. She'd been searching for him for years with the help of her adopted mother, the grandma you've known your whole life, and was able to locate his family, who in turn, got in touch with him. They had planned to have a family reunion as soon as he got home which was supposed to be soon because he had gotten injured, broken his ankle, and was being processed to be sent home.

Before your grandmother even had the opportunity to give your mother the good news, she found out that his Medi-Vac had been shot down by RPG's and he and everyone on board had been killed. It was hard enough for your grandmother to tell your mother that her brother, who she had spent years searching for and had finally found, had died, let alone tragically. And you know what? Based on what your grandparents have told me, your mother was never really the same since.

I believe that she holds guilt in her heart for not having found him sooner. She feels guilty for not being able to protect her little brother and as a result she fights and screams and yells and would kill to protect all of you."

None of them was sensitive enough to admit that tears had welled in their eyes as Terrence told Denise's story, but that was all right, it wasn't something that needed to be said out loud.

"I get that she had a hard life." Nate said. "But shouldn't that be all the more reason to listen more when her children are trying to tell her that something is wrong?"

"She tries Nate. But you have to take responsibility for your actions in this too. It's hard to listen when the decisions that you make don't take into consideration how they affect everyone around you. I'm sure it would be different if you actually asked your mother if she was willing to sit down and have a conversation with you rather than her having to show up at your school or at a police station or have her riding the streets for hours searching for you." Terrence told him.

"Yeah but…" Nate started.

"This is not a 'yeah but' type of situation." Terrence said sternly, more firmly than he had ever spoken to any of the children. "Your mother loves you and it kills her to see you hurt, or upset, or confused, or lost in any way.

Because of what she's been through as a child, when you were younger and even now her main concern is that you always have food to eat and that you guys know that she is always here. You have no idea the things your mother has gone without just to make sure that you guys had more than enough." He was starting to sound almost angry, but you could tell he was doing his best to keep his composure.

Terrence loved his mother and was just as protective of her as she was of all of them. Nate understood the strained sound of his voice as he tried to keep a lid on his frustration.

"Where on earth have you been?!" The front door swung open wide, barely allowing the words to escape from the house. His mother stood in the doorway with heavy bags under her eyes; looking as though she'd barely slept. She wore a worried expression that he could see beginning to morph into a mix of anger and frustration. She looked over at Trevor sitting with them on the porch and made an effort to compose herself.

"I have been looking for you for hours." She continued.

Terrence put his hand up to quiet her. "He's been here on the porch with me for a while now. We've been having a little man to man," He looked over at Trevor, "to man. Can you give us another minute to finish up and I'll send him in the house?"

As she stood there the expression on her face had slightly changed from worried frustration to almost shock at being hushed.

"Whatever." She said, turned and let the door slam behind her.

"See." Nate turned back to Terrence. "This is exactly what I was talking about, before you can even get a word in edge wise, she's already started."

Terrence shook his head again. "You know Nate, not being a parent, it's probably hard for you to see this from her point of view. Again, it wouldn't be the first time you've run away, and it wouldn't be the first time that you caused your mother to worry. We can't pretend that there is no history for her to base her feelings on. Stuff like this doesn't get better every time something happens, it only gets worse. Which means it's up to you to change that. You ever heard the expression 'walk a mile in someone else's shoes'?"

"Yeah, I guess so." Nate said.

"Well try walking a mile in your mother's shoes. That means loving something more than you've ever loved anything or anyone else, including yourself. You're still young and to be honest, you've never experienced that type of love in your life. You've been loved that way, but you've never loved anything that way. The flings that you have with these young ladies will come and go. What you have to remember is that these situations are supposed to educate you on the things that you want and don't want in your relationships. You only have one heart, and you can't let every female that you date or call your girlfriend, or that you hang around and refer to as your friend, snatch that heart out your chest.

You have to save it and keep it protected until you find someone who truly deserves it. At this stage, young man, the only woman that you should be giving your heart to that way is your mother, the lady that sacrifices for you, she deprives herself for you, she breaks her neck for you and would do anything for you. I mean come on; your mom went and got you a dog because she thought maybe it would help you develop an emotional attachment to something. She was hoping that you would learn what it means to care about something other than yourself."

He looked at both of the boys sitting on the porch with him. "Parents work hard trying to give their children everything that we never had, when the reality is we wouldn't be who we are today if we hadn't gone through the things that we went through in our lives. When you've never gone through anything, you never have to sacrifice anything. When you never have to worry about risking or losing anything, you don't learn to appreciate things. You guys understand what I'm trying to say here?"

"Yes, sir." Trevor said, thinking about his own parents and how they must have felt losing Jake.

Nate's head was hung as he listened. "Yeah, I know what you're saying."

He didn't feel like there was any reason in arguing the point now. It was like a grown-up thing to tell kids that they were unappreciative and undeserving. An argument would've been pointless and perhaps there was something that he was missing that years of experience would eventually teach him. Today though, he felt like he always did, which everyone around him was missing. He didn't have that experience yet; he was still learning how to deal with situations and how to cope with his emotions. Being yelled at and told that he was unappreciative and selfish wasn't teaching him to cope with his emotions. What it was doing was enforcing his feeling of worthlessness.

"Don't worry man." Terrence said, giving Nate a hearty pat on the back. "You're going to get this. I promise you. When I was your age, I thought I was in love with every girl I talked to and one day I realized that they never really loved me back. They were only with me for what I could give them or try to buy for them because I was always working. I got into my twenties, and I basically swore off love.

I told myself I'd never be in love with any woman and that if they were going to use me then two could play that game. I wasted years and years and years of my life stuck in that mentality and you know what changed that?" He asked Nate.

"What's that?" Nate replied even though he had a feeling that he knew what Terrence was going to say. It didn't change the fact that he was still curious, not to mention it prolonged him having to face his mother.

"Everything changed when I met your mom. That lady doesn't take crap from any man and wasn't planning to allow one to waste her time. No matter how much I told myself that I wasn't in love with her, the truth was I couldn't imagine my life without her. When you see me doing things for your mother it's because I appreciate everything that she's ever done for me.

The way she pushed me, and she supported me and the way she encourages me. It didn't take me long at all to realize that the only thing that she was doing for me was what she does for you all every single day. She tells you that you are great at things, and don't tell me your mother never told you that because I've seen her. She's always encouraging your talents. Every time you show the slightest interest in something she's behind you 100%."

Nate thought about the weight set that she got him when she'd seen him going outside every day for his walks or to work out in the front yard. He'd only mentioned once that he wanted to start lifting weights to get in shape. He had a dream of going into the military one day and wanted to be ready and in shape when he was old enough to be enlisted. He thought about the guitar that at that very moment was sitting next to his closet door in his bedroom. He and a friend of his had decided they wanted to learn to play the guitar. His friend already had one so when Nate would go to spend the night, they would take turns practicing on his. Like before, he'd only mentioned it to her once and it was under the tree that Christmas.

He heard what Terrence was saying and he knew that his mother loved him and worried about him. He knew this like he knew his name, but when things got dark in his mind, all of that knowing washed away like chalk on a sidewalk. All he could see and hear was that he wasn't enough. He wasn't smart enough or fast enough or strong enough. He just wasn't enough.

"Nate." Terrence said, trying to draw him from his thoughts. "Go inside and talk to your mom. Try to understand why she's so upset. And before you start losing your shit," He smiled at him then. "Take a deep breath and try to think about what we talked about. Walking a mile in your mom's shoes is not as easy as she makes it look."

Nate stood up from his spot on the steps and dusted himself off a bit. He took the last two steps onto the porch and headed for the door.

"Hey, one more thing." Terrence called to him.

"Yeah?" Nate turned.

"Do I want to know about the stool?" He shot a look at Reisun, who had jumped up and was waiting patiently at the door with his little nub wagging from side to side anxiously, and then back to Nate.

"Another story for another day?" Nate shrugged.

"Good enough for me." Terrence said. He turned to look back across the yard. The grass was still slightly wet with dew which was drying rapidly in the quickly warming air. There were still birds singing their morning song. It was truly a beautiful day.

"Ya'll staying out here? Nate asked Trevor and Terrence as he opened the door.

"Maybe for just a bit. You go ahead and I'll be in shortly. Trev and I will give you and your mom some time to talk alone."

Nate shrugged. "Thanks for that," he said and went into the house.

Terrence chuckled a little bit and then said to Trevor. "There is no way that I'm stepping into the middle of that poop fest right now."

Trevor smiled.

PART NINETEEN

Pearls

When they walked into the house Denise was sitting at the kitchen table waiting with a cup of tea in front of her.

"Hey." Nate said walking over to where she was.

"Where were you?" She disregarded his greeting. "I was worried sick about you, and I don't even know why, because this is just what you do. As soon as things get a little hard, or as soon as you have to face the consequences of your actions, you disappear and run. How on earth do you ever expect to become a man handling your problems like a little boy?" Her voice was rising steadily as she spoke.

Nate's head had already started to throb. He tried doing what Terrence said and took a deep breath as he waited for her to finish.

"Well," she said. "What do you have to say for yourself? I grounded you last night, Nate! You had no business leaving this house to go anywhere! It's like you go out of your way to be blatantly disrespectful! I'm your mother and I expect you to respect the rules of this house and if you can't do that…then."

she paused. "I just don't know, maybe you don't need to be here."

"Wow." Nate thought.

That was his mother's go to line. 'Can't respect the rules of my house then you don't need to be here.'

"Can I say something now?" He asked.

"Please, say something. Say something that makes all of this makes sense, Nathaniel."

Ah man. She'd resorted to using full names. At least she hadn't used his middle and last name.

"I wasn't trying to be disrespectful," he started. I just needed to get some air and the dog needed to be let out. We just walked up the road and walked back. I'm sorry." Nate told her sincerely.

Walk a mile in her shoes.

"Oh, and it was just so hard for you to come and knock on my door and let me know you were going to go do that? I mean at least let me know!" She'd begun to rub her temples.

"It was early. I didn't want to wake anybody." He told her.

He grabbed a chair at the other end of the table and sat down across from his mother. He kept the conversation he and Terrence had in the forefront of his mind. He just had to walk a mile in her shoes so he could understand why she was so upset. His right mind told him to try and understand, while his left mind screamed back, 'Maybe it's time for her to understand why you're so upset!'

"Hush!" He screamed at himself internally, trying to quiet his consciousness.

"Mom." He said, "Can we like, really talk? Like without the screaming and hollering and you being angry at me for everything that I do?"

She gave him a surprised look. "I'm not angry at you for everything that you do. Nate, why is it so hard for you to understand that I love you? Because I love you, I worry about you."

"I get that," Nate said. "And every time I find myself in a dark place, I try to remember that, but sometimes it's like falling into a hole that's so dark at the bottom. You look up and you see some light, but no matter what you do and no matter how hard you try there is just no way to get out. Then you start screaming and hollering before I can tell you anything."

"Then tell me now, Nate. I'm listening." She leaned toward him on the table. "Okay? I'm sitting right here and I'm listening. Tell me now. What's the problem? Is it something that I'm not doing or something that you need me to be doing more?"

"No!" Nate said, shaking his head, trying to organize his thoughts.

"It's not you, it's me. It's like there's something wrong with me." He was wracking his brain trying to explain to her how he felt on an almost daily basis.

"There's nothing wrong with you. You just need to think before you do things." Her words were starting to blend into a long line of sounds that were similar to how the teachers talked in all the old Charlie Brown cartoons his mother made them watch every

Christmas.

"Mom, what I'm trying to say is..." The throb that had started in his head was steadily growing bigger and louder. He just knew that if she looked hard enough, she'd probably see his temples trembling with frustration, confusion and hurt. He rubbed his own temples now, trying to quiet the chaos.

Before he was able to finish his sentence Reisun placed a paw on Nate's right foot and looked up at him.

"Help?"

He barely heard it through his throbbing head, but it was a question and then it was an action. He lifted his eyes and looked across the table at his mother who was sitting with both palms planted flat and her eyes wide. Tears had already begun to spill over the rims of her eyes and her mouth was moving, but no words were coming out.

"Mom?" Nate said, looking at her, at her expression. The expression she wore was exactly how he'd felt yesterday when Reisun had allowed him to feel her pain, but this time it was working the other way. This time, Reisun was allowing his mother to feel <u>his</u> pain, his hurt, his sorrow, his confusion all mixed up into a blur of emotions and sensations that were so overwhelming sometimes you just want to stop feeling. He knew what she was feeling from him at that moment; worthless, sorrowful, desperate, physically in pain from the inability to sort out and make sense of everything all at the same time.

"Reisun." He whispered. He watched as her body slackened along with her expression.

"Baby." She choked out the word and began to sob. She got up from her place at the table and almost ran to him, grabbing him up and pulling him into her arms.

"I love you so much." She cried. "I thought I said it enough, maybe I don't, but please never forget that. Not just me, but your entire family loves you so much."

"Mom are you okay?" Nate asked smothered in her embrace.

"I don't know." She said. "I really don't know."

"I do." He told her. He returned her hug. "Believe me, I definitely know the feeling.

She kissed his left cheek and then his right and then his forehead the way she used to when she put him to bed at night as a small boy.

"Nate," she said pulling away slightly. "If you are ever feeling confused, or scared or worthless you can just come and sit with me. We don't even have to talk if you don't want, but baby please understand I'm always here for you no matter what."

"Okay." He answered quietly.

"I know I get angry sometimes it's only because I love you and you scare the crap out of me. I believe we can get through this if we do it together. Can we please try, Nate?"

"Yeah." Again, the answer was barely whispered. Nate had begun to feel a little weepy himself but blinked back the tears.

"That's all I ask. That we try together." She gave him another quick hug and turned away from him to wipe her face. She didn't like them to see her cry, something about never wanting them to worry when they were little.

"So," Nate said trying to lighten the mood. "Does this mean that I'm no longer grounded?"

She smirked. "Actually, what this means is that maybe I'll think about giving you your phone back next weekend instead of next month which is far better than what I was planning to do with it."

"What were you planning to do with it?" Nate just had to know.

"Well, if you must know. I woke up this morning and you were gone, and I had this vision of me in the driveway running over your phone and then handing you back the pieces." She smiled.

"Wow Mom, that would've been dirty." He shook his head. He knew she would have actually done it.

"That wouldn't have been dirty, that would've been real life. You know I have no patience for disrespect, and I am still not one to reward misbehavior. We can talk all day, but out of line is out of line, even if you do sometimes feel like it's a bit out of your control. At some point we've all got to learn to sit on our demons before they overtake us, and we become their footstools." She added profoundly.

Yet another one of his mother's 'words of wisdom' and she had enough of those little pearls to last him a lifetime.

"You can, however, use the house phone to call the rest of your friends and let them know that game night has been cancelled. Since Trevor is already here, he's welcome to stay. Don't want to punish him because we had a…" She considered it for a moment. "Situation."

"Thanks Ma." Nate said, watching her as she sat back down and started sipping her tea, staring blankly into space. He wondered if she was trying to make sense of what she'd experienced only moments ago.

They had both had enough for today and Nate decided that he and Trev would spend the rest of the day inside. They spent the afternoon playing video games and watching YouTube. When Nate's mom started rattling around in the kitchen they offered to help with dinner. Both the boys found themselves enjoying a normal family meal with no talk of disobedience, defiance or loss. They laughed about old TV shows and talked about movies they were looking forward to seeing together. They were all sure to include Trevor in the conversation as they joked and reminisced.

"If you're going to be a part of this family you have to talk." Olivia told Trevor. "Our whole family is jokey that's why we thought Nate was an alien 'cause sometimes he be acting like he can't talk."

"Whatever." Nate tossed a pea onto Olivia's plate.

"Wow." She rolled her eyes. "He's resorted to throwing food. Real mature."

"Food Fight!" David stood up with a fork full of food cocked and loaded.

"I wish you would." Denise gave him a look that slid him sheepishly back into his seat.

"Boom!" Olivia laughed. "Mom-blocked! More wars could probably be ended if they just sent in everyone's moms."

Nate laughed and added. "Right. Their moms would be like, 'Didn't I tell you to leave that other country alone? Now get your tail in this house.'"

"Aww man. But mom they started it." Terrence jumped in pretending to be the other country.

They all got a good laugh from the idea of countries being punished by their mothers.

Nate looked over at Trevor who had been thoroughly enjoying the conversation and nodded toward his room. Trevor gave him an acknowledging nod in return.

Nate jumped up from his seat and started to clear his place. "Well, we're finished. We're going to go chill in my room." He gestured for Trevor to get up.

"Glad you're done." Denise said. "However, the dishes are not. Olivia, you clear the table. David, you've got floor duty and Nate and Trevor can tag team the dishes."

"Dang. So close." Nate shrugged and headed into the kitchen with Trevor to wash dishes.

Olivia cleared the table and dropped the dishes into the warm soapy water Nate had run in the sink. The boys waited for David to finish sweeping the floor and they had the kitchen to themselves before they started. Nate took his place in front of the sink and tossed Trevor a dish towel to dry.

"Your family is pretty cool." Trevor said quietly, drying plates and placing them in a stack on the counter.

"They're alright when they want to be." Nate was working on a frying pan with the brillo pad. He knew his mom would check to make sure it was clean and make him come back and do it over if it wasn't.

"I don't really talk with my folks." Trevor moved on to drying silverware, placing them in the drawer he'd help to get them out of earlier.

"Because of your brother?" Nate asked.

"Pretty much." Trevor opened a couple of cabinets until he found the dishes and placed the stack he'd dried on the shelf.

"What happened to your brother?" A voice said from behind them. Olivia had made her way back into the kitchen.

"Nunya!" Nate turned and snapped at her. "Why are you so nosey?"

"Whatever. I just came in here to get my charger for my phone. Dang, I just asked a question." She unplugged the cable from an outlet near the kitchen table and swung her head, so all of her braids fanned out in a circle.

"Well mind your business because this is none of yours." He told his little sister.

"I don't care. Ya'll over there whispering like ya'll got some big secret or something. Don't nobody even care what ya'll are talking about." She stormed off in the direction of her room.

"Annoying little sisters are something else you have to deal with as part of this family." Nate laughed.

"She looked like she was mad." Trevor placed the last glass in the cabinet and folded up the dish towel.

"Nah, she's alright. Watch this." Nate let the water out of the sink and rinsed out the remaining soap. When he was finished, he called down the hall to Olivia.

"Hey Olive, we're about to watch a movie, come make the popcorn!"

Olivia popped her head out of her room. "What movie is it?"

"I don't know, one of the new ones mom just got." He told her, giving Trevor a sly smile.

"Hang on, I'm coming." She slid back into her room and grabbed her phone.

"She's my sister." He explained to Trevor. "She'll be mad for a second and don't care the next. That's how it works."

"That's how it works around here." Olivia leapt into the room and gave Nate a smack on the back of the head. "That's for calling me nosey. Now turn the movie on."

She was out of reach before Nate could think to grab her and at the microwave tossing in a bag of popcorn.

Trevor found himself smiling again; this house was so different from his own. He remembered a time when his family got along like Nate's, but that time seemed so long ago. He was glad to be included and even called a part of this silly, strange, hysterical, complicated, magical family.

David joined them in the den to watch the movie and they spent the rest of the evening eating popcorn and talking. Nate had already decided that tomorrow he, Trevor and Reisun would go back to the woods. Tomorrow they would learn more about the new furry addition to his family.

He elbowed Trevor in the side. "Tomorrow." He whispered and motioned toward Reisun.

Trevor nodded in agreement.

Olivia watched the interaction suspiciously but said nothing.

"So, what's going on tomorrow that has to do with the dog?" She thought to herself. She looked over at the dog that she still knew as Blackie and found him waiting patiently to meet her gaze.

"Blackie, you are so weird." She told him.

"It's not Blackie anymore." Nate corrected her. "It's Reisun."

"What kind of name is that?" Olivia said with a smirk. "You making up names for the dog?"

"Nope. That's just his name." Nate continued watching the movie without further explanation.

"You act like he told you what his name was or something." she teased.

Nate only shrugged and replied, "He did."

"Whatever." Olivia twisted back around in her seat to face the TV better. "If he told you his name then we're all gonna be rich."

Nate shot Trevor a quick look which he caught knowingly.

"If you only knew." Nate thought. "If you only knew."

PART TWENTY

The Stranger

The dirt spit and flew from under the truck's tires as he stomped on the gas petal and tore out of the gravel driveway. He was pissed to say the least. He'd fed that damn dog and gave it shelter. How dare it betray him! He punched the steering wheel for emphasis as he turned onto the dirt road that led away from his concealed property in the woods.

"A week outside tied to that fence post with no food and water will teach that ungrateful animal to listen." He growled to himself. "Maybe two."

He turned on to the main road with the truck tires still spinning. "$50,000. I paid $50,000 for that beast. I should have just taken them like I started to. Listening to that old man and his nonsense about destiny. Should have killed the old man and just taken all the dogs. $50,0000 down the drain."

When he was just a child his father told him stories of a mythical animal that only gave birth to a new litter every 25 years under a silver full moon. His father had chased the legend of these dogs his entire life. Leaving for months at a time with each new piece of information he would receive about their location or the location of a new litter.

These animals had magical powers and whoever owned one could take on the powers of the animal as their own.

Stories that he still recalled to this day. The only difference was that his father was weak and stupid. He left his family time and time again promising to return and change their lives for the better. The last time his father left he was 16 years old and hadn't even said goodbye. By that point he had stopped caring if he stayed or went, and his mother was so withdrawn and disillusioned that she had completely shut down and lost touch with the real world. Every day that his father was gone he'd feed his mother and make sure she took her medication. He blamed his father for his mother's condition, and he blamed those dogs for his father's obsession.

When his father walked out the door for that final time, he assured them that this was it. He knew where to find them, and he would return home this time triumphant. He never did though. There was no letter of explanation or phone call for his family to come join him. His father was just gone, and he didn't care.

His mother didn't last much longer after that. She wasn't able to work, they had no other family to reach out to and his father... He did his best to find odd jobs to help support them, but he was just a boy, and it was never enough. When his mother passed away several months later the doctors said she'd suffered a stroke, but he knew better. She had loved her husband. The husband that had abandoned her in her time of need. Yes, he knew that she hadn't died as a result of a stroke, though she may have suffered one. His mother had died of a broken heart and for this he blamed his father as well.

As the EMS wheeled his mother's lifeless body from their home, he overheard the police officers discussing calling child services to pick him up. He was officially an orphan since there was no way of reaching his father or of knowing if he was even still alive and that meant he would become a ward of the state and be placed in a boy's home or hallway house of some kind. This would not do. Under the guise of returning to his room to collect his things, he gathered clothes and supplies into a backpack along with what little money he had remaining and slipped out his bedroom window. He would be his own man from then on. A better man than his father had been, a stronger, smarter man.

The road was pitch dark with not a streetlight to be seen and it had started to rain. He hit a switch to turn on the blinding bar light that he had attached to the front of his truck to illuminate his way. It lit up the road for at least a mile ahead of him.

No one travelled this back road without reason and as far as he knew he was the only person that really had any business back here. So, blinding an oncoming car was the last thing that he cared about. He was headed for his primary domicile, what the average person would have referred to as home, but for him was no more than a front, a façade to fool anyone that might be searching for him.

"If it still won't turn over its powers by the time I get back, I'll just get rid of it and then do what I started to do in the first place, get rid of the old man and get me a refund. He owes me that much for selling me a faulty animal." By now his wipers were beating rapidly against the pounding rain.

A family of deer debated crossing the road as he approached. Deciding to risk it they took off for the other side through the blinding lights of his pickup. He saw their desperate attempt as target practice and hit the gas once more, aiming for the smallest of the group. He imagined what he could remember to be his father's face on them as he mowed them over with his truck and continued on his way.

Draya

Draya had been listening to the rain all night. It beat on the roof and windows, playing a percussion lullaby that paved her way to dreamland. She didn't fight the sandman's soft song but embraced it. She'd finished packing her bags and was looking forward to getting on the road in the morning after the rain stopped. She'd intended to head back to school that evening, but the rain and her parents had had other plans. It was only Sunday, and she didn't have classes scheduled till 2 tomorrow afternoon, so she could stay, have breakfast with the folks early Monday morning and be back on campus by lunch.

She closed her eyes for what felt like only a few minutes and awoke to the sun shining through her bedroom window. It was 5:30 and she could smell bacon and coffee. It was incredible and she was hungry. She enjoyed breakfast and conversation with her mother and father and then started to say her farewells as her dad carried her bags to the car.

"Alright, Pumkin. You drive safely heading back and don't let that gas hand get under a quarter of a tank. You know how far apart the gas stations are headed back that way." Her father told her.

"I know daddy, I'll be careful, and I'll call as soon as I get back." She gave him a huge hug and a kiss on the cheek.

Her mother handed her an obsidian stone. "For protection my special girl." She pulled Draya into an embrace and kissed her face several times. "Keep all of your eyes open sweetheart. Had a dream last night about you."

"Oh, yeah?" Draya raised an eyebrow. Her mother was very sensitive to spiritual things and believed in listening to the spirits speak through dreams and signs. She'd always referred to Draya as her extra special girl, saying that she had these gifts as well, but so far, the only gifts Draya was aware of was retaining mundane information and useless facts that might come in handy if she were to ever be a contestant on Jeopardy.

"Just be open, be aware and be safe baby." Her mother placed a kiss on her forehead.

"All eyes open." Draya assured her mother with a quick tap to a spot on her forehead just between her eyes.

In the car she watched as her parents stood together, arms around each other's waist, waving and shrinking in the rear-view mirror. When they were completely out of sight, she turned up the radio and prepared to settle in for her 4-hour ride back to campus and her life as a first-year college student.

After about two hours of driving her stomach had begun to remind her of the coffee she'd had for breakfast, and she needed to go bad. It would be at least another hour before she made it back to the main road and public restrooms, but this was not going to wait. She pulled her car off the road and into the grass along the roadside and hopped out. She ran around to the other side of the car and opened the passenger side door, squatting between the door and the car to relieve herself. It definitely wouldn't have waited.

She stood, straightened her clothes and took this opportunity to stretch. She looked down the road in the direction she'd just come from and then further up the road in the direction she was going. Not a single car in sight coming or going. She could have probably pee'd in the middle of the street with no interruptions or passing traffic. But that was country living for you. Her parents had always been the types to live off the grid somewhat and the back roads in the country could see you driving for several hours before encountering another motorist.

She reached into the car on the passenger side and grabbed a Slim Jim out of her travel snacks bag. She opened it up and bit off a big piece. She was flexing her toes and bending her legs at the knee to encourage circulation as she leaned against the small SUV eating her Slim Jim and enjoying the afternoon sun. When she was done, she took a swig from her bottle of water, tossed it back onto the passenger seat and closed the door on that side of the car. She started to head around to the driver's side when she felt something brushing against the side of her face.

She raised her hand to touch the place on her cheek where she'd felt it and looked around for what may have done it. A leaf, a feather…there wasn't much of a breeze, but she'd definitely felt something. Her hair was done in long burgundy and black braids that ran down her back, but she'd had those pulled up into a messy bun and all of those strands were tucked away. She started walking toward the driver side of the car again when she heard something this time. A small voice, barely a whisper, but she had heard it clear as day….in her mind. A small voice that had said, 'Please'.

She froze then. Had she really h…'Please…hear…me.' The small fading voice called out.

'Keep all of your eyes open.' She recalled her mother telling her before she'd left. ALL of your eyes.

She closed her eyes and listened for the voice again. It came again quickly, yet fainter than before. 'Please…' this time she reached with her mind for the voice that she heard.

"Who are you?" She asked with her mind, "Where are you?"

A burst of white light washed over her as the answer came with exuberance. "HERE!"

In her mind she saw a golden beam of light leading into the trees, the light followed a dirt road that opened into a clearing where a brown cabin was seated just inside the tree line.

"Here! Please…please…" The voice faded and the intensity of that white light had begun to fade as well. There was no time to waste, she knew this, she could feel it. Someone needed her, they needed her to hear them, and they needed her to help them.

She ran over to the trunk of her car and opened it. She kept a baseball bat in there that her best friend had given her for protection.

"Just in case. Can never be too prepared." Her friend had told her with a huge, make them regret they ever messed with you, grin.

She grabbed the bat from the truck and turned to look back in the direction that the golden beam of light had led. She started out slowly at first, but something in her was urgent. Her steps became faster as she headed into the trees and down the dirt road. Before she knew it, she had started to run, bat in hand, heart racing, in the direction that she knew the voice had come from.

When she reached the end of the dirt road it did open into a clearing where she saw a rundown, old brown cabin sitting. She looked everywhere expecting to see a person lying somewhere injured on the ground.

"Where are you?" She said the words out loud, but low as not to attract any unwanted attention from anyone who might be inside the cabin.

But there was no reply. She thought for a moment and then asked the same question, this time pushing it out with her mind. She closed her eyes and asked the question again, "Where are you?"

"Here." The voice slipped through her mind in a sliver and was gone just as quickly.

She heard a chain rattle just off to her right and could see that there was one attached to a fence about 500 yards away. She made her way over to the fence where the chain hung, with the bat protruding out in front of her for safety. Her steps were slow and cautious as she approached, not knowing exactly what to expect. When she finally came in to view of what was connected to the end of the chain she drew in a deep breath. There lying on the ground was a huge black dog. It was emaciated. It looked as though it had been outside for some time chained to the fence with a huge truck chain wrapped and dead bolted around its neck.

She let the bat fall to the ground and knelt down by the poor creature. She placed one hand over its head and was relieved when it opened its eye and looked up at her.

"Oh, my goodness," she exclaimed. "Who would do something like this to a poor animal?" It looked as though the poor creature hadn't been fed in a long time, it's body more bones than anything.

"I'm gonna get you out of here." she told him softly, stroking the top of his head. She picked up the heavy deadbolt and examined it. It was huge, as big as her hand, with a basic key lock. It had started to rust slightly from exposure to the elements, but she was sure she could still open it. She definitely had a head full of trivial information and among that information included how to pick a lock. Her mother had taught her how to many years ago, "Just for the heck of it." her mother told her. "You can never know too much, and there's no such thing as having too much information."

Another nifty tidbit that her mother was good for reminding her of was making sure that she always had a Bobby pin on her.

"My mom can be a little strange sometimes, but she made sure that I am definitely always prepared." She smiled to herself as she pulled the Bobby pin from her hair. She used her teeth to straighten the Bobby pin and then jammed it into the keyhole of the deadbolt lock and began to wiggle and twist the Bobby pin until she heard something click. The latch popped and she twisted it and dropped it to the ground allowing the chain to fall free from around the dog's neck.

"OK," she said with a breath of relief. "let's get you out of here and someplace safe and dry." She looked up at the sky and could see the heft of the clouds overhead. It would be raining again soon, and she'd rather be in the car when it started.

She slid one hand underneath the dog and tried to wrap her other around his chest and lift him from the ground. He may have only been skin and bones, but he was still very heavy.

"Man, you are a heavy guy. Maybe I should go back and get my truck and drive it up here. There is no way I'm gonna be able to carry you all the way back." She stood and placed her hands on her hips considering.

What felt like a breath of air blew over her and she could hear the soft sound of that faint voice again in her mind saying, "I help."

Suddenly she felt energized and strong. She knelt down again and slid both her arms beneath the dog's body and lifted. This time he was light as a feather, and she was surprised at her own strength. She recognized that it felt as though there were small leaves and debris circling them in a cyclone of mist, but her primary concern was getting this dog back to her vehicle before the rain started.

She wasn't exactly sure where the faint small voice was coming from that had led her to the dog. Or if it had come from the dog itself, which was the only insanely logical explanation for everything that was happening. But what she did know was that the urgency that she felt was real. There was something wrong and dangerous and evil here and they needed to get away from it as quickly as possible.

She made it back to her SUV quickly and used the hand that was pressed against the side of the dog's body to open the back passenger side door. She slid the big dog onto the back seat, still sopping wet from the previous night's rain, and slammed the door shut. She ran around to the driver's side and jumped in, starting the engine and turning up the heat to blow directly into the back of the SUV.

"OK, now what do I do? I can't take you back to campus with me and as sick and injured as you are we definitely need to find a vet or something." She sat considering her location compared to the closest vet or Animal Hospital. "There's nothing around here for hours. What do I do?"

The voice came again whispering softly in her mind, "shelter." it's sang lowly.

She turned around in the driver's seat and looked back at the pile of fur that was beginning to dry in her back seat. "Is that you that I'm hearing in my head?"

"Yes." Came the voice softly.

"But how is that even possible? How is it possible for you to not only be talking to me, but to be talking to me in my mind?"

"Only few." Came the soft response. "Must hurry."

"Right. The shelter, right?"

"Shelter." The voice in her head agreed.

She turned back around in her seat and thought to herself, "what shelters are close to here?"

"Not far." The voice said. "Not far."

She thought for a moment and then recalled that there was an animal shelter not far from them about 45 more minutes up the road. She could see the shelter in her mind having had gone there several times with her family to visit the animals. She had never been able to have a pet of her own due to her father's allergies, but they would take her to the shelter and let her visit the animals and make an entire day out of the trip.

"Yes." The voice agreed. "There..." it reacted as though it were able to see the image that she held in her mind of the shelter.

"Alright. We'll head to the shelter." she assured the voice in her mind. Though Draya knew she should have found all of this to be incredibly peculiar she was only shaken by the deep-rooted feeling that this was a bad place that they had to get away from. She threw the car into drive and pulled back onto the main road headed for the shelter.

It was still pretty early when they arrived at the turn to the dirt road leading up to the animal shelter. The rain had started to fall heavier now, becoming a steady trickle, just enough for her to have turned her windshield wipers on low. As she pulled slowly up to the gate leading to the animal shelter, she found it was still locked and chained shut.

"It's still early." she said out loud. "Doesn't look like anyone's arrived here yet."

She turned in her seat again and looked back at the pile of black fur curled up on her back seat. "Looks like we're gonna be just sitting here until somebody arrives. or I can just pick the lock and we can wait outside the animal shelter."

"No," the small voice floated through her head again. "Not safe. You go."

"Wait? What?" she started, surprised. "I can't just leave you out here it's starting to rain again and there's no telling how long it'll be before someone finally arrives. I can take you all the way up to the shelter there's probably at least someplace safe and dry I can leave you there…" she started to explain to the bundle of fur who's breathing had become a bit shallower.

"Not safe," the voice said again. "Eyes that remember."

"What?" She said confused.

There was a flash then in her mind of a huge man swiping his hand across a table knocking dishes and glasses onto the floor, shattering them. He was angry, shouting something about surveillance cameras recording his license plate. Then just as fast as it had appeared it was gone.

"Wow, that guy was intense." She was still watching the shallow rising and falling of the dog's chest as she spoke. "Scary guy." She said, "If I were you, I'd want to get away from him too. I guess once he realizes that you're gone he's probably gonna be looking for you huh?"

"Yes." The dog breathed. "Not safe. Eyes that remember."

"The cameras. You think he'll come here looking for you and see my car on the cameras and then come looking for me."

"Don't think….know. Bad man."

"Ok, I get the bad man part. But you are hurt and there's no telling how long it'll be before…"

"Soon…" The dog interrupted her. "Be here soon. Must go."

She didn't want to leave the injured animal there on the damp ground near the chained gate, but she wasn't able to just hear this enchanted animal, she was also able to feel him. He sent her waves of urgency and danger and not safe.

Draya jumped out of the front seat and proceeded to open the back door where Reisun lay still slightly damp and limp. She looked at the poor creature and reached her hand over stroking him gently on the head.

"You are something else." She told him. "I'm going to trust what you say, but I will be back to make sure you are alright."

She did her best to express feelings of trust, caring, concern and love to him before removing her hand and searching her vehicle for something she could lay him on and make him comfortable as he waited. Or at least as comfortable as possible. She found one of her school hoodies in the back of the SUV and stuffed it under her arm.

"Gonna need your help again if you have it in you." she said, beginning to slide her arms underneath the dog.

"Together." Reisun sighed in her mind.

"Together." She responded out loud to him.

She lifted then and carried him over to the fence when there was a patch of soft moss stretching across the ground. She kneeled there and lowered him gently, being sure to not let any part of him fall too heavily. Taking the hoodie from under her arm, she placed it lie a pillow under Reisun's head.

"This is insane. I don't want to just leave you, but I know you really want me to. How can I know you'll be alright?" She had started to cry now, but the increasingly heavy rain washed the tears from her face as quickly as they fell.

"See you.... again." Reisun assured her. "Go now."

Draya leaned down and placed a soft kiss atop the dog's head deep into the wet black fur. "I'll see you soon."

She stood and ran back to her SUV, jumping into the driver's seat and throwing the car into reverse. She was forcing herself to move because she knew that his she didn't there was no way she would be able to tear herself from that spot. She had been a part of a miracle, something amazing and unexpected. Something that most people would never experience in their lifetime, and she had been a part of it.

She carefully backed down the drive until she was able to find a place where she could turn around. When she was back on the main road headed for school, the tears were still falling. She wiped them away as she recalled Reisuns words. "See you soon."

"Yes, you will black dog. You most definitely will."

PART TWENTY-ONE

Lost and Found

A week passed before the strangers' impatience got the better of him and he was headed back to the cabin. He knows that by now that dog would be weak and desperate for food. They were certainly a hardy breed and could survive months without food or water in the right conditions, and he knew the dog would not succumb to the elements. It was magic after all and had to be destroyed in a very specific way; otherwise, they were known to live for hundreds of years.

It had rained for several days after he'd chained the dog to the fence, but today was clear. The weather was a mild 78 degrees with blue skies and a sparse sprinkling of fluffy white clouds. Perhaps he would be generous today and feed the beast that had attempted to attack him with such disrespect.

The stranger arrived at the cabin expecting to find the animal chained and humbled. His boots fell heavy on the gravel as he jumped from the truck and began to make his way over to where the dog lay.

"What the-," His eyes narrowed in frustration as he surveyed the area. The dog was gone! He rushed over and began searching desperately. "Dog!" he shouted; his voice filled with aggravation.

There was no sound, no sign of the dog having escaped or dragging itself off in any direction. But there was something there, faintly in the dirt along the fence there appeared to be tread marks from a small set of sneakers. Someone had been there and helped the dog escape. Someone had stolen from him, and he was furious. He turned and hurried back to the truck. He reached in and grabbed the sack filled with the items given to him when he bought the dog. Retrieving the collar from the bag, he held it up in front of him and said in a deep rumbling voice, "Find the beast to which you are tied." The collar warmed in his hand and began to glow a soft, silver glow. The warmth of the collar in his hand began to draw the stranger to the right toward the road.

"You think you got away, dog." He said as he jumped back into the driver seat of his truck. "But I will find you and you will obey."

He started the engine and stomped on the gas, heading back to the main road. An hour later he found himself pulling up to the sign for the animal shelter. The collar's glow was solid, and its warmth pulled toward the driveway of the shelter. He smiled to himself and began to make his way slowly up the drive and through the gate. As he passed through the gate the warmth of the collar suddenly went cold and the glow dimmed to nothing. He hit the brakes and looked hard at the collar, shaking it as he did.

"Find the beast to which you are tied." He roared at the collar. "Find the beast to which you are tied!!"

No matter how much he shouted the collar did not respond. The stranger looked around himself then. Focusing, he could almost see the fine mist of enchantment that he had driven into as he entered the shelters gate.

"It appears that this place is protected." He mumbled to himself. "No matter, you can't hide from me."

He continued down the rest of the drive to the shelter and was greeted by the receptionist's eager smile.

"Well, hello there. How can I help you today?" she asked cheerfully.

He put on his best and most charming grin as he approached the desk. "Yes, perhaps you can help me. My dog seems to have gone missing and I was hoping that someone may have brought him in." He explained as casually as possible.

"Oh dear," she said with a sympathetic nod. "Do you have a picture of your dog? Perhaps I can have someone check in the back."

He hadn't cared enough about the dog to have ever taken a picture with it, let alone of it, so he stumbled just a bit as he said, "No, no not one me at the moment. This just happened within the past couple of days. I was so concerned I just started looking. I probably should stop by home and grab a photo."

"Oh, no worries." She reassured him. What does your dog look like, I'll have someone take a look."

The receptionist had already reached for the phone and called Adam to the desk before The Stranger had an opportunity to object and suggest he go have a look for himself. Adam floated through the double doors that led back to the kennels. He was wearing a bright smile as he made his way to the reception desk until he saw who was waiting there. Adam sensed immediately the danger this man presented. He could see the darkness of the aura that seemed to roll off of the man like a black cloak.

"How can I..." Adams voice left him as he tried to greet their unexpected visitor. He didn't need to finish the line; he already knew why the man was here. The receptionist went on without missing a beat.

"It appears that we have a missing dog. He was just about to tell me what our missing pup looks like." The stranger held Adam's gaze with a chilling understanding of who he was.

"Yes, solid black, white chest marking." He stated pointedly with no inflection or tone to his voice. It was flat and knowing.

"Oh, that sou-," The receptionist started.

"No!" Adam interrupted quickly. "Haven't received any animals fitting that description." He gave the receptionist a quick pleading glace before going on. "You're welcome to leave your information ad we can give you a call if anything comes in fitting that description."

The Strangers eyes narrowed at Adam with a burning desire to make him eat the words he had just said. "I'll do that. Thank you." He practically snarled at Adam. Adam stood there for another few moments seeming to be waiting for the man to leave. "I'll leave my info with the receptionist. I'm sure you are very busy, and I'd hate to keep you from your work." His upper lip had begun to curl over his upper teeth in a visible snarl.

"Of course." Adam stammered out and quickly left the room back through the double doors.

"I'm...I'm so sorry we couldn't be of more help." The receptionists' demeanor had changed with the exchange between Adam and the stranger. She had begun to sense the danger that Adam had been immediately aware of upon entering the reception area.

"Perhaps you can be of more help than you know." The stranger said leaning on the desk toward her.

He looked her deep in the eyes and said slowly, "I need you to show me the surveillance video for the last two weeks."

Her eyes glazed over as she repeated the words back to him.

"Show you the surveillance video." She mumbled blankly.

She turned in her chair and began to run the video back for the past two weeks as he had requested. She moved slowly in her haze as she adjusted the speed to allow the video to play quickly through.

"There!" He told her. "Roll that part back there, where he's carrying in something." The video clip in question was the morning Adam had found the large black dog lying on the ground, wet from the rain. He had rushed the dog into the shelter without thinking, but knowing full well that this special animal would be safe. The stranger leaned in closer as he examined the video of Adam carrying in a large dog wrapped in towels. Just as he had become convinced that the little sprite of a man had lied, his conviction was shattered by the appearance of a fluffy white tail falling from beneath the towels.

"Dammit!" He pounded his fist on the desk leaving a deep scar in the wood.

The receptionist was completely unphased by the sudden outburst, still lost in her mesmerized state. He composed himself and stood up straight.

"Thank you. You have been a great help." He waved his hand slightly and she began to shake her head with confusion.

"Yes, um, of course." He left the shelter quickly, determined to find his property. The shelter may not have yielded the reward he was seeking, but it would only be a matter of time before he found his little lost pup, as the receptionist had called him.

"Time for you to come home little pup. You can't hide from me."

PART TWENTY-TWO

New Tricks

The next morning Nate was anxious to get out the door. He waited in his room until he heard his mother moving around in the kitchen and the tell-tale smells of coffee and toast filled the air.

He gave Trevor a nudge with his foot.

"My mom's up. Let's go." He said.

"Where we going?" Trevor sat up wiping sleep from his eyes.

"Back out in the wood with Reisun." He gave Trevor a 'you should know this' look.

"Oh yeah." Trev looked over at the dog lying at the foot of Nate's bed on the floor. "I'm ready."

They'd slept in their clothes so they wouldn't have to waste any time getting out the door this morning. Nate just wanted to ensure that he kept his mother happy by abiding by her request to let her know before he left the house.

He crawled over to the end of the bed and called down the hall to her.

"Hey mom!"

He waited for her to respond as he leaned over and grabbed his shoes.

"Good morning, sweetheart." She called back.

Perfect, she sounded like she was in a pretty good mood. He grabbed his hoodie from the foot of the bed and started to jump up but was surprised to feel that there was some resistance. Nate gave the hoodie a tug and the hoodie tugged back.

"Nate." Trevor said pointing down.

"What the…," Nate pulled again. He could see tension as he pulled. "Must be caught on something."

"Nope, not on something." Trevor told him, still pointing down.

He tried to shake it loose from the end of the bed where he assumed it was stuck on or under something on the floor. A soft growl came from the foot of the bed. He leaned forward to look over the footboard and found Reisun lying on the floor holding one end of the hoodie in his mouth.

"Hey!" Nate scolded him. "Let go. What are you doing?" He tugged harder and Reisun tugged back in return with just a nod of his head.

"Dude, we are so, not playing tug-of-war with my hoodie. It's my lucky hoodie Reisun, I need it!" He was starting to get upset. He felt like someone was threatening his sense of security. Anxiety was starting to build in his chest at the idea of Reisun destroying his hoodie. He needed it, it kept him safe and allowed him to block out all the chaos of the world while wallowing in his own misery.

"Dude, help me." He looked over at Trevor.

Trevor went over to where Nate was now standing and took hold of the hoodie along with him, giving it a hard tug.

Reisun stood up and took a couple steps back with the hoodie still held tight in his mouth as though he'd heard Nate's unshared thoughts. He started to pull harder, a low growl rolling in his throat.

"You're gonna rip it!" Nate was trying to yell without raising his voice and attracting his mother's attention. He leaned back for better leverage. For just a second yesterday's events had slipped his mind and Reisun became just another dog about to destroy something he loved…for just a second.

"No need!" The words rumbled through him making his teeth click as it did.

"Do need!" Nate shouted back, out loud.

Trevor couldn't hear what Reisun was saying, but he had a sense of what was being said based on Nate's reactions.

Reisun adjusted his grip on the hoodie, sinking his teeth in. Nate and Trevor pulled back and heard a quick rip.

"Ah man! You're ripping it!" He almost cried.

Reisun was wagging his little nub mischievously. "Rip rip rip rip rip." Reisun teased.

"Fine." Nate said letting go. Trevor released his hold on the hoodie as well.

Reisun, quite pleased with his conquest, was shaking the hoodie back and forth.

His mother opened the door then only giving a couple taps as a warning. She had a very clear rule about locked doors and walking in whenever she wanted. 'My house, my rules.' She liked to say.

"Hey you guys. What's going on in here?" She asked.

"Nothing." Nate sat back on the bed heavily.

"You're up and dressed early." She stepped into the room holding her coffee cup in her hand and taking a sip. "Were you planning on going somewhere?"

"I was actually waiting for you to get up." He explained. He shot a dirty look over at Reisun, who had tucked the black hoodie into a corner and was now sitting on it.

She looked at Reisun sitting in the corner. "Is that the black jacket you always have on?"

He shot another glance at Reisun and replied, "It's supposed to be warm out today, didn't really think I needed it. I just wanted to ask though, if it was okay if we took the dog out for a quick walk." He gave her his best puppy dog eyes.

"Sure sweetie." She rolled her eyes. Her mood had changed significantly.

"Walking a mile in someone else's shoes sure can make a world of difference." Nate thought.

"I think me, and Terrence are just going to kinda chill out today and binge watch a series on Netflix." She told him.

Sunday was the only day of the week that they both didn't have to work so they usually spent it together doing something or nothing, it really didn't matter. During the spring and summer, they would all go spend the day at the lake fishing. When the weather got a bit cooler it was the movies or a buffet where they would all spend hours laughing, talking and eating. She never had to force anyone to take part in these family outings because they all enjoyed them so much.

She turned to leave and then stopped, reaching into the pocket of her robe. "It's easier for me to keep track of you when you actually have this." She handed him back his cell phone and walked away without another word.

"Well, Reisun, I don't know what else you can do, but you are obviously a miracle worker." Nate shrugged. "Yesterday she was saying that she planned to run over my phone. I was actually still expecting to get back in pieces. I didn't even have to wait a week, pretty awesome."

He turned the phone on and immediately it began to chime wildly with his missed notifications and text messages. There had been at least 20 messages and seven or eight missed calls since he had turned his phone over to his mother Friday night. Normally he would spend hours returning calls and catching up on his missed text and social media notifications, but he had other things on his mind right now. The last thing he wanted was to start looking at messages and spiraling back down the rabbit hole of self-doubt and depression. Nate tucked the phone into his back pocket and gave Reisun a nod toward the door.

They headed out, down the porch, across the long front yard and onto the dirt road. They reached the hunters path that led into the woods and to the clearing within a few minutes, this time Nate and Trevor followed Reisun who appeared to already know where they were going. There was no particular rush to get there so Nate let his mind wander through the unbelievable events of yesterday's discovery. He still had questions and his curiosity about Reisun had only grown.

A twig snapped behind them causing both boys to pause. Nate looked back through the trees expecting to see a deer or rabbit rushing off in the distance. Reisun only turned for a moment, sniffed the air and wagged before resuming his role as leader of their little safari. After a few moments of silence Nate and Trevor continued on as well.

"Reisun, the miracle worker," Nate started as they entered the clearing.

"So, Mr. Miracle worker. You've managed to get my mother to see things from a different point of view, what else do you have up your doggy sleeves?"

Trevor looked around the clearing and then up at the rope that was still tied to the limb above where the stool had set. He found himself feeling a sense of comfort knowing that the rope still hung, waiting patiently to serve its intended purpose.

Reisun barked.

"I'm not thinking about doing anything crazy. I was just looking, you know?" He told Reisun in a hushed voice.

The dog barked again.

"Be nice to have someplace to sit out here." Nate said sarcastically.

Reisun sat, indicating that sitting on the ground worked just fine.

"Right." Nate said rolling his eyes. He and Trevor sat cross-legged on the ground in front of the dog.

"Soooo here we are," Nate said. "I've decided that I'm not crazy and yesterday definitely happened. So, what else can you do?"

Nate leaned forward, looking Reisun squarely in the eye expecting to see it filled with a silver glow like he'd seen in the vision. "Well, your eye isn't glowing. Maybe I imagined that part. Is that possible? Can I imagine stuff in the images that you show me?"

"Memories," Reisun expressed to them.

"Your memories, right?" Trevor asked.

Reisun shifted in agreement, shuffling his front paws one after the other.

"Okay so, you showed us your memories. There was a man in your memories, like a real douche bag, that said something about powers. Did he mean like right now, us talking...I mean...thinking to each other?" Nate asked him.

"No," came Reisun's answer. "More."

"Well like what, dude? I mean, tell me something...show me something. We're out here talking to you so obviously we believe you, but as screwed up as my life has been lately; maybe I'm just ready to believe anything." He picked up a pebble from the ground next to him and rolled it around between his fingers.

"Throw," Reisun told him silently.

"You want to play fetch now?" Nate asked. "Well, you are a dog; I guess that's like your thing, right?"

"Throw!" Reisun's tail had started to wag, and he was doing his two-leg shuffle again.

"Alright." Nate reared his arm back and tossed the pebble toward the lake. "Go get..." Before he could get the words completely out there was a rustle of leaves and Reisun was dropping the pebble that Nate had thrown back to the ground in front of him.

"What the what?" Nate said with his mouth hung wide. "You barely moved."

"I was looking right at him." Trevor said with an awed expression. "It's like he flickered or something."

"Fast." Reason said, once again pleased with himself. His little nub was wagging feverishly now, and he was ready to go again. "Throw." He was bouncing with excitement.

"You throw it this time." He told Trevor to hand him the pebble.

Trevor looked at the small stone, examining it thoroughly, trying to memorize the look and feel of it. It was a simple grey stone with little slivers of white running through it. On the back of the stone there was a small white spot that reminded him of one of his freckles. He'd remember that spot if it wasn't on the stone that Reisun brought back.

Nate was determined to keep his eyes on Reisun and catch the movement for himself this time. Trevor gave it a hard toss in the direction of the lake, he wasn't watching where he threw the pebble, he was watching Reisun, who'd become a blur for only a second before he was again dropping the pebble on the ground in front of Nate.

"Fast is definitely an understatement." Nate said.

"Wow." Trevor agreed.

He looked in the direction of the lake and could see small circular ripples extending five feet or more out into the water. He reached out and touched one of Reisun's front paws.

Now both Nate's eyes and mouth were wide. "Did you just run on water? Because that would be freaking insane!"

"Fast," Reason reminded him. Nate could feel the joy infused in the word as it washed over him.

The boys took turns throwing the pebble a couple more times so Reisun could chase and retrieve it.

"Just an average day playing fetch with my dog." Nate had to smile at the irony in that thought.

Reisun was so fast that he barely left a mark on the ground as he retrieved the pebble. Each time he became a blur of himself, appearing to vibrate with movement.

"You know." Nate said, looking at Trevor. "It's almost like The Flash.

He moves so fast it's like everything else is standing still. That's pretty cool."

He gave Reisun a few scratches on the top of his head. "So, do you think you're as fast as The Flash?"

"Flash?" Reason tilted his head, confused.

"He's a superhero," Nate explained. "You know, like Superman, Ironman, Wonder Woman. Those are Superheroes."

"Super. Heroes." There was still confusion in the expression of words from Reisun.

"Okay like, people who have powers, like yours, that use them to help other people." Nate elaborated.

"You superheroes?" Reisun questioned.

"That I am not." Nate told him. "I don't have any superpowers. I can't fly or run fast like you or whatever else it is that you can do. The only thing I have the power to do is basically tic people off and I seem to be really good at that. I'm also pretty good at making people leave. I've pretty much mastered that one."

"I no leave." Reisun said. "Friend."

"Got that right buddy. We're nothing like that guy that had you when you were a puppy. He was not a good guy."

"No superheroes." Reisun growled.

"Right," Nate agreed. "He was more of the super villain type.

"Super villain." Nate could see Reisun's eagerness to know these words.

"Yeah, the bad guy, like the man in in your memory. He's a bad guy."

"Bad guy," He growled again.

"Yeah, bad guy." Nate did his best growling sound.

Trevor sat and watched the interaction between the two with fascinated wonder. He could hear the conversation this time as it was being shared with him and was excited to learn what else Reisun could do. He'd never in his life seen anything like what this amazing creature was sharing with them. He knew that Reisun had to trust Nate in order to share such a secret and in turn Nate had to trust that Trevor would keep their secret as well.

Reisun's ears perked at the sound of Nate's attempt at growling and cocked his head.

"You superheroes." Reisun said. This time it wasn't a question, it was a statement. "Powers. Show you."

"How?" Nate asked, ready for whatever Reisun had in store for him.

"Stand. Show you." He kicked the pebble toward Nate.

Nate picked it up, standing as he did and looked over his shoulder at Trevor who shrugged.

"Okay, so what are we doing?" Nate looked back at Reisun.

"You throw. You catch." Reisun pranced and bounced happily.

Nate tossed the stone into the air and caught it in his hand. Making a grand gesture of the toss.

"Ta da." He bowed holding up the stone to show them he'd caught it.

Reisun barked at this mockery. "Throw!" The force of the word pushed against Nate. "You catch.

"If you say so." Nate said, "But you know I'm nowhere near as fast as you are, right?"

"Throw," Reisun demanded again. "Catch."

"Fine." Nate turned toward the lake and reared back to give the stone a toss. He didn't put as much effort into this toss as he did when he was throwing the stone for Reisun. He felt silly trying to show his dog that he couldn't move anywhere near as fast as him. He knew he couldn't move as fast as an average dog let alone a supernatural one.

He gave the stone a toss in the direction of the lake and then lifted his foot to chase after. In a blink he could feel wind whipping across his face and he found himself on the other side of the lake just in time to hear the stone plop gently into the water.

"What...the..." Nate said. "How the freak did I get over here?"

Trevor was on his feet waving his hands in the air on the other side. Nate could hear him shouting, "Holy crap!" Reisun was barking and spinning with excitement. In a flash he was at Nate's side on the other side of the lake.

"Are you serious?" Nate leaned over and grabbed the dog's face. "Are you freaking serious?! I can run as fast as you?"

"I give you." Reisun said happily. "Share."

"Holy crap! Do it again!" Nate said filled with adrenaline and excitement.

"Run." Reason said still bouncing. "Run fast."

This time there was no throwing stones. Wordlessly they began to run, side-by-side, through the trees. Everything whizzed past them in a blur. He could feel the wind on his face and hear Reisun breathing heavily at his side as he kept pace with him. Trevor did his best to watch them as they flew through the woods, running this way and that. Mostly he only caught glimpses of bushes moving, or leaves being kicked up as they passed. He watched until the tells of their movements disappeared into the distance.

They ran through the trees, jumping across large ditches, over fallen logs and into the fields on the other side of the forest. They'd covered the distance in less than a minute. When they reached the other side of the farming fields, they stopped.

"That was awesome!" Nate screamed out loud.

There was no one around here, but his heart was racing, and his adrenaline was up, and he just needed to scream the words for the world to hear.

"You superheroes like The Flash." Nate said, repeating Reisun's way of saying the words so he'd understand.

"Flash." Reisun agreed. "Flash! Flash! Run more?"

"Sure, we can run some more." Nate told him, assuming that was what he meant. "This time let's race. I'm sure Trev is trying to figure out where we are."

Nate knelt in a racer's stance. "First one back to the clearing is a rotten egg."

"Race, race, race." Reisun was barking merrily.

Nate took off running again with Reisun hot on his tail, still barking. They slid back into the clearing at the same time, kicking up dirt as they did.

"Ah man! This is insane!" He ran over to where Trevor was standing. "Dude, tell me you saw that?"

"Yeah...I mean, I kind of saw it. You guys were moving super-fast." Trevor said, beaming at him.

"Man, we were moving so fast that we made it all the way to the other side of the woods and back." Nate was beside himself with excitement.

"Seriously?" Trevor looked at his watch. "You were only gone for like a minute. How far away was that?"

"Like five miles at least!" Nate grabbed Trevor by the shoulders and shook him as he said this.

He turned his attention back to Reisun. "So, is there more?" He asked. "Like what else can you do? Can me and Trevor both do it? Like when we can both hear you?"

"Only you." Reisun expressed to them. "Only master."

"Well, as crazy as all of this is, that does kind of make sense." Trevor said. He was a little disappointed, but he understood. It was like in the vison they'd seen. The stranger said that the dog could share its powers with its owner.

"Dang." Nate was a bit disappointed too, but also secretly pleased that this was something only he and Reisun would share.

Reisun sensed this and eagerly looked around the little clearing. He spotted a fallen log just to the left of them deeper into the woods.

"Throw." He told him.

Nate followed Reisun's gaze into the woods, spotting the fallen log and instantly knowing that's what he was referring to.

"Throw that? Seriously?" He thought about it for a moment. "Could I really?"

"Throw!" Reisun said. It was as if he was having the most fun, he'd ever had, and they could see the puppy in him as he danced and bounced around barking happily.

"All right." Nate found himself smiling at the dog's jubilance. "Let's give it a go."

He walked into the woods and gave the fallen tree a once over. It had obviously been there for some time; moss grew across the bark and the tree itself was so wide that if it were still standing both Nate and Trevor together, wouldn't have been able to wrap their arms around it.

"He wants me to throw this." Nate thought to himself. He'd already run faster than the Road Runner through these woods with Reisun, so why not?

He planted his feet firmly on the ground, placed both hands on the fallen tree and gave it a little push. It moved easily, sliding about two feet from its fallen position and stopping heavily against several trees behind it.

"Holy crap!" He was staring at his hands and then turned to look back at Reisun and Trev.

"Give you." Reisun told him.

Nate walked up to the tree and lifted it with one hand effortlessly. He turned so that he was aiming between a gap in the woods and tossed the tree in that direction. It sailed up and through the treetops, spinning end over end until it was no longer visible. They all listened as it landed heavily off in the distance.

"Wooo hooo!" He howled with excitement.

He was already looking around for something else to pick up, it didn't matter what it was at this point, the strength was intoxicating, and he wanted to do it again. He found another fallen tree a little further into the woods and sped over to it. He lifted it easily and tossed it playfully from hand to hand before throwing it with all his might. The tree became a rocket, flying through the air like a shot.

Trevor watched until it was out of sight. "Wonder where that's gonna land." He called to Nate.

In a rush of wind, Nate was back at his side. "I threw it toward the field. So, it shouldn't hit anything but the ground. It was easy, like tossing a ball of paper or like throwing the rock. I barely even had to try."

"Okay, so he's telepathic, which is why we can talk to each other without saying anything. He's superfast and he's super-strong. That is pretty awesome." Trevor said.

"Yeah, and he can give those powers to me." Nate added.

"Share," Reisun clarified.

"Oh, right. You can share that with me. So, like, if you can do it, then I can do it. We share." Nate was starting to understand more, but he still had questions.

"So, can I run really fast and pick up heavy stuff when you're not around?" He asked.

"No share." Reisun expressed sadly.

"So, you have to be near me or something like that?"

"Yes." Reisun could see the understanding in Nate's face, and it pleased him. He'd found his bond in Nate and it had opened up a flood gate within him. He was happy to share his abilities with the young boy who he had sensed, on meeting his mother, was missing something deep within himself as well. The confidence that now radiated from the young man was contagious and Reisun was tempted to show him that their shared abilities were limitless, but it was too soon, and he was still learning for himself the true degree of their power's limitless ability.

"Well, that's not too bad. I guess that's what that bad guy, the super villain, was trying to get you to do, right?" He wanted you to share your powers with him."

Reisun growled. "Douche bag."

"He was definitely a douche bag." Nate agreed, smiling at Reisun.

"Listen." Reisun said. His ears were cocked, twitching and trembling as they collected the sounds around them.

"Listen." Reisun pushed into Nate's mind with hushed expression.

There was a scurrying sound of hurried scratching coming from somewhere. Nate looked down at his feet and saw a beetle hurrying by on the ground, leaving the slightest trail as it did. Nate could see the intricate detail of the trail the insect's small skittering feet made in the dirt and could hear the little beetle, no bigger than a ladybug, as it moved across the ground.

Reisun turned his head to the right and repeated, "Listen."

This time the sound came from further away. It was the sound of a car engine running in their yard. It wasn't his mother's or Terrence's truck. Somehow Nate could tell just by the heavier sound of the engine that it was more than likely a pickup of some kind.

"See." He could hear Reisun expressing to him.

"What is it?" Trevor was looking in the same direction they were but didn't hear or see anything unusual.

Nate turned in the direction of the house and did his best to focus on the sound he was hearing. His eyes caught every space, crack and hole among the trees and leaves until he could see all the way back to the house. There was a dark green F150 sitting at the end of their driveway idling.

"Mail man must have gotten a new truck." Nate said.

Reisun only growled.

The truck sat for several minutes. It didn't pull completely up to the house or stop at the mailbox. It only sat idling at the end of the driveway. Nate saw Terence come out of the house heading for the shop. He paused, looking down the drive at the truck sitting there. He raised a hand to wave the person into the yard, but it continued to sit. They watched as Terence began to head down the driveway to approach the truck. The driver must have also seen this and began to back up onto the main dirt road and pulled off in a cloud of kicked up dust.

"That was weird." Nate said. He looked over at Trevor who was waiting patiently for an answer to his earlier question. "There was a random truck sitting in our driveway. My dad started to go see who it was, and it pulled off."

"You could see all that from here?" Trevor said looking in the direction they'd been looking in before.

"Clear as if I were standing right there." Nate smiled.

He paused again. "I hear something else."

Reisun had obviously heard it too. His head was already turned in the direction of the new sound with his ears perked.

"Sounds like," Nate started, listening in the same direction. "Sounds like footsteps coming from the other side of the lake."

Now they were all looking in the direction that Nate had indicated.

"You think someone else is here?" Trevor whispered.

"I'm looking." Nate replied in an equally hushed tone.

PART TWENTY-THREE

Sis and the Gator

Olivia had finally managed to track the boys down. She'd tried to stay far enough behind that they wouldn't notice that she'd been following them, but that had only resulted in her getting herself lost in the woods. She'd stayed on the faint path that she'd seen them take into the trees and listened for the sound of them talking and the dog barking ahead of her. When she arrived near the clearing, she could see them standing around looking off in the opposite direction. She eased closer to where they were standing, doing her best not to step on anything that might give her away.

She made her way to a large tree that was just wide enough to hide behind and peeked around it watching them. She was surprised to finally see the lake that Nate had been telling them about and just how big it actually was but looked around the clearing unimpressed.

"This is where he keeps sneaking off to?" She thought to herself. "He is so weird."

The breeze had started to pick up again and she heard Trevor ask Nate a question and then turn his own attention to something above his head. He seemed to be mesmerized by it. She followed his gaze and saw what had captured his attention, swinging lazily in the breeze.

"What the…" She mouthed the words she'd heard her brother say a million times.

Hanging there, just above him, was a rope tied into a noose, like you see on TV. Olivia blinked a couple of times to make sure she was actually seeing what she thought she saw.

"This can't be real life right now." She said, starting to step out from behind the tree.

She felt like she was stuck in some insane television series. Watching her brother and his friend, staring up at the noose that swung loosely from a tree limb only feet above their head, it was all too surreal. She couldn't believe how fast her heart was racing. She put her hand to her chest to try to hold it in and felt like it would burst out at any moment. She felt like they'd somehow found themselves in the Upside-down.

"So, what do you see?" Trevor asked him.

"Nothing actually." Nate said, turning his attention back to Trevor and Reisun. "It sounded like footsteps, but it stopped, and I don't see anyone."

Reisun's little nub was wagging feverishly with recognition, but he remained silent, allowing Olivia to stay hidden behind the tree a few yards from them.

"So, what's next?" Nate asked Reisun. "What else can we do?"

Reisun appeared to think for a moment. His powers were new to him as well and it seemed that anything he put his mind to they were capable of doing.

"Fly!" Reisun leaped into the air with ease, remained there for a moment and then landed lightly back on all fours.

"Yesssss! I knew it!" Nate shouted. "I knew it!"

"This I've got to see." Trevor said, sharing in their excitement.

"Let's do it!" Nate exclaimed.

Olivia was still watching them from her hiding place behind the tree. "Are they talking to the dog or each other?" She thought. Her heart was still racing as she watched them.

Nate was standing on his toes and jumping up and down.

"How do I do this?" he asked, looking at Reisun.

"He's talking to the dog." Olivia said out loud. My brother has actually lost his mind for real."

Reisun looked at Nate and then up at the noose that hung from the tree above them.

"Tell me how and I'll take it down." Nate told him.

"Fly." Reisun said, pleased.

Nate looked up, focusing on the rope and the limb that it was tied to. He felt an electric sensation surge through him, and he began to rise off the ground. Trevor took a couple of steps back to give him room. Olivia stood watching from behind the tree. He rose slowly at first, making it look like he was standing on his tip toes and then she could see the dirt falling from his shoes as he began to rise higher and higher toward the swinging rope. He was flying.

She strained to see from the distance she stood from them and couldn't quite tell if this was some kind of trick or if he was climbing something. His hands weren't moving; they remained at his sides, until he was face to face with the noose. He reached up to grab the rope just where it met the limb it was tied to, but she'd seen all she needed to see. She burst out from behind the tree screaming for him.

"No!" She screamed. "Don't do it!"

She'd taken two steps, rushing toward her brother and suddenly found her left foot caught in a tangle of vines. Before she realized what was happening, she was lying face down in the dirt. She looked back at the tangle of abrasive vegetation wrapped around her ankle and foot and then turned to sit up. Reaching down, she began snatching at the vines, only to find them full of thorns and brambles. They dug deep into her hands and stung her.

"Dammit," she said, shaking her hand and placed one of her cut fingers into her mouth.

"Nate, wait! I'm coming!" She yelled. She pulled at the vines with her leg trying to snatch her foot loose. The thorns dug deep into her ankles and scraped away bits of skin as she pulled. She yelled again, but this time in pain. There was a splash from the water just off to her left, Olivia glanced over briefly, saw nothing and went back to tugging at the vines.

She looked around for a stick or something sharp that she could use to free herself and get to her brother before he did something terrible. Both Nate and Reisun heard the commotion that Olivia was making. She was a couple of yards away from what he could tell, and he used his higher vantage point to get a better look at where she was.

She wasn't quite on the other side of the lake, but she was some distance away. He could see that she'd fallen and gotten tangled up, which was pretty easy to do out here. He willed himself to drift back down to the ground hurriedly.

"Olivia followed us out here." He said landing softly.

Reisun knew Olivia had been following them and he'd been keeping his ear on her just as he kept an eye on Nate. He even knew why she'd followed them out into the woods. She was worried about her brother and was trying to find out for herself exactly what was going on. Nate's entire family had been worried about him in their own way, but Reisun was confident that soon their worries would be diminished. He could feel the change in Nate and how much lighter his spirit had become. Their shared powers and abilities had given him a sense of purpose.

There was a huge splash from the lake. They all turned at the sound. It had been so loud that you wouldn't have needed super hearing to catch it, Nate had heard that sound tons of times. The first time he and his friends had been trying to push an old rowboat into the lake. They'd been so surprised and excited that they'd rushed home and told his mom all about it. It had been huge then and that had been over a year ago.

Nate's annoyance at the fact that his little sister had followed them would have to wait. He was definitely a little annoyed but there was no time for that now, there was something much worse to be concerned with. Something sinister had set its sights on a vulnerable prize that now lay tangled in vines by the water's edge, and it was moving fast.

Reisun barked, looking over at Nate. This wasn't like Lassie trying to tell his humans that Timmy had fallen into a well, far from it. It appeared that the longer Nate and Reisun were connected, the stronger their bond grew. Without a word they both knew what needed to be done.

"Holy crap!" Trevor exclaimed. "What the heck was that?

"Gator. And not a small one either. "Nate said matter-of-factly.

He concentrated his focus across the water to where his sister lay on the bank tugging at the vines. The water was moving in a swift shallow wave in her direction.

"I see it." Trevor said pointing.

He was looking farther out where two more lines of rippling water had begun to move in her direction. There were more of them headed toward her. There was no time to waste. Nate looked at Reisun and gave him a quick nod. Reisun took off full sprint around the banks of the lake headed for Olivia. Nate chose a more direct path across the lake, flying effortlessly over the water.

He reached the largest of the ripples; it was definitely a gator, and it was huge. Nate flew over the monstrous reptile, which had to be at least three and 1/2 times his own length, to get a better look. It was scary to look at, but even scarier considering where it was headed. Its body was long and muscular, covered in moss and algae that had collected there over the years. It moved effortlessly through the water with no more than a deliberate swish of its tree trunk size tail. This would be his first true test sharing Reisun's powers.

He met Reisun on the far side of the lake, just as the first gator broke the water's surface. Olivia screamed as the water sprayed in every direction. The gator roared at Nate, revealing a mouthful of razor-sharp teeth. Nate could smell the stench of old fish and rotted meat and knew this gator was used to eating well. He stepped between the gator and his little sister.

"Nate, no!" Olivia screamed.

He looked over his shoulder at her. "Don't worry, I got this." He assured her.

"This is not TV, Nate!" She yelled.

Nate gave Reisun another nod and turned his attention back to the gator. It had drawn back into the water and appeared to be considering the scene it was witnessing. He took a step forward watching it and noting that the other two smaller ripples were now barely visible logs floating nearby, waiting to join in on a free meal. The largest of them, still facing Nate, let out a low rumbling sound that trembled the water around it.

"Anytime now would be great! "He called over his shoulder.

Reisun had begun snatching out the vines that had wrapped themselves around Olivia's ankles, pulling them up effortlessly.

"Almost got it." Olivia told him.

Trevor came crashing through the trees carrying a long stick he'd broken off to a pointed end. The sudden noise cued the gator, which sprang out of the water in an attempt to snag a distracted morsel.

"Nate! "Trevor yelled, starting to rush towards him with his pointed stick raised.

Nate grabbed the gator by the top of its mouth and bottom jaw, holding it open wide.

"No." Nate stopped Trevor mid step. "Help my sister."

"Ok." Trevor turned and ran to Olivia's side, taking her by the arm to help her up. Reisun stepped out of the way with the last vines still hanging from his mouth. She pulled her foot loose, bringing a tangle of vines with her as she did, and got to her feet with Trevor's help.

"Thanks," she said hugging Trevor and then kneeling to hug Reisun. She stood and looked for Nate, who was holding a monster of a gator by the mouth with his bare hands. She blinked a couple of times and rubbed her eyes, not quite believing what she was seeing. The gator shook its massive head back and forth violently, but Nate continued to hold it steady. It reared up on its hind legs and came crashing back down onto its side going into a roll. Nate allowed himself to be pulled up off the ground.

He slammed the gator's jaws shut and wrapped an arm around its neck, swinging his legs around its shoulders, preparing for the roll. He'd seen this on Animal Planet a million times, the infamous death roll.

It rolled three or four times to the left and then several more times to the right before rearing up once more and falling back, with Nate, into the water.

"Nate!!" Olivia and Trevor both shouted.

The water thrashed and foamed with an unseen struggle that appeared to be taking place just beneath the surface. Olivia, now free from entanglement, started for the water.

"Wait. "Trevor caught her by the hand.

"Get off of me!" She snatched her hand away. "We have to do something!"

Trevor looked at Reisun. "Help him." He pleaded.

Reisun replied with an understanding nod and headed for the water's edge.

"And what the heck is he supposed to do, get eaten too?!" Olivia was frantic.

"Cover." Reisun said looking back at them.

The words rang in Olivia's head for a moment, and she could see a clear picture of them covering their ears.

"Wha… "She started.

"Cover your ears!" Trevor told her, already covering his.

She could see that Reisun was clearly waiting for her, so she placed her hands over her ears and pressed them there.

She swore she saw him smile as he turned back to the water. He inhaled deeply and barked three times, shaking the ground and sending a shockwave across the surface of the lake.

Both Trevor and Olivia cringed at the immensity of the sound, pressing their hands tighter to their ears. Olivia turned into Trevor's shoulder, who did his best to shield her. After a few moments had passed they looked up and realized that everything around them was now completely silent. There were no birds singing, no rustling from within the trees, the wind even appeared to have died down. Olivia joined Reisun at the water's edge. The lake stretched out in front of them, still and quiet.

"Where is he?" she asked Reisun, fully expecting an answer.

Reisun groaned and sat down still looking out over the water. Olivia followed his gaze and waited.

One by one fish began to rise to the water's surface until hundreds could be seen floating across the lake. They'd been stunned, mouths gaping and fins waving slowly at the equally stunned children standing at the water's edge.

"Something's wrong." Olivia said. "No one can hold their breath that long."

She started for the water again. "We have to do something!"

Reisun reached out with his paw at that moment and Olivia was washed in the sensation of what she understood to be, "No."

"Watch." Reisun expressed to her soothingly.

She was still completely perplexed to how this dog their mother had adopted from the animal shelter was now communicating with her in a way that was completely understandable, but she listened and continued to watch the water.

The stillness of the water was now being disrupted by tiny bubbles rising in a circle. She could see that some of the fish were shaking off their stunned state and retreating back into the depths of the lake as the rising bubbles grew larger and larger in size. The water began to roll over itself now, as if it were being boiled, until finally there was an explosion and Nate could be seen rising above the water's surface now holding the gator by its tail.

Water rained down all around them, soaking them to the bone.

"Well, that was fun big guy." Nate told the gator he held. "Now go find something else to eat."

He swung around several times building up momentum and released the big gator, sending it sailing further off into the lake. He watched as it landed in the water some distance away, shook off the impact and swam away in defeat.

Nate floated over to the bank where everyone was standing and shook off the water from his own drenched clothes like a dog fresh out the bath.

"Hey!" Trevor said with a relieved smile.

"Oh, my bad." Nate laughed, realizing that he was shaking the water off and onto everyone else.

Reisun took the cue and began to shake as well.

"Hey!" Olivia was the unfortunate victim this time.

"I'm bad." Reisun shared with them and then began to pant happily.

"First of all, it's, 'My Bad', and second of all…what in the H…E…double hockey sticks, is going on Nate?" She said, grabbing him by the front of his shirt.

Nate was still looking out over the surface of the water for the other two smaller gators he's seen as he was flying over. He could see the very tip of the snouts poking ever so slightly from the water, followed by two sets of peering eyes, that had been watching the events that took place on the bank, as they turned slowly and sank back beneath the surface. Now that he knew they were safe he allowed his sister to shake him by his shirt in frustration.

He grabbed her hands and removed them from his shirt. "You good?" he asked, giving her a quick look over and only finding some scrapes and scratches.

"I'm fine. Are you good? Since when can you fly and stuff? Is that why ya'll are always out here in the woods? And what's up with the rope in the tree over there?" Her questions poured out one after the other.

"Oh no you don't." Nate put up a hand to stop her. "First of all, what are you doing out here?" He asked her.

She rolled her eyes, "Duh, I'm following you stupid." she said.

"Whatever, Olivia. Why are you following me?" He clarified.

"I wanted to see what you are out here doing. You be disappearing for hours at a time, mom's around the house all worried and crying and stuff and you know that ain't even like her. Mom's from New Jersey and it takes a lot to get to her. So, I came to see for myself." She explained.

Nate could see the concern in his sister's eyes. She's been worried too and looked as if she were still on the brink of tears.

"Put your arms up." He said.

"What? What does that have to do with any…" She started.

"Stop talking so much and just put your hands up, dang." He grabbed her wrist and raised her arms above her head. "Trev, you too."

Trevor raised his hands without question. Nate flinched and then was a blur of himself as he ran circles around both Trevor and Olivia. They were caught up in a whirlwind that blew through their clothes and hair until they were completely dry.

"Holy crap!" Olivia exclaimed.

When Nate stopped, he was standing directly in front of her again. He reached out and pulled her into his arms. "If you're going to feed the gators like in that movie Lake Placid, how about use something other than yourself next time." He laughed.

Olivia gave him a punch and wrapped her arms around his neck. "I was so scared for you." She told him.

"You didn't have to be. I had that gator under control." He assured her.

"Not just that." She had tried to hold her tears back and failed. She buried her face into Nate's shirt as she continued. "I saw the rope hanging in the tree and I thought you were about to…"

"I know." He started.

"No, you don't know!" She balled. "You have to stop acting crazy Nate! There's nothing wrong with you. I thought you were about to kill yourself! We black, we don't do stuff like this!"

Nate pulled Olivia back and held her at arm's length. "First of all, you had no business following us out here." He said. "Second of all, being black has nothing to do with nothing and third of all I know and I'm sorry, my bad. It's just that, you know for a long time I had been feeling really crazy. You know, like I'm just mad all the time and I don't know why I'm mad. Sometimes I just didn't know what to do about it, but everything is going be okay." he said sincerely. He wiped the tears that had soaked her cheeks. Olivia had always tried to be strong like their mom, but also like their mother, she was scared for him, and the tears continued to flow.

"So, what's with the rope?" She sniffled.

Trevor stood silently with Reisun, not wanting to disrupt such a sensitive moment between brother and sister.

"OK, I'll be honest with you. Every day when ya'll would see me leave to go walking with my backpack and my jacket on, I was coming out here. Every day I would sit out here looking at that rope when I was feeling really bad, and I admit that I thought about using it. I would weigh just how bad I felt and then decide if I should just go home and think about it some more. Then I'd come back and see how I felt the next day. That's what I did every day for like a year. But when we came out here today with Reisun it wasn't about that. When we realized you were in trouble, I was about to take the rope down." Nate explained. "Reisun is the one who told me that you were on the other side of the lake about to get eaten by some alligators. I told you it was dangerous out here."

"Well, now I know." She said wiping the back of her hand across her face.

"I bet." He laughed and hugged her again before letting her go. "And I better not catch you ever coming out here again."

"You definitely don't have to worry about that." They both laughed at this.

"And you don't have to worry. I'm all good." He reassured her again.

Olivia gave Nate a final hug, squeezing him tightly as she did and then pushed him away as though she were completely repulsed by the idea of hugging her brother.

"Now, do you want to explain the rest of what happened here?" she asked with one eyebrow raised.

He looked away playfully as though he had no idea what she was referring to. "Ummm, you mean with the gators or ...."

"You know exactly what I mean. You thought I wasn't going to see the super speed running dog and my brother flying across the lake coming to my rescue? I mean, come on, he talked to me, and I understood it." Olivia said letting the events replay in her mind like a movie. "I know this has something to do with this guy." She leaned over and gave Reisun a few scratches behind his ears.

"Well, if you want to keep knowing, it's got to be our secret." Nate said. Trevor came and joined them then.

"So, I take it you knew about this too?" Olivia asked Trev.

"Kinda." He replied quietly.

"I feel like I'm always the last to know everything." she said, shaking her head.

"Well, you know now." Nate said. "And this definitely has to be our little secret, can we trust you with this?"

"Duh," She rolled her eyes again. "We're family, aren't we? So, tell me."

"It's kind of a long story." Nate explained. He shared with Olivia everything that Reisun had told them. Each boy took a turn telling part of the story excitedly. "Reisun is just like a super awesome dog, and he chose me." Nate finished.

Olivia looked over at Reisun and smiled. "Yeah, he is pretty cool."

"I think we've been out here long enough." Nate stretched and looked around. He extended a hand to Olivia, who took it without question. "Grab Trev's hand too," He gestures in Trevor's direction with his head.

She reaches for Trevor's hand and holds it tightly. "You sure you know what you're doing?"

Nate looks at Reisun, who barks happily and then becomes a blur, rushing through the trees toward home.

"You guys ready?" Nate teased.

"Ready," Trevor said.

"I guess." Olivia took a deep breath, not quite sure what to expect. She closed her eyes and before she realized it, they were weightless, soaring through the air toward home.

PART TWENTY-FOUR

Trevor

Olivia watched as the trees passed beneath her and found herself believing that this must be what it feels like to be a bird every day. She looked over at Trevor, how had his one free hand extended out in front of him 'superman' style. His eyes were wide with awe and excitement.

"This is awesome!" Olivia shouted.

"Woooohooo!" Trevor howled in agreement.

Nate smiled. "We're going to come down behind the house. Hold on." He told them.

They could already hear Reisun barking excitedly somewhere on the ground beneath them. He'd beaten them there and was celebrating his victory.

"First, first, first." Reisun sang in Nate's head.

"I was taking my time." Nate said lowering into the trees and settling them all safely on the ground.

"That was so cool." Olivia said breathlessly.

"I thought he could only share with you?" Trevor was watching Reisun intently as he tossed the random thought out.

"Yeah. It's weird. I kind of felt like if I concentrated hard enough, I could hold you guys up, so we gave it a try and it worked. I didn't even know we could do that." Nate scratched his head as he considered this.

He'd just known that they could do it. Just like he somehow knew that there were few limits to exactly what they were capable of doing, perhaps no limits at all.

"We have got the coolest dog ever!" Olivia grabbed Reisun's face and gave it a squeeze, flopping his ears as she did.

"Cool!" Reisun expressed to all of them with genuine love and excitement.

"I can feel your happy." Olivia giggled, wrapping her arms around her waist. The sensation rushed through her like a flurry of tiny tickling fingers that raced down her ribcage and up her spine.

"Yes, you are." Nate had to agree with a smile.

"Well, my super nose is telling me that mom's making fried chicken." Olivia turned in the direction of the house and pretended to sniff the air.

"Last one back…" Nate started to say.

Olivia took off running as fast as she could. "You guys are gonna be rotten eggs!" She called back to them. Reisun was keeping pace with her as they carefully dashed through the trees.

"When in Rome." Trevor said and took off running in the direction Olivia and Reisun had gone."

"Wow, guys really?" Nate called before taking off after them.

Even at his normal rate of speed, Nate was pretty quick and caught up with Trevor easily. Olivia and Reisun came bursting through the tree line into their yard first with Nate and Trevor close behind. They came out just behind their stepdad's shop.

Olivia had slowed to a jog now as she passed Terrence who was leaned over a motorcycle reconnecting wires and hoses.

"Hey dad." She gave him a quick wave as she passed. "Might want to hold your nose, there's some rotten eggs behind me."

Nate and Trevor pretended to roll their eyes the way Olivia was known to do. "We let you win." Nate said.

"You wish you let me win!" Olivia was already on the driveway headed for the house with Reisun still on her heels. There was the promise of sharing chicken with Olivia, and he wasn't going to miss out on that.

Terrence dropped the wrench he'd been using on a pile of tools he had sitting next to him. He grabbed an old rag from his back pocket and began to wipe his hands with it.

"So, I take it you guys are the rotten eggs huh?" He smiled.

"Looks that way." Nate returned the smile and gave Trevor a nudge with his elbow.

"Yeah." Trevor agreed quickly and then added, "But she kind of cheated though."

Terrence shook his head clearly amused, "Smells like dinner is about ready."

"Yeah, that's what brought us back too." Nate said. "We were headed in."

"Sounds like a plan." Terrence joined the boys as they made their way down the driveway toward the house. He threw his arm around

Nate's shoulder and listened as they talked about walking through the woods, all the deer they'd seen and the gators in the lake.

Both Nate and Trevor were careful about the details they shared, being sure not to mention that Olivia was almost eaten, the dog could talk telepathically, and Nate could fly. It was actually surprisingly easy. They weren't lying about anything, simply not elaborating on specific details the way they'd seen politicians and celebrities do for years. Nate knew that just like in those situations, there was a chance they'd be found out, but hopefully it wouldn't be until he had an opportunity to come up with a better story to explain it all.

Sure enough, when they reached the house, the air was filled with the aroma of dinner. They could smell fried chicken, fresh baked cornbread, seasoned rice and vegetables.

"Please tell me dinner is done." Nate said, entering the kitchen. "I'm starvin' like Marvin!"

Denise smiled, "You guys go get washed up and we can eat."

The boys ran back to the bathroom to wash their hands and met Olivia coming out.

"Dang, I beat ya'll again." She stuck out her tongue playfully.

"I bet you won't beat us at eating." Nate pushed by her and slid into the bathroom.

"You eat like you have six stomachs." Olivia said, "I wouldn't even want to try with your greedy behind."

She waited by the bathroom door for them to finish and they made their way back into the kitchen together.

Olivia knocked on David's door on their way by. "Dinners ready." She yelled through the door.

It flew open. "I know," David said standing in the doorway. "I could smell it in my dreams."

He joined them as they headed to the kitchen.

When dinner was over, and the table had been cleared Denise leaned back and glanced over at the time on the stove.

"It's starting to get late, and it'll be dark soon. Is someone coming to pick you up Trev?" She asked him.

Trevor appeared to have been caught off guard by the question. He actually hadn't been thinking about the fact that he would eventually have to go home and start getting ready for school tomorrow. He'd been enjoying himself so much that he honestly wished he didn't have to leave.

"Ummm…, I'll have to call and see." he said hesitantly.

"No problem." Denise said. "Just let me know and if they can't I don't mind dropping you off."

"Thank you." Trevor excused himself from the table and headed back to Nate's room to make his call.

"They probably aren't there." Nate told her. "They usually aren't."

"That's a shame." Denise looked down the hall in the direction he'd gone. "Does he have any other brothers or sisters?"

"Nah," Nate answered without going into any detail.

"Must be lonely." Terrence added. "It's nice that you hang out with him."

"Trevor is cool. He's just kinda quiet and keeps to himself most of the time." Nate added.

Denise considered this for a moment. She'd had a chance to observe Trevor and could clearly see that he was dealing with his own issues. He was very quiet, but also very polite. His eyes were sad, often betraying the tone of his voice and he went out of his way to avoid eye contact though she often caught him staring intently at them until he was noticed doing so. He always looked as if he were trying to figure them out, like watching animals in the zoo.

"Well," She finally said. "If he's not able to reach anyone then he's welcome to stay tonight and I'll just take you both to the bus stop in the morning."

"Ok, cool." Nate popped up out of his seat and headed for his room.

Reisun, belly full of fried chicken dropped for him by Olivia during dinner, followed Nate. Trevor was standing with his back turned to the door when they entered. His backpack was open on the bed, and he was looking out the bedroom window with his phone pressed tight to his ear.

Nate fell heavily onto the bed with a bounce sending the backpack tumbling to the floor and spilling its contents.

"Dang, my bad." Nate said getting up to pick up the bag.

Trevor turned at the sound and quickly slid his phone into his back pocket, dropping it to his knees before Nate could touch anything. "I've got it." Trevor said using his body to block Nate from getting any closer.

"It's no problem." Nate reached down to help him pick up his things from the floor.

"I've got it!" Trevor snapped and then added softly, "Its ok. I don't mind."

Nate stood staring at him for a long moment, caught off guard. "Ok." He finally managed and sat back down to kick off his shoes, sending them sailing toward the closet door but not quite making it in.

"Were you able to get anyone? What did they say?" Nate asked him.

Trevor shook his head, "I just left a message." He said shoving the last of his 'things' into his bag.

"Well, my mom said you can stay the night again and she'll just take us to the bus stop in the morning. You think they'd be ok with that?" Nate had been watching Trevor pick up his stuff as he spoke.

"That's cool." Trevor stood up and swung his bag over his shoulder. "I'm going to use the rest room real quick.

"Aight." Nate grabbed his phone and began searching his social media for funny videos to watch.

Reisun whimpered a little when Trevor left the room and got up from where he'd been lying in the corner and walked over to Nate's bed. He placed his head on the mattress and looked over at Nate.

"Sad." Reisun said in Nate's head.

"What?" Nate looked over at Reisun and then sat up to face him fully. "No, I'm good. I'm not sad." He gave Reisun a pat on the head and started to go back to scrolling on his phone.

Reisun slid his head from the mattress and began searching around on the floor. He came back up with a small notebook and placed it on the bed.

"Friend sad." He pressed the words into Nate's head.

"What's this?" He said taking it.

"Trevor." Reisun motioned to the notebook.

PART TWENTY-FIVE

Trevor's List

Trevor opened his mouth to explain but was interrupted by a knock on the door before he could start. Denise peeked her head in the door then.

"You guys good in here?" She asked.

The air was thick with tension but both boys nodded, and Trevor walked over and took a seat on the edge of the bed.

"Umm, ok," She raised an eyebrow as she looked from one boy to the other. "I want to stop by the feed store tomorrow and grab our boy some high protein food, so you guys try to be up and ready on time in the morning." Trevor was staring down at his feet, so Nate stepped over to the door where his mother stood.

"Gotcha. We'll be up." He placed his hand on the doorknob then.

"Is that your way of telling me to leave? Because you know I'll stand here all night." She gave him a poke in the side.

"Nah ma," Nate swatted her hand away. "You can stay as long as you want." He shot a quick glance at Trevor that told her that they needed some quiet time.

Denise had seen that thousand mile stare many times in Nate's face when he would start to shut down emotionally. To see that he was able to recognize that need in another made her heart swell.

"Nope, I always feel like something is going to reach out and grab me any time I'm in your room." She laughed. "Nite you guys."

"Nite ma." Nate started to slowly push the door shut.

"Nite." She barely heard the soft whisper of Trevor just as the door closed. She was worried about that young man, but she hoped his friendship with Nate would help build both of them up.

She headed to her room with thoughts of Trevor and Nate on her mind. She knew her son already had the odds stacked against him as a young Black man in America, but to also be dealing with an issue as taboo in the Black community only made life harder for him. Especially when so few people even took mental health into account when young people like him...and Trevor, begin acting out.

While his mother was in her room worrying as a mother often does, Nate had turned to confront Trevor about the notebook that had fallen out of his bag.

"Trev, what the hell man?" he asked, lowering his voice and walking over to join Trevor on the bed. "What's up with the notepad and why is my sister's name in it with scratches through it?"

There was a long pause before Trevor said anything. He took a deep breath and looked down at the book in his hand.

"I guess it's like my security blanket. I was never really a fighter and after Jake..." He faded off at his brother's name and had to wipe his face and clear his throat before he began again.

"After...what happened. Everything was terrible. Everywhere was terrible. They teased me and beat me up. They stole my stuff and called me names..."

He squeezed the book in both his hands until it rolled into a small tight tube. "And every time they did, I wrote their name down. I wrote down what they had done to me and how it made me feel. I numbered each one and sometimes I would reorder the names. They were going to pay for what they'd done to me. How they treated me. They were all going to pay."

His voice was small and low as he said this. Nate sat quietly, listening without judgment. He waited until Trevor had stopped talking and was again wiping moisture from his eyes.

"But why is Olivia's name in there?" He leaned forward and asked.

"No!" Trevor's head snapped around to face Nate now. "It's in there but I scratched it off. I mean, it was before I knew...anybody. I'm sorry."

The tears were running freely down his face now. He didn't remember having ever cried in front of a friend before. But then, he hadn't really ever had very many friends to begin with. They sat quietly again for several minutes. Trevor taking the time to compose himself and Nate trying to decide just how he felt about what Trevor had told him.

Finally, he said, "So, all the names on your list...you were going to...?"

Trevor shrugged, "Yeah. I had a plan and all. What day I was going to do it, what time, how. All of it. And then I met you...and Reisun."

At the sound of his name Reisun stepped over to where Trevor sat and rested his head on his lap. The room began to fill with the smell of fresh baked cookies and sweet warm breezes that seemed to embrace their bodies as well as their senses. Trevor actually smiled then as he placed a hand on Reisun's head and began to pet him gently.

"Exactly my point." he said waving his other hand around. "I was so angry all the time and then I meet you guys and your family, and you treat me like...a normal person." He drops his hand back to the bed as if defeated.

"Dawg, you are a normal person." Nate reassured him. "Nobody's perfect and we all get mad, or sad or lonely sometimes. If that doesn't make us normal, then who's normal? And for that matter, what is normal anyway?"

"That's what I mean." Trevor said still petting Reisun. "I tell you that I keep a list of people's names that I wanted to hurt, and you say, 'nobody's perfect', while your magical dog changes the entire environment of the room to try and make me feel better."

Reisun's head popped up then and his mouth dropped open in a heavy pant as if to say, 'I'm just trying to do my part'.

"You my people." Nate told him. "I been in a messed-up place for a long time too and I know how it can be when stuff starts to get dark." He paused for a moment and then asked, "Do you still feel like that?" Trevor didn't hesitate, "No." he said quickly. "I mean, like maybe I did early on in the month, but...I mean, like, how can I still feel that way knowing there is actual magic out there? Like, not only did I make a new friend, but you trusted me with Reisun's secret. I want to be here to help protect it."

"That's what's up, bro." Nate said, reaching out to do their handshake.

Trevor met him halfway and they shook. Reisun gave a quick bark and the loving haze in the room began to clear.

"Man, hush R before you get us in trouble." Nate said in a hushed voice. Reisun dropped to the floor and rolled onto his back, covering his face with his paws. At this the tension in the room had been completely lifted and both the boys began to laugh out loud.

From down the hall Denise could hear the boys in the room seemingly having a good time. She got up from the bed and stepped to her door, opening it just a crack.

"You've got an early morning! Good night you guys!" She called down the hall to them.

"NITE!" They called back simultaneously and then broke out into another round of laughter.

"Hey," Nate said once they had settled down.

"Yeah," Trevor responded.

"You know what you have to do now right?" Nate asked him.

"Burn it." Trevor answered knowing what his friend was referring to.

"Yup. We'll do it tonight in the burn can in the back yard."

"Cool."

They chatted quietly for several hours waiting for the clock to strike twelve. Seemed like as good a time as any to set flame to the past and be reborn to a new chapter. Perhaps a happier chapter.

PART TWENTY-SIX

Small Talk with the Devil

The stranger's trip to the college to try and track down the likely culprit that had stolen his property had proven to be fruitless. He'd lurked around the campus for several days attempting to use the sweatshirt he had found to track its owner with no luck. Asking students wasn't an option as many of them were already looking at him as though he didn't belong there.

He was able to gain access to the girls' volleyball practice but with no more to go on than a lost sweatshirt, he had no way of knowing who it belonged to. What he hadn't been aware of, however, was that one of the students had noticed him. Not only had she noticed him, but she had seen him before in a dream, or a vision shown to her by a very special friend. That same student had made up her mind that day to return to the shelter as soon as she could to make sure her friend was safe. With no other leads the stranger decided that the collar was his only option for finding the dog, but he had to use it sparingly.

Using the collar to track the animal was draining it rapidly and the glow had begun to dim slightly. It would need to be placed back around the dog's neck to be re-energized. He hung the collar from his rear-view mirror and stomped on the gas in the direction that the collar indicated. Three hours later he was pulling up in front of a feed store in what appeared to be a small rural town. The collar's glow had dimmed to practically nothing as he pulled into the store's parking lot.

"Must be someone in here that can lead me to my friend." He said out loud to himself. He grabbed the collar and tucked it into his coat before leaving the truck and heading into the store.

Denise had seen the boys safely to their bus and was headed to the feed store just as she had planned the night before. For some reason she felt like Reisun would prefer a hardier food with a higher protein content and the feed store offered several varieties. She smiled as she thought of the boys joining their friends this morning at the bus. They had been in such a good mood. Even Trevor had been more talkative than she had ever seen him. Perhaps the dynamic of Nate, Trevor and Reisun, the three musketeers, was good for all of them.

Denise walked through the aisles of the small feed store, lost in thought, comparing different brands and prices of food, when she heard a voice behind her.

"Excuse me, miss. Do you know if this brand is good for puppies?" The man's voice was a bit gruff, but polite.

Denise turned around to see a tall, husky man with sharp features and a cold smile. His eyes were piercing, and she felt a chill run down her spine. She hesitated for a moment before answering.

"Yes, I think that's a good one. But you might want to check with the store owner to be sure." Denise tried to keep her tone neutral, not wanting to encourage the stranger any further.

The man nodded and walked away, but Denise felt his eyes on her as she continued to browse. She couldn't shake the feeling that he was watching her, waiting for something. As she was about to leave the store, the man approached her again.

"I couldn't help but notice you have a dog of your own," he said, his smile growing wider. "Do you have a picture of him?"

Denise hesitated, but eventually pulled out her phone and showed him a picture of her dog with her son sitting under their favorite tree. The man's eyes lit up, and Denise immediately regretted showing him the photo. As they spoke, Denise felt like something was off about the man. He seemed too interested in her dog, too eager to know more and he was standing way too close.

"He is quite the big boy." The man said as Denise slid her phone back into her bag.

"Yes, he is. I'm sorry but I have an appointment shortly and just wanted to grab a couple of things beforehand, so-," She made a quick excuse in an effort to escape the uncomfortable encounter.

"It was a pleasure." He said extending his hand to her.

She extended her own hand in return and shook his. As they shook, he was sure to also touch her arm on the side she held her purse on, dropping a small black stone into her bag. Denise released his and abruptly and turned, walking off with hurried steps, away from the stranger with greedy eyes, feeling relieved to be away from him.

The stranger left the store with a huge grin on his face. The stone he had dropped into her bag was an enchanted stone used for tracking over short distances. It gave off a blue light that he is able to see with his naked eye while it remains invisible to others. This light will leave a trail leading back to wherever she goes. His mouth practically watered as he thought about just how close he was. He was closer than he had ever been to finding his missing canine, and he would have him back. Even if it meant destroying anyone that got in his way.

PART TWENTY-SEVEN

Strange Vehicle

With everything that had happened over the past couple of weeks Nate was content to be sitting quietly in the front yard with Reisun. It was Saturday and they'd been out there all morning watching the birds and enjoying the breeze. There were only a couple more days of school left, and his mother had been frantically trying to get his brother ready for graduation. She had already gone for the morning shopping for his graduation suit and shoes. Both David and Olivia had gone with her, he had opted to sleep a little while longer and spend the day outside.

He wasn't exactly interested in spending his entire Saturday hopping from store to store with his mom. Terrence was gone for the day as well. He got an emergency call from one of the bike clubs and had gone to pick up two bikes to work on.

"Well, Reisun, maybe this time next year I'll be the one graduating." He said hopefully.

He leaned back against the tree and then sat up quickly and turned to look behind him. He'd had a bad experience with ants crawling into his clothes when he'd drifted off to sleep outside one day, so he looked back to ensure he wasn't leaning on a trail of them. When he was satisfied that the tree was clear he leaned back again and crossed his arms over his chest. Reisun had rolled onto his back with his feet kicked up in the air enjoying the early summer sun. Nate could hear him snoring a little as he dozed. "You look comfortable." Nate laughed.

Then he turned his face upward toward the sun and closed his own eyes. Perhaps he would take a quick nap too. As the heavy sensation of sleep began to take over his consciousness, both he and Reisun were alerted to the sound of big tires rolling down the dirt road. Their senses were synced and even with his eyes closed Nate could tell several things about the approaching vehicle. He could tell that it was a truck, mud tires and stank of diesel.

There was something else about the truck as well, like a nostalgia that they both knew but only Reisun was able to fully recall. He was at once weary and the hair on the back of his neck stood straight up with furious intent. He knew that sound.

He knew that smell. He knew that truck. The sudden shock of realization had also caused Nate's eyes to fly open and as soon as he saw the approaching vehicle, which was still several hundred yards away, he knew exactly who it was. The stranger. But how? How could this man that had been no more than a vison from Reisun's past now be coming down his dirt road heading toward his home? How had he found them? Nate thought and Reisun received these thoughts as if they were of one mind.

"Collar." Reisun stood and the word resonated from him.

Nate stood as well. "He can use the collar to find you?" he said with a bit of fear, beginning to take hold in his voice.

"Yes, collar." Reisun expressed to him. "Coming for me."

"He'll have to go through me first." Nate was searching the ground for anything that he could use as a weapon. There was no way he was letting this man take his dog. It didn't matter if Reisun did have powers, he was a part of their family and family sticks together, no matter what.

He found a long limb that had fallen from one of the trees and picked it up as the truck pulled into their driveway, stopping halfway between the mailbox and the house. Nate and Reisun were both on their feet at this point, bracing themselves to do whatever they had to do to protect their home and one another. They watched as the driver's side door slowly opened and one heavy boot was placed on the ground, followed by the other.

A large man, maybe 6 feet or better, stepped out of the truck. He left the engine running and didn't seem at all concerned that he had also left the driver's side door wide open. He took a couple steps in their direction, waving his hand in the air.

"Hey there," he called to them. "Are your parents' home?"

He was looking further up the driveway as he asked this, as though to assure himself that there were no other cars parked there. Nate didn't answer. Just watched the man, slowly approaching. Reisun took a couple steps forward as well. His head hung low, and the hair still raised cautiously on his back, but now he had begun a slow and steady growl.

"Doesn't look like anybody's home." The man called to him again, but he'd ceased his steady approach. Nate still had not replied, instead he shifted the limb that he found, holding it vertically in both hands, like a sword or a baseball bat.

"That's a nice dog you got there." The stranger continued from where he stood. "Looks like he's pretty protective of you. Guess I'll just stand my ground here." He gave a half-hearted chuckle at that.

"Or you could leave," Nate replied.

The man smiled slightly. "It's almost as if you know who I am."

The smile on his face seemed to falter a bit as he tried to maintain his faux friendly persona. This obvious ploy to hide his true intentions would have been far more successful had the stranger had had any real idea of what Reisun was truly capable of. Reisun stepped forward now in response to the man's last statement.

This brought an even more vile grin to The Stranger's face.

"Oh, I am sure you know and remember me well young pup." The stranger planted his feet and the small grains of gravel around them begam to vibrate.

Before either of them was aware there was a sudden wash of energy pushing against them in a flood. Sound was too loud, light was too bright, the ground felt unstable under their feet, it was as if he was everywhere all at once. Blasting them with heat and cold, light and sound. Nate shook his head frantically trying to clear his mind. He could feel Reisun reaching out to him in the chaos, and they connected there.

"Must focus." Reisun came through the noise as clear as if they were sitting quietly by the pond together. "We are strong together. Focus."

Nate's head was spinning and making the rest of the world feel as though it were spinning as well. He tried to focus and was bombarded with images of his family, past hurts, arguments, it was too much, how was he supposed to focus.

"I can't!" He heard himself screaming out loud.

"Focus." Reisun was ever calm, clear and present.

Nate tried again to connect with Reisun, they were already bound, but there was something there in his mind that he knew he had to reach. It was like a golden thread blowing in the breeze and all he had to do was slow down, breathe, wait for his moment and take hold of it. As he realized this, everything began to come into focus.

"I remember him from your vision." Nate pushed to Reisun.

"Yes," Reisun's head had lowered even more in anticipation. "Bad guy."

"Ha! Looks like you guys are pretty close." The stranger slapped his knee with amusement. "Almost as though you all can communicate without saying a single word." The smile was growing like mold across his face, becoming somewhat gruesome and joker-like.

"I think you should leave." Nate said.

"You know," The stranger said, "That there doggy of yours looks a lot like a dog I used to have. Been looking for my ling lost pup for a real long time. He's got some real specific identifying marks on him. Like a white patch of hair on his chest shaped somewhat like diamond. As a matter of fact, just like yours does."

"Don't really care." Nate snapped. "Only thing that matters right now is that you're trespassing. The last thing you should be worried about is what my dog looks like."

The man laughed heartily, rearing back as he did and holding his stomach with one hand as his other rested suspiciously on his hip. He brought that hand down now, exposing what he held there. It was Reisun's collar. A shiver ran through both Reisun and Nate.

"It's okay," Nate expressed to Reisun. "It's all right. Nobody is going to take you from us, nobody."

"You all having a little heart-to-heart over there." The man asked. "You know, I'm sure I've got a missing dog flyer in the truck somewhere. I handed a few of them out at the high school during their band practice. Bet all I'd have to do is contact the local authorities and let them know that I found my dog. I'm sure they'd have no problem coming over here and making sure that I got him back without issue." He taunted.

This man had basically just threatened his family and Nate was getting angry.

"Get off my property now!" Nate shouted. "We know who you are and know exactly what you want and you're not going to get it. This is my dog! This is our property! You are trespassing and you need to leave now!"

It felt as though the hair on his own neck had started to rise. "Well, young man." The Stranger said, swinging the collar in his hand loosely. "You seemed nice enough in the photo your mother showed me, but if you think you can, how about you make me."

At this the ground beneath both Reisun and Nate began to vibrate. Small pebbles began to rise from the ground as the air around them swirled violently. With an unspoken, synchronized push, they shot a huge ball of energy at the man, pushing him back and knocking him to one knee.

"Seems as though you've learned a few things since last we were together dog." He stood to his feet and raised the collar he had in his hand. "Unfortunately for you, I am your master, and you must obey."

"Never!" Reisun was awash in an electric energy that was growing exponentially.

"You will obey! Obey me! I command you as your master!" The man shouted holding the collar up before him.

The collar had begun to glow a soft silver glow. It was faint, but clear as day, even in the bright afternoon sun. Just as it seemed that things were about to clash in a most epic way, The Stranger suddenly cut his eyes over his shoulder.

"It appears that our conversation is about to be interrupted. But it is far from over boy."

The collar disappeared into the man's long coat, and he retreated to his truck. "We'll finish this another time. Perhaps when I've acquired a more persuasive bargaining chip."

With that the tires on the truck began to spin and kick up rocks and dirt. In a cloud of smoke and dust, the truck vanished down the road.

"What the heck?" Nate said out loud this time.

"Family coming." Reisun clarified.

"We've got to do something about that guy." Nate told him as he searched further down the road with enhanced vision. He could see his mom's car about a half a mile away making its way hastily toward them.

"I've got a bad feeling about the 'bargaining chip' he mentioned."

"Yes," Reisun agreed. "Family not safe."

"Yeah, family not safe." Nate agreed. "I think it's time we got the team together."

PART TWENTY-EIGHT

Codename: EndGame

Trevor glanced over at the alarm clock on his nightstand. In ten more minutes, the alarm would be sounding, so he reached over and flipped the switch off before it could. With summer right around the corner, he actually he found himself looking forward to getting up every day and more often lately, before his alarm went off.

With his plans for this Saturday being to meet with Nate and Reisun, he was even more excited to get his day off to a start. A quick shower, some breakfast and his meds and he was ready to head out the door. Without his backpack. His mother made her appearance in the kitchen not long after he'd placed the container of orange juice back in the fridge.

"Hey mom." Trevor greeted her casually.

"Hey," there was an edge of surprise in her voice and when he looked up to meet her eyes, she appeared genuinely shocked.

"You, okay?" He asked her.

"Yes...I'm, I'm good. Are you okay? Have you taken-" She stumbled to start.

"Already took my meds and had breakfast." He interrupted and then took a big swallow of orange juice. "I made you some toast and scrambled eggs. Thought you might be hungry."

He slid a second glass of OJ over to his mother. Started some coffee too. No guarantees on how good it will be though." He smiled slightly as she continued to stand in front of him, staring. "Mom, I'm ok. Really. I promise I'm -"

He was cut short by his mother rushing over to him and closing him in a tight embrace.

"I'm ok." He finished.

She kissed the side of his face softly and took the glass and plate of food before turning to head back up to her room.

"Your father should be home from his trip today. How about we all sit down and have dinner together?" she asked tentatively.

"Sounds like a plan." He nodded a tight-lipped smile in her direction, and she returned it with a pencil thin upturn of her own lips before disappearing around the corner. It was a start.

As Trevor was contemplating this interaction he'd just had with his mother, there was a frantic knock at the door. He glanced over at the clock on the microwave and saw that it was only 7:45, way too early for someone to be beating down his door like that. Unless...his dad had been gone for almost a week for a business conference. What if this was like before when they knocked on the door after...Jake. The hurried knocking came again, and Trevor rushed over to open it before his mother started to get concerned as well.

He swung the door open wide and found Nate and Reisun standing side by side on his porch. Trevor peeked his head out the door to see if he saw Nate's mother's car, but it didn't appear to be anywhere on the street. If she'd just dropped them off and left, he would have at least seen her driving away down the street.

"Um, hey." Trevor said confused.

"No time for pleasantries." Nate said like an old school cartoon hero. "We have a problem."

Trevor turned and yelled through the house to his mother. "Mom, Nate's here. We're headed out!" He didn't wait for a response before he closed the door, and the trio was headed down the walkway in from of Trevor's house.

"What's up?" He asked when they hit the sidewalk.

"Tell you everything when we get to the clearing." Nate said. "So how are we-" Trevor began. "Run." Reisun finished his thought for him.

Trevor could feel a surge of energy flow through him, and it felt as if his muscles were flexing and releasing, pumped full of adrenaline and ready to burst.

"You know how it goes," Nate smiled at his friends. "Last one there-," They all took off running before he could finish the line. While Nate was getting his team together, The Stranger was busying himself as well. He had made it his business to be a constant worrying presence around the family. Not because he felt that Nate and Reisun were truly a threat, but more to show them that they were reachable, vulnerable and well, simply because he enjoyed the insecurity that a bit of harassment could implant.

He lurked in the shadows and watched as Nate's mother, sister, and brother went about their daily routine. He had been following them for several days, taking note of their movements and actions. He knew their schedules and routines and made sure that Nate was fully aware of it. He would leave little mementos for Nate to show him that he was able to get close to his family. A threat that said, 'I could do so much more to them if I wanted to.'

When the boys arrived at the clearing, they quickly explained the situation. Trevor listened carefully. "This dude sounds insane." Trevor was shaking his head as he took it all in. "Well, we definitely can't let him get to Reisun. Did you tell your parents what's going on?"

"Nah," Nate was pacing back and forth, kicking up little puffs of dirt with each step. "I don't want to risk anybody getting hurt. Me and R were able to hold him back pretty good. With the three of us working on him..." He stopped and looked over at Trevor.

"We'll kick his ass!" Trevor stuck out his fist and waited for Nate to dap it up.

"Hell yeah!" Nate dapped his fist and they did their handshake.

"We're going to need a plan." Trevor pointed out after they shook.

"Right. We need to get him onto our ground where we'll have the upper hand." Nate agreed.

They decided to set up a trap in the woods and ambush him. If he was able to track Reisun, it should be easy enough to give him something to track. They would lure him to a trap, where they would finally have the chance to confront and defeat him.

Nate and Reisun quickly took off to set up the trap, while Trevor began to gather supplies. They worked tirelessly, setting trip wires and snares in various places throughout the woods.

"Where'd you even learn to do stuff like this?" Trevor asked Nate as he was explaining how the snares worked and how to set them up.

Nate laughed, "You'd be surprised what you can learn between boy scouts and YouTube."

They knew that The Stranger was smart, and they had to be careful not to make any mistakes. They made sure to take their time covering and hiding all of their hard work.

"We all know what parts we play. Now it's time to implement our plan, codename: Endgame." Nate said in his most militant voice. Reisun gave a soft huff of amused indifference.

"Really." Trevor said rolling his eyes.

"Hey, this is serious business. This guy is dangerous. Besides, it sounds cool."

Nate placed his hands on his hips and did his best superman pose.

"Well, can we discuss how cool it sounds at the house." Trevor walked over to him and gave him a playful push. "It's like 2:30 and all this brainstorming and planning has worked up an appetite."

"Snacks." Reisun gave an enthusiastic bark of agreement.

PART TWENTY-NINE

It's a Trap

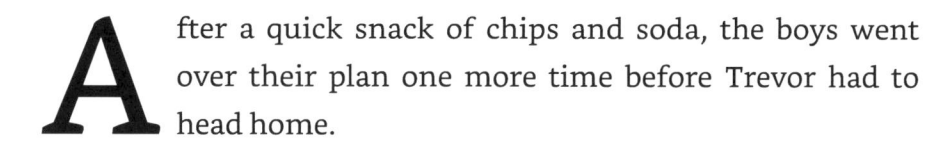

After a quick snack of chips and soda, the boys went over their plan one more time before Trevor had to head home.

"I'm having dinner with my mom and dad tonight." Trevor told them with a shrug.

"That's cool." Nate placed an assuring hand on Trevor's shoulder. "You're still going to be able to get back on time, right?"

"I should, as long as my 'Reisun juice' doesn't run out." Trev chuckled.

Nate looked over at Reisun. "Is he good to go and come back?" He wasn't 100% certain how sharing Reisun's powers worked but he felt like Trevor would be able to continue to use the one they'd shared with him, speed, for several more hours.

"Fast all night." Reisun reassured the boys without making a sound.

"Cool." Trevor gave Reisun a pat. "Well, everything is set. I'm going to head home for dinner, and I'll be back by 8."

They shook a farewell and Trevor became a puff of dust as he made his way home at top speed.

As the day wore on, Nate's family finished their daily routines and headed home. The Stranger followed them from a distance, waiting and biding his time. He knew that both Nate and Reisun would know that he was nearby and that's exactly what he wanted. He wanted them on high alert, never knowing when he was coming, or from where.

His plan had been to terrorize Nate and his family before catching them off guard and taking what he had come for. He had no idea what was waiting for him in the woods.
"He's here." Nate said looking over at Reisun from where he sat on his bed.

"Yes." Reisun stood and began to move toward the door. "Is time."

"Is time." Nate agreed and stood as well. He grabbed his black hoodie and made his way to the front door. "Taking the dog out. Be right back." He called to his mother, who was busying herself in the kitchen.

"Kay." She called back without looking.

When they were on the front porch Nate glanced at the time on his phone.

7:58.

He looked down the dirt road a ways. At the very end of the road, sitting just across the main road in a cover of trees was The Stranger. He'd pulled his truck far enough back off the road that the average passerby probably wouldn't even notice him. But both Nate and Reisun had.

"Man, where is-" Nate started.

"At your service." Trevor had come skidding to a stop just in front of the bottom porch step.

"Went around. I saw creepy truck dude sitting in the trees at the end of the road, thought he might notice me." Trevor told them in a rush.

"That was smart." Nate took the porch steps in a leap.

"Let's go. Reisun, do your thing." The ground under Reisuns' feet began to tremble and before long all four of the canine's feet were floating several inches above the ground.

"Takes a lot of energy to do that, huh." Trevor asked him.

"Yes," Reisun nodded. "Also attracts bad guys."

With that he began to rise higher and higher into the air.

"We gotta go." Nate tugged Trevor's shirt and the two of them took off running into the trees.

In the truck the collar that The Stranger had been using to track Reisun began to glow brightly. The light from the collar filled the truck bed and The Stranger had to stuff the collar back into its sack and wait several seconds before he was able to see again.

"He's getting stronger." He smiled to himself.

He stepped out of the truck and slammed the door behind him. "Time to reclaim my property."

Compelled by the translucent beam of light that led into the trees near where he knew both the dog and the boy laid their heads, The Stranger followed the hunting trail that he'd come to at the end of their dirt road, into the woods. The sun was beginning to set, and the trees were already casting long dark shadows everywhere.

"You think this is a game boy?!" The Stranger shouted into the trees. "You think you can hide from me in here? Or perhaps your plan is a surprise attack using your newly acquired powers? Powers that are rightfully mine!" He shouted to no one in particular.

Nate appeared from behind a tree. "Cliche villain much?" He said and started to laugh. "Man, you are corny."

The Stranger turned in his direction and raised a hand. As he did, small round rocks, about the size of oranges, began to shake themselves free from the ground.

"I find it interesting that you make sarcastic jokes without the full understanding that I will happily remove every digit and limb from your body while keeping you alive to enjoy life as the insect that you are!" He reared his hand back and launched the rocks in Nate's direction.

They came flying toward him like cannon balls. Smashing into the surrounding trees and splintering them into pieces. Nate dove out of the way just in time but pretended to be injured. He held his arm and rolled around on the ground moaning in pain.

"Fast, but not fast enough." The Stranger took a few steps in Nate's Direction while invisibly pulling even larger rocks from the ground and preparing to strike again.

Just as he was rearing his arm back for the next borage Reisun leaps over Nate and lands heavily in front of him, shaking the ground as he does.

"No!" Reisun barks loudly, vibrating the air and forcing the man back.

The rocks crash to the ground as he fights to remain standing. Reisun slides his head under Nate's good arm, and they take off into the trees.

The Strange gives a shout and presses his hands, palms down, toward the ground, using counter force to stabilize himself.

"Can't get away from me that easily." He snarled and took off after them at full speed.

He wasn't near as fast as Reisun and Nate, but he was fast enough to keep a general direction of which way they'd fled. He was focused on broken limbs and footprints as he ran which is why he didn't notice the trip wire until it was too late.

He stumbled forward, not exactly crashing to the ground but off balance just enough so that when the snare caught hold of the front of his boot it took him completely down.

"Yes." Trevor celebrated quietly from his perch high in the trees. "Time for phase two."

He leapt from the branch he'd been perched on and landed next to Reisun and Nate near the lake.

"We can't give him time to get back up good." Nate told them.

"Let's do it." Trevor widened his stance in preparation.

Reisun, Nate and Trevor took off in different directions and began snatching tree trunks up from the ground and launching them in The Strangers' direction. One after the other they tossed the heavy tree trunks and even pulled up some boulders of their own and tossed those as well. They continued to do this until Nate raised a hand for them to stop.

He looked over at Reisun. "You hear anything?" He asked him.

Reisun sniffed the air, cocked his head to the left and then to the right before looking back at Nate. "Close." He told his friend.

"Closer than you think!" Before any of them realized what was happening Trevor found himself being lifted up off the ground.

They had injured The Stranger, but they hadn't stopped him completely.

"Trevor!" Nate yelled.

"Get out of here, you, guys!" Trevor swung his arms and kicked his legs trying to attack the man and give his friends time to get away.

"We're not leaving you." Nate shouted back.

Reisun was growling and barking, foamy drool flying from his mouth as he did.

"Let go!" Reisun demanded.

The hair on his back stood on end, sparking with energy. The stranger laughed and looked at Trevor dangling in his hand.

"As you wish...dog." With a flick of his wrist, he sent Trevor flying.

Trevor slammed hard into a large maple tree about 30 yards away, falling to the ground in a distorted crumpled heap.

"No! Trevor!" Nate was screaming.

The air around both he and Reisun had begun to crackle with energy. It whirled and whipped, picking up rocks and dirt and debris.

"I will kill you!!" He shouted at The Stranger. "I'm going to kill you!!"

"Not if I kill you first." The Stranger smiled menacingly. "Since you and your friends seem to enjoy throwing things..." A huge tree trunk came flying at them. Reisun sprang into the air and kicked against the truck with all four feet, splitting it in half.

"You have so much to learn." The Stranger was still smiling as he said this.

From the left and the right side of them the trees began to fall in their direction.

"Run, now." Reisun expressed to Nate.

Even with their increased speed it seems that the falling trees were two steps ahead of them. They came crashing down from every direction, knocking them off balance and into boulders that had mysteriously uncovered themselves from the ground.

When they finally broke free of the tree line they collapsed onto the ground, bruised and defeated. The Stranger hadn't followed them. He had his own wounds to lick. But this meeting had not turned out the way they had thought it would. Nate looked back that the woods and thought of Trevor lying there in a heap on the ground. Tears began to fall, and his stomach clenched with pain.

"Trev." He sobbed. "We can't just leave him in there like that."

Reisun limped over to where Nate had collapsed on the ground just outside of the tree line and pressed his forehead to his.

"Friend, gone." Reisun told him.

"I know!" Nate sobbed even more.

He wiped his arm across his nose, drawing a long line of blood. He hadn't realized his nose had been bleeding until now. "That bastard killed Trev and I'm going to kill him!"

Nate began to pull himself to his feet.

"No. Look." Reisun motioned in the direction they had just run from. "Friend gone."

It was true. Nate focused his vision and searched the woods where they had been for his friend. Neither Trevor's body nor The Stranger were anywhere to be found.

"He...took him? Why would be take him?" Nate was so confused.

Not only confused, but angry and a little scared. There was no way they were going to be able to beat this guy by themselves and as much as he didn't want to, it was time to tell his family what was going on.

PART THIRTY

A Family Affair

It was a slow and steady trek back to the house. It was completely dark now and the walk seemed so much further than it usually did. Stars were just beginning to make their appearance in the sky and the almost full moon helped to light their way across the yard and onto the porch. Nate eased the front door open hoping that his mother was already in her room, and no one would see them coming into the house. Reisun had a pretty good gash on his side and was limping. Nate had several cuts and bruises across his body from being slammed into boulders and slashed by the falling branches of huge trees.

Luckily both his parents were in their room for the night watching a movie. But there was one person that had been checking for his return. Olivia.

As soon as she heard Nate's door make its familiar squeal, she popped her head out of her bedroom door.

"Hey, mom asked where you were, but I covered-," She paused and then came hurrying down the hall to him. "Oh, my gawd. What happened to you?"

He could hear the concern in her voice.

"Long story." He told her as he fell across his bed with a groan.

"You're bleeding Nate. And both of you look like you just survived a war. What happened?"

"Ok, ok. I'll tell you. I was going to tell everybody anyway." He breathed heavily.

"Hold that thought." She ran out of the room and was gone for a couple of minutes before she returned with the first aid kit, rags and peroxide and Dave, who looked concerned and afraid for his brother.

They listened as Nate told them the whole story. How the stranger had tracked Reisun and been following around them and their mother. How they had confronted him in the yard when no one was home and they tried to confront him again with Trevor in the woods. He told them what had happened to Trevor and how his body was gone and they didn't know what The Stranger had done with him. By the time he had told them everything Olivia had finished patching them both up and was wiping tears from her eyes.

"You know we have to tell mom, right?" David told him.

"Yeah, I know." Nate answered in a hushed voice.

"But I don't want her to see me like this. You know how she is. Give us a couple of hours to heal up."

"A couple of hours?" Olivia exclaimed. "Do you not see yourself? You're a mess. You're both a mess." "Heal fast." Reisun expressed this to them. "Just need rest."

"Whoa." David said, putting his hands up. "First timer here."

"Sorry." Reisun stood and walked over to place his head under

David hand.

"I knew there was something special about you." He was stroking his head gently. "We'll give you until morning. Then we need to have a family meeting before anything else happens. Doesn't sound like this guy is just going to give up." Nate said.

But his words had gone unheard. Nate was already fast asleep and Reisun wasn't far behind him. As they lay in bed, healing from their injuries, Nate and Reisun felt a deep sense of sadness and loss. They missed Trevor terribly and wished that he was still with them. But they also felt a burning desire for revenge. They knew that they had to stop The Stranger from hurting anyone else, and they were willing to do whatever it took to make that happen.

Early the next morning Nate's family had gathered around them in Nate's room. Olivia had been so concerned for Nate and Reisun's safety that she had talked David into waking their parents up so they could tell them what was going on that night. As unbelievable as their story had been, they had convinced them to wait until morning to confront Nate about everything.

When Nate finally woke, his mother was sitting on the edge of the bed next to him looking deeply worried for her son's safety. She hadn't known exactly what to believe when Olivia started telling them about the dog having powers and some maniac that wanted to kill them and take the dog back. But now as she examined the rapidly healing cuts and bruises that covered his entire body, she was ready to believe just about anything.

Reisun inched closer to her from where he had been laying at the foot of Nate's bed. He placed his head on her lap and looked up at her.

Tentatively she placed a hand on his head and said, "Hey there."

Softy Reisun expressed, "Hello."

Denise sucked in a breath at the sound of Reisun's 'voice', if you could call it that. It was more of a feeling than a sound, but she had heard it clear as day.

"Pretty cool, huh?" Olivia said.

"You heard that too?" Denise said looking around at them.

The expression of shock on Terrance's face told her all she needed to know. He had definitely felt it and was left speechless.

Denise turned her attention back to her injured son. She couldn't believe that he had been in a fight with a dangerous stranger who had killed their friend Trevor. She sat beside Nate's bed and held his hand, tears streaming down her face.

"Nate, I'm so scared of you," she said. "We should call the police and let them handle this. They'll know what to do."
Nate shook his head and sat up in the bed. "Mom, we can't call the police. The Stranger has powers that they won't be able to handle. Besides, he knows about Reisun's powers, and we can't let him get his hands on him. We have to handle this ourselves."

As she was watching, she could see the last of the wounds on Nate's face healing over and his bruises beginning to clear. His eyes were bright, and alert and he looked as if he were ready to jump up and head back out to fight. She touched his face, running a finger across one of the fading cuts.

"What's happened to you?" She asked in an awestruck voice.

Reisun eased himself off the bed and stood before her.

"We bonded. Share powers. Share abilities. Share healing."

She shook her head of Reisun's expressions and looked back at Nate. "It's going to take some time for me to get used to that." She told him.

Denise could see the determination in her son's eyes. She knew that he wouldn't give up until he had avenged Trevor and stopped The Stranger. She took a deep breath and nodded her head in agreement. "Ok, I understand. Zombie apocalypse style" she said. "But we have to be careful. We can't take any unnecessary risks."

Nate nodded, leaned forward and hugged his mother. "Zombie apocalypse style." He chuckled a little at the thought. He was relieved that his mother was on board with the plan to not call the police and take care of this themselves.

Suddenly, Reisun began to growl, drawing the attention of everyone in the room. They turned to see him standing on his hind legs, his front paws outstretched.

Olivia gasped. "What's happening? Is he okay?"

Nate smiled. "He's showing you that he trusts us to protect his secret," he said. "Watch this."

Reisun closed his eyes and concentrated, and a small ball of light appeared between his front paws. It grew brighter and brighter until it filled the entire room, illuminating everything around them. They could all feel the light seeming to fill them up until it felt like it was coming out of their fingers, toes, eyes, ears and even their mouth.

They were now all bound as one, sharing a power between them that was only made stronger by their bond. They could feel the energy radiating from him and through them and knew that he was capable of amazing things. And now, so were they. Olivia couldn't contain her excitement.

"This is so cool!" she exclaimed. "Now we can beat The Stranger with Reisun's powers!"

Nate smiled, happy to see that his family was starting to believe in their ability to stop The Stranger. "We can do it," he said. "But we have to work together. We have to train and prepare ourselves for whatever comes our way."

The family nodded in agreement, eager to do whatever it takes to keep themselves safe and stop The Stranger. They knew that it wouldn't be easy, but they were ready to face the challenge. As they continued to discuss their plans, Reisun lay down on the floor, exhausted from using his powers. But he too knew that they could do it. Together, they were a force to be reckoned with, and they wouldn't rest until The Stranger was defeated.

PART THIRTY-ONE

The Final Meeting

They sat down together and planned over breakfast. Like a well-oiled machine they all moved in sync with one another. When Denise finished the bacon and eggs, Olivia was beside her with plates that were immediately passed to David as they were prepared and then slid over to Kevin, who casually bumped them into place with his pinky finger.

"This is something else." Terrance said with a huge grin. "Feel like I could lift an elephant."

"I know, right." David took his seat at the table. "I ran to check the mail just now and nobody even noticed that I'd left. Gone and back in a flash."

Denise joined them at the table. "Well as fun as all this may be, we still have a very serious issue to deal with."

"Right." They all agreed.

Olivia looked over at Nate. "So, we need to practice right? Learn how to use our powers?"

All of their eyes were on him now. "No," he said standing up from the table. "You'll just know what to do. Besides, -"

Nate walked over to the door and called back over his shoulder, "doesn't look like there's gonna be time to practice."

They all sensed the change in the atmosphere now. There was a pressure resonating from outside and it was taunting them.

"You guys ready for this?" He had turned to face them now.

"Nobody messes with one of ours." David said, coming to stand next to Nate.

"Right." Reisun pushed to them.

"Let's do this," Kevin beat his chest in an effort to hype himself up.

Nate grabbed the doorknob and swung it open.

He and his family were determined to protect Reisun from The Stranger at all costs. They stood shoulder to shoulder with the brave dog, ready to fight for his freedom.

He stood just in the driveway a few yards from the house. The tail of his long trench coat being lifted and billowed by some invisible breeze.

"Ahh, has this become a family thing?" He called to them. "I was just going to kill you, but it would be more fun to make you a sibling less orphan!" The air crackled with energy as The Stranger attacked, but the family held their ground.

They used their powers in unison, working together with Reisun to defend against their enemy's attacks. Then, as if by magic, Reisun began to glow with an otherworldly light. It was as if the power within him had been ignited by the love and support of his family. Both of his eyes blazed with intensity, and Nate could feel the ground trembling beneath his feet. Then, for just a moment, both Nate and Reisun were caught up in a whirlwind of lightning, flashes and light. When his feet finally returned to the ground, he could see that Reisun was now substantially larger, about the size of a cow, and he himself felt even more...well, buff.

"Well dang." Olivia smirked from where she stood holding a car transmission with one hand, ready to throw.

The Stranger seemed to sense the change in the air, and he hesitated for just a moment. That was all it took for Reisun to unleash his full power. With a mighty roar, Reisun unleashed a burst of energy that sent The Stranger flying backward. The ground shook as waves of force emanated through each member of the family, was enhanced as it passed through Nate and into Reisun's body.

The Stranger raised his coat in a defensive manner, but it didn't appear to have any affect. He exploded into a fiery sunburst of sparks that lit up the sky. Nate shielded his eyes from the blinding light, feeling the heat of the energy wash over him.

He could hear his family screaming in triumph, and he knew that they had won. When the light finally faded, The Stranger was nowhere to be seen. He had vanished, leaving behind only a smoldering pile of ashes.

Nate and his family looked at each other in disbelief, unable to understand what had just happened. They had won, but at what cost? They had almost lost Reisun, and they had lost their dear friend Trevor. But as they turned to each other, they realized that they had won something far greater.

They had won each other's love and support, and they had proven that nothing could tear them apart. Reisun walked over to them, wagging his tail happily. His eyes were bright, and Nate could sense the pride emanating from him.

"We did it," Reisun said.

"Together, we defeated The Stranger and protected our family." Nate hugged Reisun tightly, feeling tears streaming down his face.

Tears of triumph and of frustration. He cried for his friend and for the relief he felt that his family was safe. He knew that they would never forget this moment, his family was something special.

PART THIRTY-TWO

Graduation Day Hijinks

David's graduation had come around far quicker than any of them had actually been prepared for and they found themselves rushing around the house, graduation day, in order to make it to the ceremony on time. Reisun was eager to come along, but they were informed that no dogs were allowed on school grounds during the graduation. He had no intention of letting that stop him from attending a celebration of a member of his family though. He would simply race the car to the school and sit quietly outside the fence of the field where the ceremony was being held.

He was quite proud of the plan he'd come up with and was turning to share his idea with Nate when his ear twitched. As if they had been summoned, the entire family entered the kitchen at once.

"Everything good?" David asked.

"Yeah, you guys go ahead so you're not late. We've got this." With a quick glance from his mother, Nate stepped outside to investigate with Reisun at his side.

Reisun's ear twitched again. This time Nate was tuned in to exactly what Reisun was hearing. About a mile down the road an injured deer had wandered into the middle of the road. A few cars had swerved to miss it, but it didn't appear that the last car was controlling the last-minute swerve at the speed it was travelling. It had only barely missed the deer but was now swerving out of control and into oncoming traffic.

It was headed straight for a minivan containing a family who was on their way to the same graduation ceremony as Nate and his family. Nate's heart raced as he realized the gravity of the situation. He and Reisun raced towards the impending accident. As they approached everything appeared to be happening in slow motion. They saw the family in the van screaming in terror. The young woman driving the car with the college sticker on the back windshield, was frozen with fear, unable to take control of her vehicle. Even the small deer sat frozen in the middle of the road.

Using their super speed and strength, Nate and Reisun worked together to prevent the accident. Nate grabbed the deer and dragged it off the road, while Reisun pushed the car out of the way of the oncoming van. With their combined efforts, they were able to redirect the cars to a safe stop, saving the lives of the people in both vehicles. As the dust settled, Draya, the young woman who had saved Reisun and brought him to the animal shelter, emerged from the car, shaken but unharmed.

She looked up and saw a young, relatively attractive black man and his dog standing there, on the side of the road, ready to help. The dog that was with the young man looked so familiar to her. For just a moment she thought, 'Could it be?' Overwhelmed with gratitude however, she pushed the thought aside and thanked them for saving her life again. The young man just shrugged and patted his dog on the head.

None of the parties from either car were actually able to say what happened, but they did know that Nate and his dog had been there to ensure that everyone was alright.

Draya looked away to check her car for any damage. Not seeing any immediate damage, she turned her attention back to the young man and his dog. However, when she did, they and the injured deer were all gone.

Later that day, at the graduation ceremony, Draya saw Nate sitting in the bleachers with his family. She looked around just knowing that the dog was here somewhere as well. She wasn't wrong. On the far side of the field, sitting on the other side of the fence, was the big, dark silhouette of a dog.

When the ceremony ended, she wasted no time catching up to the young man she'd seen on the road. She approached him to express her gratitude once more.

"Hey there stranger." She waved as she approached.

"Hi." Nate said with a raised eyebrow.

"I'm Draya, from the accident earlier." She extended her hand.

"Nate," He shook her hand. "Yeah, I remember you."

They started walking toward the parking lot.

"I just wanted to say thank you again." She told him as they walked.

"Yeah, you said that earlier. So, who graduated?" Nate brushed aside the gratitude as humbly as he could. They had all seen him there, but they don't know what he did or what part Reisun played in it, and he wanted to keep it that way.

"Oh, um, my cousin. Kind of promised my mom I'd come to her graduation. But that's not the only reason I wanted to catch up with you again." She told him, trying to keep her purpose on track. "Your dog. Where'd you get him from?"

She tried to seem casual as she asked this, but after recent events, anyone asking too many questions about Reisun made the whole family suspicious.

"He's adopted." Nate raised an eyebrow. "Why do you ask?

Just then Reisun came bombing out of the trees on the side of the field and through the parking lot to where they stood.

"Friend!" He was expressing excitedly. "Friend! Friend Draya!"

"It is you!" Draya dropped to her knees and threw open her arms. Reisun came crashing into her, sending them both tumbling to the ground. Nate smiled.

"Well, this explains a little bit, but I'm sure there's way more to this story." He reached down and took Draya by the hand, helping her up. "How about dinner with me and my family?"

"Do they know how special he is?" She asked in a whisper.

"Oh yeah, they know." Nate laughed as they made their way across the lot to Draya's car.

The End

Afterword

Nate sat at the kitchen table with the rest of his family and their new friend, Draya, enjoying his brother's graduation dinner. They were all laughing at a story that Olivia was telling about when they were younger when there was a knock at the door.

"I wonder who that could be?" Denise said, starting to get up from her seat.

Reisun jumped up next to her and began to bark frantically. The entire room fell silent then.

"You don't think he came back, do you?" Olivia looked over at Nate with concern in her face.

"He's gone. No way." Nate said, waving her off. "Besides, pretty sure he wouldn't knock."

"Open!" Reisun practically shouted the word in their heads.

"Okay, okay." Nate stood up from the table now. "You don't have to yell."

"Nate." His mother was also looking at him concerned. "It's ok mom. I have a feeling we know who it is." He went over and opened the door, swinging it wide so they could all see who was standing there.

The man standing at the door was thin and spritely. He wore a huge smile has he lifted his hand in a friendly wave.

"Hi, ummm, I didn't mean to interrupt. My name is-" He started.

Before he could finish his greeting both Denise and Draya said with surprise, "-Adam!"

"What are you doing here?" Denise asked curiously.

Once again Adam opened his mouth to speak and was interrupted.

"Perhaps it would be better if I were to explain." Came a voice just to the left of where Adam stood.

Adam stepped to the side and the door was filled by a small man of Asian descent and two large canines, one a deep black and the other a stunning silver grey.

"His parents." Olivia said with true awe in her voice.

Reisun whimpered with joy and was at the door in a flash. The dogs took off into the yard running and barking excitedly. The family all joined Adam and the man on the porch as the watched the dogs frolicking together in the grass. Nate came to stand by the man on his right side and Adam took his place on the left.

"I take it you're not here just for the family reunion." Nate inquired calmly.

"You would be correct." The man told him. "We have much to discuss young man.

"Sounds like the punctuation changed." Olivia said, heading down the steps and out to where the dogs were.

"What's that mean." Dave asked her.

"You know, " She called over her shoulder. "Like when a movie is over and it says, 'END'. Only instead of a period now our 'end' has a question mark."

"I guess you're right." Dave said looking over at his mother.

"Definitely seems like these adventures got a few more chapters left in it." Denise said, heading back into the house. "Can I offer you something to eat or drink Mr.-"

"Jin."

"Mr. Jin. It's a pleasure to meet you." She gestured for him to come into the house.

"Yes. We shall see if your sentiment remains once we have spoken." He smiled slyly to himself as he said this.

"Oh man, here we go." Nate gave Dave a jab in the arm as they followed the others into the house. "You ready?"

"Do I have a choice?" Dave replied sarcastically.

"Nope."

The End?

Reasons To Stay

If you need reasons to stay with me
reasons why you shouldn't go so soon.
I've got the biggest one of all.
I love you, from here to the moon.

Now multiply that by infinity
that's how much love I have for you.
and if you were no longer here
I wouldn't know what to do.

Who would laugh at all my jokes?
and tell me I'm a corn.
or tell the best scary stories.
during the height of a thunderstorm

I need to hear your voice.
telling me that I can do it, you know I can.
I need more than just the memories.
a view from way back when

Only you know my deepest secrets.
only in you can I confide.
you're the only one who understands.
I wasn't always sad when I cried.

I need you to stay because you're funny.
I need you to stay because you have the greatest laugh.
I need you to stay because you're talented.
I need you to stay because you're built Ford tough.
I need you to stay because you're super smart.
because you have the best hair, nose, ears and eyes.
I need you to stay because you make the best sweet potato pies.

I need you to stay because you're innocent

and still have so much to see.

I need you to stay because you're special, especially to me.

I want you to stay because somewhere out there

there's somebody just for you.

and if you were no longer here, what on earth
would your soulmate do?

I want to stay because sometimes I need help too.
When things get tough no one else is better
at figuring out just what to do.

I'd miss your singing in the shower.
and tipping, soaking wet to your room
I'd miss your adventurous spirit in a world filled with gloom.
You can't go before your time you have too much to do.
you've touched far too many lives, all of whom would miss you too.

If I knew it would keep you here, I'd give you 100 reasons to stay.
Starting with I love you; I love you; I love you, I love you.
and I'd remind you of this every day.

Follow Us on Social Media

🐦 @NDBossie

🤖 @NDBossiethaAuthor

🎵 @NDBossiethaAuthor

📘 @NDBossie

Send us an email and let us know how our book as affected your life or just to talk and vent. We'd love to hear from you.

📧 Reisunthenovel@gmail.com

Made in the USA
Columbia, SC
06 June 2023

836f216e-790c-4bc6-92a5-7b25b3de2ceeR01